A Perilous Circumstance

Gentlemen of London

Laura Beers

Chapter One

England, 1813

William Cobbett, the Earl of Grenton, did not like most people. He found them bothersome, which is why he preferred to be alone. Yet people did not have the good sense to leave him be.

He watched his solicitor wipe sweat from his brow as he rambled off excuses about how he had failed at the simplest task. Mr. Mason was a small man with a thin face and was the type of man that most people would dismiss as unimportant, but he had come highly recommended. Up to this point, he had been competent at his job.

Having heard enough, William leaned back in his chair. "Why are you wasting my time, Mr. Mason?"

The solicitor grimaced. "You must give me more time."

"I already gave you three months," William replied. "Do you not believe that should be sufficient time to secure a head-mistress for the orphanage?"

"Under most circumstances, yes, but you are asking for the impossible."

"I don't think I am."

Mr. Mason reached down and pulled out a piece of paper from a brown satchel. "You have requested a lady who is of high rank, well educated—but not a bluestocking, and is comfortable with living in the rookeries."

"Is that an issue?"

"I daresay it is," Mr. Mason replied with consternation. "I have posted an advertisement in the morning newssheets, but no one has responded."

"That is where you went wrong. Any respectable lady would not be reading the newssheets."

"I have exhausted my search, but there is not one lady that fits your description," Mr. Mason said. "I have, however, sent you a few names of women that would be qualified for the position as headmistress."

"They didn't suit."

"Some of them might have been older—" Mr. Mason began

William cut him off. "I didn't take issue with their age," he said. "I took issue with *them.*"

"Why was that, my lord?"

"They were not a good fit for the orphanage. They were much too common."

Mr. Mason frowned, and he was clearly agitated. "Women of worth do not run orphanages," he stated. "They are much too busy trying to secure an advantageous marriage."

"My mother had a vision for this orphanage, and she wanted it run by a woman of worth. She felt that only a lady would be able to bring her vision to fruition."

"Forgive me, but your mother wasn't lucid towards the end," Mr. Mason remarked. "Perhaps her expectations were too lofty."

William narrowed his eyes, and his voice grew steely. "I would proceed cautiously, Mr. Mason."

Mr. Mason shifted in his seat, showing discomfort. "I

mean no disrespect, but orphanages are generally run by older, unmarried women. It is hard work, and ladies are not up to that task."

"There must be someone," William said.

"I contend there is not," Mr. Mason responded. "Right now, Mrs. Hughes is running the orphanage, and she has been doing a fine job. It might be best if you just continue to let her do so."

"Do you intend to tell me what to do?" William asked.

"I would never do something so bold. I am merely offering a solution."

William shoved his desk chair back and rose. "Your solution is not one that I would consider," he stated. "You have failed me, and I do not stand for incompetence."

"Sir, if I may…"

William raised his hand, stilling the solicitor's words. "I have heard enough. I will give you one more month to bring me someone to run the orphanage. If you do not, you will no longer be in my employ."

"If you would broaden your requirements, then I might have more success finding someone."

"I tire of your excuses," William barked. "Just do your job."

Mr. Mason rose. "I am doing my job, but I contend that the woman you are looking for does not exist."

"She does," William replied. "You just haven't found her yet."

"The pay is generous, but any lady who accepts this position has committed herself to a life of spinsterhood."

"Not every lady is fortunate enough to find a match."

"That is true, but they can become a governess to a respectable family," Mr. Mason pointed out, "whereas you are asking someone to willingly live in the rookeries."

William came around his desk. "I am late for a meeting, and we are going in circles," he said.

"I will do my best."

"Do better," William urged. "I have no use for ineptitude."

Mr. Mason tipped his head. "I understand, my lord." He picked up his satchel. "I will make this my utmost priority, and hope to report back to you with good news."

"I hope so, as well, for your sake."

After Mr. Mason departed from his study, William walked out and saw his butler standing in the entry hall. Thorne was a tall man with a rounded face and a big nose, his once-black hair now peppered with white.

Thorne stepped forward and announced, "Your coach is waiting out front, my lord."

"Thank you for seeing to that."

"It was my pleasure," Thorne said, extending a black top hat. "I do hope you have a pleasant time at White's."

William stifled a groan before it could cross his lips. His friends had been adamant that he join them for a drink tonight, despite his many excuses, but they had been relentless, and he'd eventually run out of reasons for not attending.

Thorne opened the door, and William stepped out of his townhouse and into his coach. He had been fortunate enough to have developed these friendships at Eton many years ago, but lately, he found their outings to be tedious.

He knew they were worried about him. Ever since his mother died nearly a year ago, he had craved solitude. Being alone was comfortable. It was familiar, and he didn't want to weigh anyone else down with the overwhelming grief that he felt. It was all-consuming, taking with it nearly every ounce of joy he had once possessed.

The coach jerked forward and started rolling down the crowded street, which was surprisingly busy despite the late hour.

William pulled open the drapes and stared up at the night sky. What wouldn't he give for a moment of reprieve?

When had life become so hard? It wasn't simply the

passing of his mother, as these feelings had settled upon him before then. He had watched her wither away until he hardly recognized her. She'd grown so thin, so weak. All he could do was watch as the life drained out of her. He couldn't help her; no one could.

And then she was gone. The one constant in his life just… left.

How did one move past tragedy? Did the numbness in your heart ever truly go away? Or would he be left with unrelenting grief for the rest of his life?

The coach came to a stop in front of White's and a footman stepped off his perch. The door opened and William stepped out onto the pavement. He stared up at the gentlemen's club and debated about climbing back into the coach and returning home.

The opportunity disappeared, however, when his friend, Lord Hawthorne, approached him with an obnoxious smile on his lips. "Grenton," Hawthorne greeted, "you came!"

"Did I have a choice?" William grumbled.

Hawthorne chuckled. "You always had a choice."

William relaxed a little. "Did I?" he questioned. "Because you made it nearly impossible to refuse."

"It was for your own good," Hawthorne said, clapping a hand on William's shoulder before leading the way inside.

William followed his friend, weaving his way through the crowded hall until they found the others tucked back in a corner.

Lord Haddington raised his glass when he saw him. "Grenton," he greeted.

William acknowledged him with a tip of his head before turning his attention towards Lord Hugh. "Good evening," he said as he pulled out a chair.

After he was situated, a server approached the table and asked, "Would you care for something to drink, sir?"

"Brandy, and do keep them coming," William replied.

The server left to do his bidding, and William looked up, baffled to see his companions eyeing him, concerned looks on their faces.

"May I ask why you are all staring at me?" William asked.

Unrepentant, Hawthorne shrugged. "You seem more despondent than normal."

"I assure you that is not the case," William replied.

"But you admit that you are despondent?" Hawthorne pressed.

William glanced skyward and shook his head. "Why did I ever agree to spend time with you?"

Hawthorne smiled. "Because we are the only friends you have."

"Pity, that," William replied. "I suppose I do find you somewhat tolerable."

"Only somewhat?" Haddington asked.

"If you must know, I just came from a meeting with my solicitor," William shared. "He has yet to secure a head-mistress for the orphanage."

"I fear it is a fool's errand," Hawthorne said.

"Why do you say that?"

Hawthorne gave him a knowing look. "You gave him an impossible set of demands," he remarked. "No lady would lower herself to work as a headmistress at an orphanage."

"It only takes one," William said as he reached for the glass that had just been placed in front of him.

"Why a lady?" Hugh asked. "Why does it have to be a member of the *ton*?"

William took a sip of his drink before responding. "It was my mother's idea. She thought it would be beneficial for the girls."

"Have you ever considered that she might be wrong?" Haddington asked.

William clenched his jaw. "I have not."

"I just worry you are setting yourself up for failure,"

Haddington continued. "A lady does not sully herself with work like that."

"Let me worry about that," William said.

Haddington turned towards Hugh. "What are your thoughts on that matter?"

Hugh shrugged. "I have none," he replied. "I trust that Grenton knows what he is doing."

"Thank you," William said. "It would appear that Hugh is the only one of my friends that has a lick of sense."

"Graylocke would agree with Hawthorne and I, but he is on his wedding tour," Haddington stated.

"Another good man has fallen into the parson's mouse-trap," Hugh mockingly mourned.

"I think Graylocke would disagree with you," Hawthorne interjected. "He appeared blissfully happy at his wedding."

"At least this time he didn't show up to the chapel drunk," Hugh joked.

"He is a smart enough man to have learned from his mistake," Haddington said.

William tossed back the rest of his drink, letting his friends continue their banter without him. He didn't feel much like conversing this evening. Besides, his friends were wrong. There had to be a lady who would be willing to work as a head-mistress at his mother's orphanage. He just had to find her.

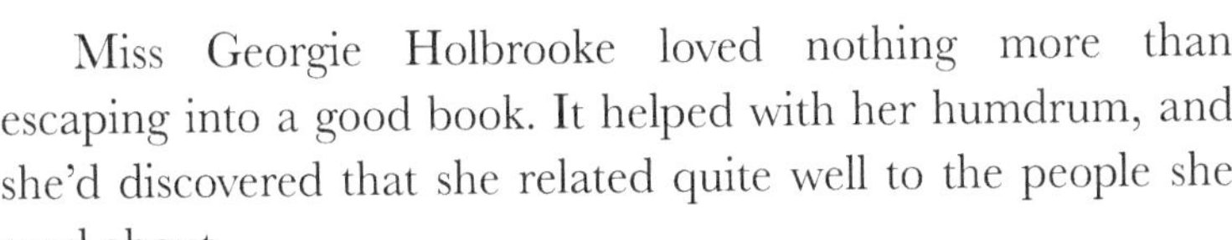

Miss Georgie Holbrooke loved nothing more than escaping into a good book. It helped with her humdrum, and she'd discovered that she related quite well to the people she read about.

She had always been a voracious reader, driving her older brother mad. He felt that she read too much and had grown far too opinionated for her own good. Normally she discounted what her brother said, but he was her guardian now that her parents had both passed, and was not one to be dismissed so easily.

Georgie released a quiet sigh. She missed her parents. Her mother passed on nearly five years ago, but her father's heart had only recently given out. She was most fortunate that they had been kind, loving parents who doted on her. For the past three months, however, she'd been forced to contend with her brother, who only seemed to view her as a useless female.

The door to her bedchamber opened and her petite lady's maid stepped into the room with a pale pink dress draped over her arm. "Lord Wakefield requested that you wear something more lively this evening," Alice announced.

Georgie glanced down at her black crepe gown. "But I am still in mourning."

"I am aware, but he invited Lord Ransdale to dine with you this evening," Alice revealed.

Georgie let out an unladylike groan. "I cannot abide Lord Ransdale. He always looks at me as though he plans to devour me whole."

"Surely that cannot be true."

"I'm afraid it is," Georgie said as she closed her book and set it on the settee next to her. "It has been that way for many years now."

Alice walked over to the bed and laid out the dress. "Regardless, you must not do anything to incite Lord Wakefield's anger."

"You are right about that." Georgie unconsciously put a hand up to her cheek. She should have known better than to bother her brother last night when he was drinking with his friends. "Do you think he would take issue with me wearing a lavender gown?"

Alice looked unsure. "Lavender isn't very lively, and you risk his ire for disobeying him."

"You are right, of course," Georgie said dejectedly. "I

wouldn't want to give him another reason to hit me." At least the gown was pale in color rather than vibrant.

"I should say not," Alice said. "Shall we style your hair? After all, you wouldn't want to keep him waiting."

"No, I most assuredly do not," Georgie agreed as she left the settee and took a seat in front of the dressing table.

Alice removed the pins from her hair, setting them on the dressing table and taking up a brush. "Did you spend the entire day in your bedchamber?" she asked as she worked.

"I did," Georgie replied. "I was trying to avoid my brother."

"I assumed as much."

Georgie met her lady's maid's gaze in the mirror. "Charles and I have never been particularly close, but he is starting to strike me for the slightest infraction now. Frankly, it scares me," she admitted.

"You do not deserve such ill treatment."

"I agree, but there is nothing that can be done about it," Georgie said. "He is my guardian until I turn twenty-one and receive my inheritance. Then I can go far away from this place."

"Fortunately, that is only a few months away."

"I am counting down the days."

"Where will you go?"

"Frankly, any place is better than remaining under Charles's rule," Georgie replied. "But I do intend to take up residence at the estate my grandmother left me. I know it is small, but it does turn a slight profit. Perhaps I could even take up gardening while I live there."

"Gardening?" Alice asked. "But you hate getting your hands dirty."

"True, but I will need to find something to occupy my time besides reading."

"You could always marry," Alice suggested.

Georgie shook her head. "I have no designs on matrimony.

I want to control my own destiny and not rely on someone else's good graces anymore."

The dinner bell rang downstairs, beckoning her to the drawing room.

Alice jumped back and rushed to the bed. "We must get you dressed!"

A knock came at the door just as the last ribbon was tied. Alice hurried over and opened the door, revealing Georgie's brother.

Charles remained in the hallway, his eyes perusing the length of her. "You look lovely," he acknowledged. "I am glad you are wearing that dress. Dark colors make you look drab."

Her brother looked so much like their father, with his dark hair and strong jaw, but the similarities stopped there. Her father had been warm, kind and inviting, whereas Charles was domineering, his eyes cold and unfeeling. Reaching into the pocket of his jacket, he pulled out a necklace.

"I thought you might want to wear Mother's pearl necklace this evening," he said.

Georgie was surprised by his thoughtfulness. He wasn't one to do kind things for her. What was he about? Realizing that her brother was still waiting for a response, she said, "I would love to."

Charles stepped into the room and indicated that she should turn around. He looped the pearls around her neck and fastened them in place.

"Thank you, Charles." Georgie fingered the strand of pearls as she turned back around to face him. Memories of her mother came flooding back to her, and she blinked back tears. She knew how her brother felt about her crying in front of him, and she didn't want to upset him.

Charles offered his arm and asked, "May I escort you to dinner?"

Georgie allowed him to lead her out of her bedchamber.

"I wanted to apologize for striking you last night," Charles said, glancing over at her as they walked down the hall. "That was in bad form."

Georgie remained silent, unsure of what to say. What about all the other times he had hit her without provocation? Did he have remorse for those times, as well?

"I do not take pleasure in hitting you, mind you," Charles continued, "but sometimes I feel that it is the only way you will listen."

"I listen to you," she attempted.

Charles frowned. "Not well enough. You are much too headstrong for a woman of your station."

"I disagree," she replied. "Mother and Father raised me to have a voice."

"They were wrong to do so," Charles stated. "Women are meant to be seen, but not heard."

"How archaic of you, brother."

Charles tensed, and Georgie feared that she had pushed him too far, which was something she was doing far too often lately.

"It would serve you well to learn how to bite your tongue," he warned.

"I know how to behave."

"Then prove it to me," Charles said as they started descending the stairs. "I want you to be most attentive to our guest this evening."

"Why did you invite Lord Ransdale?"

"He is my friend and just arrived in Town," Charles said. "It is in your best interest to behave, or else I can assure you that you will not like the consequences." His words had grown curt, and she had little doubt that he was in earnest.

"I understand," she murmured. She knew there was no point in arguing with him, not when he got like this.

Charles led her through the entry hall and Georgie felt dread fill her steps at the thought of seeing Lord Ransdale again. She detested this man and how he made her feel: small, inferior, less than—all of that and more.

She stepped into the drawing room and saw Lord Ransdale standing by the window, looking bored. He had a narrow jaw, a slightly crooked nose, and his ears fanned out from his face.

He turned to face her and smiled, and her skin crawled in response. "Miss Holbrooke," he said as he slid his gaze possessively up and down the length of her. "You look lovely."

Knowing what was expected of her, she replied, "That is kind of you to say."

Lord Ransdale approached and came to a stop in front of her. "You will discover that I value punctuality. I do not like to be kept waiting."

Her brother interjected, "Georgie is usually very punctual. It is one of her greatest strengths."

Georgie snuck a glance at her brother, wondering why he would say something so utterly ridiculous. Was Lord Ransdale insinuating that she, who'd come down with the master of the house, was late to her own dinner?

"I am glad to hear that," Lord Ransdale said. "Without punctuality, we are no better than the animals."

Her brother lowered his arm and stepped away from her. "Shall we adjourn to the dining room?"

"I think that is a splendid idea," Georgie said. She would agree to anything if it meant speeding this evening up.

Lord Ransdale offered his arm and asked, "May I escort you?"

Georgie hesitated as she looked down at his arm. To refuse him would be rude, and she would be severely punished if she did so.

With great reluctance, she placed her hand on his and tried to ignore the sickly feeling that she felt in the pit of her stomach.

Lord Ransdale reached for her hand and secured it in the crook of his arm. "I prefer you closer, my dear."

Georgie wished she was anywhere but here. She was well aware that the gossips whispered about how Lord Ransdale took advantage of his female servants, abandoning them when they started increasing. He was not a man she cared to spend any time with, much less be associated with.

They didn't speak as Lord Ransdale led her into the dining room, for which she was most grateful. She had nothing to say to him. He waved off the footman and pulled her chair out. After she sat down, he pushed her chair in and claimed the seat next to her.

Lord Ransdale reached for her linen napkin and draped it on her lap. "We wouldn't want you to soil your pretty gown," he said.

Charles sat at the head of the table, appearing unconcerned by Lord Ransdale's familiar behavior.

Georgie reached for her glass and took a sip. She knew she just needed to get through this night and hoped she wouldn't have to see Lord Ransdale ever again.

"I was saddened to hear about the death of your father," Lord Ransdale said.

Charles reached for his glass. "It was most fortunate that he didn't suffer like my mother did. He didn't want that."

"Have you taken up your seat in the House of Lords?" Lord Ransdale asked.

"Not yet," Charles replied, "but that is why we are in London for the Season."

Lord Ransdale shifted his gaze towards Georgie. "It is a shame that you are in mourning, and you haven't been able to enjoy the Season."

"It is an honor to mourn my father," Georgie stated.

Lord Ransdale reached out and laid a hand on her sleeve. "I am glad that you chose to forego your mourning gown this evening," he said. "Dare I hope that you wore this gown for me?"

"My brother requested that I wear this gown," she informed him.

"It is true," Charles said. "My sister looks much too drab in dark colors."

Lord Ransdale removed his hand when a servant placed a bowl of soup in front of him. "I agree," he remarked. "You are much too beautiful to hide behind mourning clothes."

"I am not hiding," she contended. "When one loses a parent, they are expected to mourn for six months."

"A foolish tradition, if you ask me," Lord Ransdale said as he reached for his spoon.

Georgie bit her tongue, knowing her brother would not approve if she insulted their guest. Instead, she started to eat her soup, hoping they would converse with one another and leave her be. But she was not so lucky.

"Georgie is quite accomplished," her brother announced. "My parents saw to that, sending her to Mrs. Perry's Finishing School for her education."

"That is a fine school." Lord Ransdale waved his spoon in the air as he spoke. "My mother preferred that my sister remained at home with a governess."

"That is a respectable choice," Georgie said.

"Not in my eyes," Lord Ransdale responded. "My sister is much too coddled. She needs to learn how to become a dutiful wife and run a household. The most efficient way for that to happen is for her to be sent away."

"May I ask how old your sister is?" Georgie asked.

"She is thirteen."

"She is young. There is still time," Georgie remarked.

Lord Ransdale placed his spoon down and waved the footman over. "Inform the cook that I did not enjoy the pea soup. It was much too bland for my tastes." He turned his attention towards Charles. "It is my fault, really. My French cook can rival any chef at the palace, ruining me for any cook that is subpar."

Charles flicked his wrist at the footman. "I have had enough, as well," he said. "I have been meaning to hire a new cook."

Georgie let out a small gasp. "But Mrs. Peters has been with us since we were children!"

"Yes, and we have dealt with her poor cooking for far too long," Charles remarked in a bored tone.

"But Charles—"

He spoke over her. "Save your breath, Georgie," he stated, his tone brooking no argument. "I have made my decision."

Georgie lowered her gaze as a footman came to collect her bowl. Her chest felt heavy. Mrs. Peters held a special place in her heart, and she couldn't imagine not having her in her life. She spent a great deal of time conversing with the cook over the years, especially after her mother died.

She had to convince Charles to change his mind. But how would she accomplish such a feat?

Chapter Two

Georgie was having the most delightful dream when she was awakened by the sound of her door closing. She reluctantly opened her eyes to the sight of her lady's maid pacing the floor, looking distressed.

"Whatever is the matter?" Georgie asked.

"I just heard the most distressing news."

Georgie moved to rest her back against the wall. "Which is?"

Alice stopped pacing and turned to face her. "You would want to know the truth, even if it was life altering. Wouldn't you?"

"I would."

With a frown on her lips, Alice sat near her on the bed. "I didn't hear this firsthand, mind you, but I heard it from Wilson, who heard it from Brown."

"What are you trying to tell me?"

Alice held her breath a moment before revealing, "Lord Wakefield has arranged a marriage for you."

"With whom?" Georgie asked as her heart dropped to her stomach.

"Lord Ransdale."

Georgie shot up straight in her bed. "Please say that is not so."

"I wish I could, but Brown overheard it this morning. He walked by Lord Wakefield's study this morning when he was meeting with his solicitor."

"This cannot be," Georgie stated, bringing a hand to her head. "I refuse to marry that horrid man."

"What choice do you have?" Alice asked.

Georgie threw the covers off and slid her legs over the side of the bed. "I will go speak to Charles at once," she said. "With any luck, he will listen to what I have to say."

"And what if he doesn't?"

"I don't rightly know," Georgie sighed as she rose, "but I can't marry Lord Ransdale. I would be utterly miserable for the rest of my days."

"Perhaps it wouldn't be that bad," Alice said. "He is an earl."

"I wouldn't care if he was a prince." Georgie retrieved her white wrapper from where it was draped over the back of the settee. "I will not marry a man that makes my skin crawl."

"How do you intend to convince Lord Wakefield of that?"

"I am hoping he will be somewhat reasonable, and we can talk rationally about it," Georgie replied as she tied the wrapper on.

"He is not known for his flexibility."

"I have to try," Georgie said as she walked over to the door. "Wish me luck."

Alice rose from the bed. "Do try to avoid making him angry."

"I don't intend to."

Georgie opened the door and stepped out into the hall. She had to convince her brother that she would never suit with Lord Ransdale. He was vain, pretentious, and entirely wrong for her. She could hardly stand being in the same room as him; how would she ever survive being his wife?

As she approached the study, she tried to calm her growing nerves. The last thing she needed was for Charles to accuse her of hysterical behavior. She knew this would be a most difficult conversation, but she refused to do nothing and accept her fate. Surely, she thought, my brother wouldn't wish for me to be forever miserable.

Georgie stepped into the study, where her brother was sitting at his desk. He glanced up when she stepped into the room.

"Ah, Georgie. I'm glad you are here," he said.

"You are?" She faltered. She had not expected that reaction.

He nodded. "Come here and sign these documents."

"What would you have me sign?"

Charles reached for the quill. "The details should hardly matter to you."

"But they do," Georgie said as she came to a stop in front of the desk and peered at the papers atop it. "I want to know what I am signing."

Lowering the quill, Charles replied, "It is your marriage contract to Lord Ransdale."

Georgie straightened and squared her shoulders. "I do not want to sign it."

Charles gave her an uninterested look. "Why is that?" he asked.

"Lord Ransdale and I would never suit." There. That was the truth.

"Why does that matter?"

Georgie pursed her lips. "I do not want to marry a man that I detest," she said after a moment.

"Detest is such a strong word," Charles said. "Pray tell, what has Lord Ransdale done to earn your ire?"

"His possessive stare bores into me and it makes me uncomfortable."

"He is just admiring you."

"It is more than that," Georgie said. "He doesn't value my opinion."

"Why should he?"

Georgie moved to sit on the upholstered armchair facing the desk, then changed her mind and stood behind it instead. "I would like my husband to appreciate my mind."

"That would be trivial," Charles remarked. "Women have one duty, and that is to bear heirs."

"What of love?"

Charles scoffed. "Love?" he said. "That is a useless emotion."

"Mother and Father loved each other," Georgie contested.

"Yes, and where did it get them?" Charles demanded. "Father became a shell of the man he once was after Mother died."

"He was grieving for her."

"He was weak, and he didn't focus on what was truly important."

"Which was?"

Charles stood and leaned forward over the desk. "Making sure our estate was profitable. If Father hadn't died when he did, we might have lost everything."

Georgie's brows wrinkled. "Surely it wasn't that bad."

"It was," Charles said. "It takes hard work to run an estate, and Father was too busy staring at Mother's portrait, focusing entirely too much on his past."

"You are being unfair to him."

"I am not. You are just a woman and cannot possibly understand the complexities of running an estate."

"You could teach me."

Charles guffawed. "Why would I do that?" he asked. "That is like asking a pig to provide me with milk."

Georgie tensed. "It is hardly the same."

"It is just as ludicrous," Charles responded. "You spend

your days in useless pursuits; nothing you do is of real importance."

"I can do more with my life. I just need to be given the opportunity."

Charles shook his head. "Father and Mother indulged you far too much. You have a sense of grandeur about you that I find disconcerting."

"Father thought it was important that I know my own mind."

"Well, Father is not here," Charles said, "is he?"

Georgie grew silent. "I wish he was," she murmured.

Charles walked around the desk and came to stand in front of her. "You will do your duty and marry Lord Ransdale."

"I will not."

"I beg your pardon?" Charles asked, his tone taking on an edge.

Georgie tilted her chin up even as her knuckles turned white where they gripped the chair. "I do not want to marry Lord Ransdale."

"I already signed the contract," Charles said through gritted teeth. "Your signature is not truly necessary, but I thought it was a nice gesture."

"Lord Ransdale and I do not suit."

"That matters little to me. Lord Ransdale wants to marry you, and you should be grateful to be securing such an auspicious marriage."

"Regardless, I am in mourning, and it is entirely inappropriate for me to wed."

Charles flicked his wrist derisively. "The *ton* will be forgiving once they see how much you adore your husband."

"I will never love him."

"It doesn't matter if you do or not," Charles said, "but when you are at social events, you will be mindful to behave, or else your husband will have no choice but to discipline you."

"Father never disciplined Mother."

Charles grabbed her chin and yanked it down. "He was a fool not to," he stated, "and I am not weak like Father."

With a shaky voice, Georgie pressed, "I won't marry him."

Charles released her chin and slapped her hard across the cheek, causing the chair to wobble from the force that shook her. "You will marry him!"

Georgie stared at the document on the desk as she cradled her face. "No. You can't force me."

Charles grabbed her shoulders and shook forcefully as he turned her to face him.

"Why do you make me hurt you?" he demanded. "This is all your fault. You just have to be difficult!"

"I won't throw my life away by marrying Lord Ransdale."

"You will be a countess," he growled.

"I don't care!"

Charles grabbed her arm and wrenched her out from behind the chair. "I apologize if I gave you the impression that you had a choice in the matter," he snarled.

Finding strength inside of her that she didn't know she had, she shouted, "I won't ever agree to this union!"

Charles's eyes narrowed, and he struck her so hard that she fell to the ground. "I don't need your permission, dear sister," he hissed as he loomed over her.

She'd braced herself for another blow when the butler appeared in the doorway. "Your coach is waiting out front, my lord," Wilson informed him in a tone that seemed too normal to Georgie's ears.

"I am busy at the moment!" Charles bellowed.

Wilson remained in the doorway. "I understand, but you do not want to be late to the House of Lords."

Indecision crossed Charles's face before it grew hard again. "You are right. I have commitments to uphold."

Charles crouched down next to Georgie, and she flinched. "We will continue this conversation later," he said, his voice lowered, "when there are no prying ears to save you."

Charles rose and departed from the room without another word. Georgie sat up and saw the tall, broad-shouldered butler come stand next to her.

Wilson put his hand out. "May I help you, Miss?"

"Thank you," she replied, gratefully accepting his assistance.

Once she was standing, she removed her hand from his and brought it up to her cheek. "How does it look?" she asked.

Wilson's eyes held compassion. "I'm afraid it is rather red."

Georgie sighed. "I assumed as much. He hit me rather hard this time," she said. "Thank you for saving me when you did."

"I wish I could do more."

Georgie attempted to smile but the pain in her cheek prevented her from doing so. "You did enough," she assured him.

"Would you like me to retrieve Alice for you?"

"That won't be necessary," Georgie replied. "I think it might be best if I go lie down for a while."

"I will go to the kitchen and find something to help with the swelling."

Tears came to Georgie's eyes. "It's getting worse," she admitted.

"Aye," Wilson replied in a solemn voice. "That it is."

"If you hadn't come when you did… I fear what my brother could be capable of, especially since I had no intention of relenting."

"You are much too stubborn for your own good." Wilson smiled to soften his words.

Georgie reached up and wiped a tear that was rolling down her cheek. "I won't marry Lord Ransdale."

Wilson's smile slipped. "Then he will kill you."

"I wish I could disagree."

"What are you going to do?"

Georgie shrugged. "What can I do?" she asked. "I have nowhere to go that Charles couldn't find me."

"That is what I am worried about."

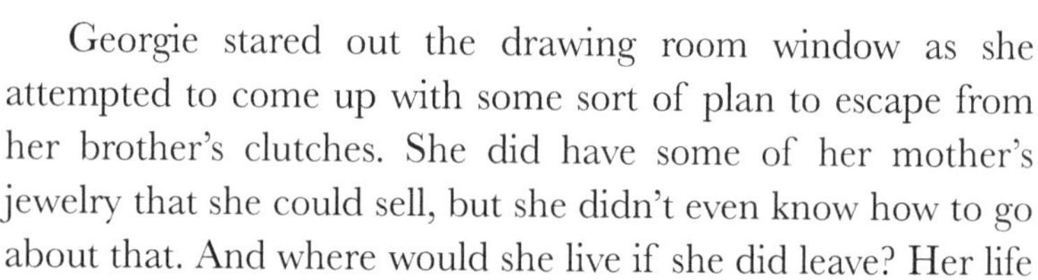

Georgie stared out the drawing room window as she attempted to come up with some sort of plan to escape from her brother's clutches. She did have some of her mother's jewelry that she could sell, but she didn't even know how to go about that. And where would she live if she did leave? Her life was far too sheltered for her to even begin to believe that she could manage to live on her own.

She was trapped in a gilded cage, and she hated it. How she wished she had the strength to run away and defy her brother! But that required knowledge of the streets that she did not possess. She was brought up to be a lady, not to live like a pauper.

The door opened and Alice stepped into the room. "You need to come with me," she ordered.

"Where?"

"To the servant's quarters," Alice replied before she disappeared back into the hall.

The strange behavior piqued her curiosity, and Georgie followed Alice into the hall. They walked in silence as Georgie hurried to keep up with Alice's quick pace. Once they arrived at the red door that led to the servant's stairs, Alice opened it and stood to the side.

Georgie put her hand on the railing and carefully descended the rickety stairs. Once she was at the bottom, she saw a group of servants standing around the kitchen, all of them intently watching her.

Alice brushed past her and said, "Come along."

Georgie walked towards the kitchen and saw the rounded Mrs. Peters standing next to Wilson. "What is all of this?" she asked.

Mrs. Peters frowned when her eyes landed on her face. "He hurt you really bad, didn't he?"

Georgie placed a hand to her swollen cheek and winced. "He did, but it is nothing that won't heal."

"This time," Mrs. Peters said. "Which is why we have come up with a plan to help you."

Georgie gave her a weak smile. "That is kind of you, of all of you, but I'm afraid no one can help me."

Mrs. Peters gestured towards a stool. "Have a seat and we will tell you of our plan," she said. "We think it is quite brilliant, and have been busy crafting it all morning."

Curious, Georgie sat down. There was no harm in listening, especially since they had gone through all of the trouble to attempt to help her.

Mrs. Peters's hands grew animated as she spoke. "My brother is a solicitor and has just informed me that his employer is looking for a lady to work as headmistress of an orphanage, and I took the liberty of speaking to him about you this morning."

Georgie's brows shot up. "You cannot be in earnest," she said. "I know nothing about being a headmistress."

"I know, but his employer is very insistent that the headmistress must be a lady. My brother is confident that your lack of experience is not as important as your status."

"I do not know what to say," Georgie said. "I have never done such work a day in my life."

Mrs. Peters's eyes held understanding. "I thought of that, but you are clever. I have no doubt that you will thrive in the position."

"You have entirely too much confidence in me."

"I have watched you grow up, and I know precisely what kind of lady you are," Mrs. Peters said. "You have a kind heart and do not deserve your brother's ill treatment."

"That is kind of you to say, but I know nothing about running an orphanage."

Wilson stepped forward. "This is not a permanent situation," he said. "You will only have to do so until you reach the age of your majority."

"Which is only a few months away," Mrs. Peters remarked.

"Exactly," Wilson responded. "You can remain hidden in the rookeries, far away from Lord Wakefield's fists."

"I have never been to the rookeries before," Georgie admitted.

"The accommodations will not be what you are accustomed to, but it will keep you safe," Mrs. Peters said. "You won't be forced to do anything that you don't want to do."

"Then, when the time is right, you can claim your inheritance and move far away," Wilson remarked, "and we will go with you."

Georgie glanced around and saw the servants bobbing their heads in unison. "I appreciate what you are doing, but I fear what my brother will do to everyone once he discovers that you are complicit in this."

"Do not fear for us," Wilson stated. "We are all here now because we are concerned for your safety."

"That is most generous of everyone," Georgie said as she glanced about the room before turning her gaze back towards Mrs. Peters. "And your brother is sure that his employer will hire me?"

"He is," Mrs. Peters said. "Aaron was quite excited about the prospect of you being the headmistress. He has been looking far and wide for someone that fits your description."

Georgie knew this was her one—only—chance to escape from her brother. She didn't know anything about running an orphanage, but she was a quick learner. Besides, this was only temporary. Once she turned twenty-one, she would gain access to her inheritance, which included a small estate in Brighton. Then her brother could never hurt her again. Frankly, what did she have to lose?

Georgie squared her shoulders. "I will do it."

Mrs. Peters clasped her hands together. "Wonderful! We shall have such fun together."

"We?"

"The orphanage is also looking to hire a cook, and I was let go this morning," Mrs. Peters revealed.

"I'm sorry for that."

"Don't be," Mrs. Peters responded. "I think it is the perfect solution. Besides, I couldn't stand working for the new Lord Wakefield."

Wilson held his hand out to assist Georgie in rising. "Alice has taken the liberty of packing your trunks, and they are strapped onto the coach."

Georgie blinked. "You wish for me to leave right now?"

"It would be for the best," Wilson replied. "Lord Wakefield is at the House of Lords, and, with any luck, he won't notice your absence until dinner."

"He will be irate."

"I assume as much."

"What if he fires you?"

"Then so be it," Wilson responded. "I can't stand by in good conscience and let him continue to hurt you."

Georgie smiled up at the butler. "You are a good man, Wilson."

Wilson's eyes crinkled up at the corners as he returned her smile. "I told your father that I would watch over you, and I am just living up to the promise."

"It is more than that," Georgie said, hoping her words conveyed her appreciation. "You have always been there for me, no matter what has transpired."

"That is a job of any good butler."

Mrs. Peters motioned towards the door. "Shall we? We should depart soon if we want to arrive in the rookeries before dark."

Georgie's eyes roamed over the servants gratefully, and she smiled her thanks. "Do take care of yourselves."

As Georgie departed the servant's quarters, she saw their black coach waiting on the street for them. A footman held the door open for her and assisted her as she stepped inside. She had just situated herself when Mrs. Peters and Alice entered and sat across from her.

Georgie looked at Alice in surprise. "You're coming, too?"

Alice nodded. "I couldn't let you go to the orphanage by yourself," she replied. "Who would dress you or style your hair?"

Georgie let out a sigh of relief. "I was wondering the same thing."

The coach merged into traffic and Georgie closed her eyes, feeling a profound sense of relief the further she got away from the townhouse. With any luck, her brother would never be able to hurt her again and she would be free to do as she pleased.

Alice's voice broke through her musings. "Are you having second thoughts?"

Georgie met Alice's gaze. "I am not."

"That's good. It's too late to turn around now."

"I have no desire to ever return to my family's town-house," Georgie confessed. "It used to be filled with love and laughter, but now it is bleak."

"But it is your home."

"Not anymore. It hasn't felt like home since Father died."

Mrs. Peters leaned forward and patted her knee. "You have had a rough go of it, but it will all work out for you. You shall see."

"I just want to live quietly in Brighton."

"You will," Mrs. Peters said. "You just have to get through these next few months at the orphanage, and I will be there to help you."

"What kind of orphanage requires a lady to run it?" Georgie asked.

Mrs. Peters shrugged. "I know not, but my brother has been frantically trying to find a lady to become the head-mistress."

"Who is his employer?"

"Lord Grenton," Mrs. Peters replied. "His mother had made preparations to open the orphanage when she became sick."

"Still, is it not odd that Lord Grenton demanded a lady?" Georgie pressed. "There must be many women not of the *ton* who would be competent in running an orphanage."

"It is odd, but from what I heard, Lord Grenton can be rather demanding."

Georgie clutched her hands together in her lap. "What if Lord Grenton meets me and finds me lacking?" she asked. "He might not hire me, and then what will become of me?"

"You must not fret about that," Mrs. Peters encouraged. "I would never have recommended you if I thought you would fail."

Alice spoke up. "I did bring along some pieces of your mother's jewelry. I thought you could sell it if it came to that."

"I just might have to," Georgie said, then gagged as an awful smell wafted through the window. "What is that terrible stench?"

Alice reached over and closed the window. "We are in the rookeries now."

Georgie brought her hand up to her scrunched nose. "I don't think I have smelled anything so foul before. It's awful."

She turned her attention towards the window and saw poorly constructed, blackened dwellings crammed together. Men with patched trousers and women in shapeless, faded dresses walked along the gloomy pavements. It was a far cry from what she was accustomed to.

Alice appeared unaffected by the smell. "I grew up a few miles down the street, a few blocks from the River Thames," she shared.

"I hadn't realized that you lived in the rookeries."

"It was shortly after my sixth birthday that my mother arranged for me to work at your townhouse."

"You were only six?" Georgie asked in disbelief.

"I was, and I was lucky to find work," Alice replied. "I worked my way all the way up from a scullery maid."

Mrs. Peters nodded approvingly. "And you did a fine job at that."

"My mother still lives in the rookeries, and I try to visit her whenever I am able to," Alice said, "but I'm afraid those opportunities are scarce."

"Why didn't you say anything?" Georgie asked. "I would have gladly given you time off to visit your mother."

"I didn't want to be a bother."

"That is rubbish. You must go visit your mother more frequently now that we are in close proximity to her."

Alice gave her a grateful look. "Thank you."

The coach came to a stop in front of a two-level faded red brick building. A sign above the door announced it as the Cobbett Orphanage for Young Women. The building, though old, was well-kept, and the pavement in front had recently been swept.

A footman stepped off his perch and approached the main door. He knocked and waited for a long moment. The door was opened by a thin woman with a pointed nose. She spoke to the footman, but not before casting a disapproving look at the coach.

The footman walked over to the coach and opened the door. "I would suggest you make haste inside, miss," he advised as he offered his hand.

Georgie accepted his assistance and exited the coach. As she released his hand, she noticed grubby-looking men loitering in the alleyways near the orphanage, and she found herself shuddering at their blatant perusal.

"Do not give them any heed," Alice said as she came to stand next to her. "They are just surprised to see a lady in this part of town."

Mrs. Peters headed towards the open door of the orphanage. "Come along, then," she encouraged over her shoulder.

They walked into the brick building and stopped in the modest entry hall. The thin woman greeted them with a critical eye. "I am Mrs. Hughes, the housekeeper here," she said. "You must be Miss Lloyd."

Georgie opened her mouth to correct the housekeeper when Mrs. Peters met her gaze, her eyes urging her to remain quiet.

Mrs. Hughes continued. "Mr. Mason informed me that you would be arriving today, but your room is not ready yet," she revealed. "I'm afraid I have had more pressing issues to deal with."

"That is understandable," Georgie remarked.

"No doubt your room will not be what you are accustomed to, but you will have clean sheets," Mrs. Hughes said. "I have yet to hang the drapes, but I have rid your room of the rats."

"Rats?" Georgie asked.

Mrs. Hughes's lips twitched. "The rookeries are overrun with rats, and we have no choice but to share the space with them."

Georgie hesitantly glanced at the floor, half-expecting to see a rat scurrying around. "I understand."

Turning, Mrs. Hughes started walking down a narrow hall with yellow floral wallpaper. "I hope you don't mind, but your lady's maid will be sharing a room with you. I have put a pallet near the wall to accommodate her since we don't have any extra space."

Mrs. Hughes stepped into a small room off the hall, and they followed her in. "This is your office," she said, gesturing about the room. "I know it isn't much, but we converted this space just for you."

Georgie's eyes landed on the desk near a window that looked out into the alley. Empty bookshelves lined one wall, and a lumpy upholstered armchair sat in the corner.

Mrs. Hughes walked behind the desk and picked up a crate. She dropped it onto the desk and announced, "Up until now, Mr. Mason was handling the books for the orphanage, but that will now be your duty."

"I shall see to it," Georgie said, hoping she sounded more confident than she felt.

Mrs. Hughes shifted her gaze towards Mrs. Peters. "I understand that you are to be the cook."

"I am," Mrs. Peters replied.

"I have never heard of a headmistress bringing her own cook, much less a lady's maid before," Mrs. Hughes stated, her voice dripping with disapproval.

Mrs. Peters stepped forward, her voice steady. "My brother assured me that my assistance would be welcomed. Was he wrong to assume so?"

"He was not," Mrs. Hughes replied. "The girls will be most grateful for something other than the mush I prepare, but I must warn you that you will have limited resources here."

"You need not concern yourself with that," Mrs. Peters responded.

Mrs. Hughes forced a smile to her lips. "The girls are attending to their chores at the moment, but you shall meet them tonight at dinner."

Georgie walked over to the window and looked out. "It isn't much of a view, but it will have to do."

Mrs. Hughes dropped into an exaggerated curtsy. "If you will excuse me, I need to see to a few things before I continue the tour," she said before she departed from the room.

Once they were left alone, Georgie remarked, "I don't think Mrs. Hughes likes me very much."

"You aren't here to make friends," Mrs. Peters advised. "Your job is to run the orphanage until you reach your majority."

Georgie smoothed back her brown hair. "Then let's get to work."

Chapter Three

Georgie sat in her office as she tried to make sense of the pile of receipts that covered the desk. When she was younger, she used to watch her father as he worked on his ledgers. He had made it look so easy, so effortless. She didn't even know where to begin.

A lone candle burned on the desk, and she wondered if Charles had learned of her disappearance yet. She feared for the household staff that she'd left behind, since her brother was not a man to be trifled with. It made her appreciate their sacrifice even more. She couldn't fail them, not now. She would do whatever it took for her to succeed.

A knock came at the door.

"Enter," she ordered.

The door opened and Mrs. Peters stepped into the room with a man following close behind. "I do hope I am not intruding."

"Not at all," Georgie replied. "I could use the interruption."

Mrs. Peters gestured towards the man. "Allow me to introduce you to my brother, Mr. Aaron Mason."

Mr. Mason stepped forward and bowed. "It is a pleasure

to be meeting you," he said. "I have heard so much about you over the years that I feel as if we are already acquainted."

"You have me worried now, Mr. Mason," Georgie remarked lightly.

"I can assure you that my sister only spoke highly of you." Mr. Mason removed the satchel draped over his shoulder and placed it on the floor. "Am I safe to assume that you have settled in?"

"I have; now I am just trying to sort through all the paperwork," she said, waving her hand over the desk.

"I would be happy to render any assistance that you require," Mr. Mason offered.

"Thank you," Georgie responded. "It is most kind of you to offer."

Mrs. Peters closed the door. "I hope you do not mind, but it would be best if we continued this conversation in private."

"I concur," Mr. Mason said. "I'm afraid what I wish to discuss is a rather delicate matter."

Georgie leaned back in her seat as she waited for Mr. Mason to elaborate.

With a side glance at his sister, Mr. Mason remarked, "I hope you do not mind, but Esther spoke to me in length about your situation."

"I imagined that would have been the case."

"I want you to know that you have my deepest sympathies, and I abhor the situation that your brother placed you in," Mr. Mason said, his gaze flicking to her bruised cheek.

Georgie gave him a weak smile. "I hope it is in the past."

"Quite right," Mr. Mason agreed. "Which is why we feel it is our duty to protect you from Lord Wakefield."

Mrs. Peters bobbed her head. "He cannot ever know where you have gone, at least until you have reached your majority."

"If Lord Wakefield did discover your whereabouts, it is

within his rights as your guardian to retrieve you," Mr. Mason explained. "We would be powerless to stop him."

"I am well aware," Georgie responded dolefully.

"Furthermore, we must proceed with caution to ensure that your reputation will not suffer from you working here," Mr. Mason said.

"I do not care about my reputation," Georgie stated.

"You say that now, but you might change your mind once you have received your inheritance," Mr. Mason said. "You may decide to take your rightful place in Society."

Mrs. Peters interjected, "We believe that Lord Wakefield will not notify anyone of your disappearance for fear of damaging his own reputation."

"That is a fair assumption. My brother only seems to care about himself," Georgie stated.

Mr. Mason's eyes held compassion as he said, "Esther and I decided it would be best if no one knew your true identity while you are here."

"That is what I deduced, since I was introduced as Miss Lloyd when I arrived," Georgie remarked.

Mrs. Peters sat on the lumpy chair. "You are safe here," she assured her. "There is no reason for you to leave the safety of these walls, and Lord Wakefield will never think of looking for you in the rookeries."

"It is a wonderful feeling, to be safe," Georgie said. "I have been fearful of my brother for far too long."

Mr. Mason picked up his satchel. "Lord Grenton will wish to meet you, but you do not need to worry. I have no doubt that he will approve of you."

"Why is that?"

"Because you are a lady, and he was adamant that a lady was to run the orphanage," Mr. Mason explained.

"Did he state why he wants a lady to run the orphanage?"

"It was his mother's idea."

Georgie leaned forward in her seat and asked, "Will you inform Lord Grenton of my true identity?"

Mr. Mason shook his head. "I will not, since I think it would be for the best to limit who knows the truth."

"What will you tell him?"

"As little as I can," Mr. Mason replied. "That you are a lady who has fallen on hard times since your parents died."

"Which isn't far from the truth."

"No, it is not," Mr. Mason agreed. "With any luck, Lord Grenton will pay you little heed as you go about running the orphanage."

"That would be my wish, as well."

Mr. Mason draped the satchel over his shoulder. "Lord Grenton did provide a generous income for you, but I doubt it will be what you are accustomed to."

"That is the least of my concerns," Georgie said.

"I will request for additional funds to pay for your lady's maid, but I do not know how Lord Grenton will react to that," Mr. Mason shared.

"If it comes to it, I will pay Alice out of my own income."

Mr. Mason nodded approvingly. "If you need anything, please send word, and I will come as soon as I am able."

"Thank you, Mr. Mason."

Mr. Mason glanced down at her black crepe gown. "You have my condolences on your loss," he said. "I didn't know your father, but I was well aware that he was a champion of the poor. He fought hard to alleviate their burdens in the rookeries."

"My father took his position in the House of Lords very seriously. He wanted to help as many people as he could."

"That is a mark of a good man," Mr. Mason said as he walked over to the door. "If you will excuse me, I need to depart before it gets too late."

Mrs. Peters rose. "Thank you for coming, Aaron."

Mr. Mason exchanged a smile with her. "Good evening, sister," he said before he departed from the room.

Mrs. Peters's eyes remained on the door for a long moment. "Aaron may be my younger brother, but he has always taken care of me."

"That must be a nice feeling."

"It is," Mrs. Peters agreed, bringing her gaze back to meet Georgie's. "That is what a good brother is supposed to do."

Georgie smiled wryly. "I'm afraid Charles didn't get that message."

"No, he most definitely did not," Mrs. Peters said as she approached the desk. "How are you faring?"

"I am well."

Mrs. Peters lifted her brow. "I would prefer the truth, if you don't mind."

Georgie laughed. "I don't know why I bother trying to hide anything from you," she said. "You've always been able to see right through me."

"It is a gift."

Rising, Georgie walked over to the window. "Frankly, I don't know what to feel right now," she admitted.

"That is understandable. You have been through a lot."

"I'm angry at my brother," she said, her voice rising. "I'm angry that he put me in this situation."

"You have every right to be angry. Lord Wakefield's duty was to care for you, but he failed terribly."

Georgie huffed. "That he did," she agreed. "He has been an awful brother since my father died."

Mrs. Peters walked around the desk and approached her. "He was awful before then, too, but it is time to move forward. You must not let that anger consume you. Instead, you must use that passion to help you thrive."

With a slight grimace, Georgie admitted, "I know nothing about how to run an orphanage."

"That is a good thing," Mrs. Peters said. "You could

breathe fresh life into this place. It is far too dreary for my tastes."

"I haven't even met the girls yet. I have been holed up in this study since we first arrived."

"I did notice that, especially since you missed dinner."

"I wasn't hungry."

Mrs. Peters placed a hand on her sleeve. "You must take care of yourself first and foremost if you want to be able to help others."

Georgie bit her lower lip before she voiced her greatest fear. "What if I fail?"

"That is impossible. I know what you are capable of," Mrs. Peters said. "I have known you since you were a little girl, and you have never once disappointed me."

"I fear that you might be biased."

Lowering her hand to the side, Mrs. Peters replied, "I know I am, but it changes nothing."

Georgie gave her a grateful look. "Thank you, Mrs. Peters," she said. "You always seem to know the perfect thing to say."

A knock came at the door before it was pushed open, revealing Alice. "I have turned down your sheets and scoured the room for any signs of rats."

"Did you find any?" Georgie asked.

Alice looked hesitant. "I do not think you want to know the answer to that question."

Mrs. Peters stepped back and encouraged, "Go to bed. This work will be here for you tomorrow."

Georgie's eyes swept over the disheveled desktop. "That is a lovely thought," she murmured.

It was still dark, but Georgie was wide awake, attempting

to ignore the straw poking through her bedding. She had never slept on a straw mattress before, and it was easily the worst sleeping situation she'd experienced to date. How she missed her feather mattress!

She'd had a fitful night of sleep and saw no reason to remain in bed a moment longer. She sat up and swung her legs over the side of the bed, the only sound in the room was that of Alice lightly snoring in the corner.

Rising, Georgie walked over to the window and saw that the sun was just starting to rise, bringing with it a whole new day. She should feel elated that she was safe, far away from her brother, but all she felt was trepidation. The thought of failing weighed heavily on her conscience. These girls were depending on her, and she knew nothing about running an orphanage. And what of the servants that she had left behind? Had her brother punished them for aiding in her escape?

Georgie leaned her head against the window frame. Tears welled up in her eyes as she thought about her father. She wished that he was still alive. He had always doted on her, and she loved nothing more than spending time with him. What she wouldn't give to hear his voice one more time. No doubt he would tell her that everything would be okay, and she would have believed him, for her father had never lied to her.

A tear escaped and slid down her cheek. She reached up to wipe it away. There was no point in crying. It would solve nothing.

The sound of a floorboard creaking in the hall drew her attention. Who else was awake? She went to retrieve her wrapper and put it on, then stepped quickly to the door and opened it.

As she glanced down the hall, she saw that it was empty; but she was sure that she had heard something. She exited her bedchamber, quietly closing the door behind her, and started walking down the hall. She wasn't entirely sure where she was going, and for what purpose, but she felt an inquisitive interest, nonetheless.

The worn floorboards were cold on her feet, but she pressed on. She had just passed the stairs when she saw a silhouette in the darkness approaching her from down the hall. Fear resonated within her, and she realized she hadn't fully thought this through.

Georgie decided not to confront the person and hurried towards the closest door. She opened it and slipped inside. Once she closed the door, she saw that she was in the girl's sleeping quarters. Beds were lined up next to each other and the only light came from the lone window on the far wall.

A towheaded girl sat up in bed and looked at her with sleepy eyes. "Is it time to wake up?" she asked quietly.

"Not yet," Georgie said. "You may go back to sleep."

"I don't think I can."

"Why is that?" Georgie asked as she walked closer to the bed.

"I had a terrible dream."

Georgie sat at the foot of the bed. "Do you want to talk about it?"

The girl shook her head.

"You are safe here," Georgie assured her. "No harm will come to you."

The child didn't appear convinced. "Are you the new headmistress?"

"I am."

"Mrs. Hughes says that we aren't supposed to talk to you."

"Why is that?"

The girl lowered her gaze. "She said that you are a lady, and you don't want to associate with urchins like us."

Taken aback, Georgie said, "Mrs. Hughes was wrong. I look forward to becoming acquainted with all of you."

"You do?" the girl asked, looking up.

Georgie nodded. "I do," she replied. "What's your name?"

"Rebecca."

"That is a lovely name," Georgie acknowledged. "How old are you?"

"I'm six."

Georgie smiled. "It is nice to meet you, Rebecca. My name is Miss Hol…" Her voice stopped and she rushed to correct herself. "Miss Lloyd."

"Do you live in a castle?"

"No, I do not," Georgie said. "Only princesses live in castles."

The door opened and Mrs. Hughes stepped into the room with a candle in her hand. "Girls!" she called. "It is time to get up!"

Mrs. Hughes's eyes landed on Georgie, and she asked, "Dear heavens, what on earth are you doing in here?"

Georgie rose. "I was becoming more acquainted with Rebecca."

"You shall have more time for that later, but Rebecca is needed downstairs," Mrs. Hughes said. "Come along, now."

Rising, Rebecca groaned. "I don't want to clean out the fireplaces today."

"If you continue to complain, I will assign you additional chores," Mrs. Hughes directed. "You know the rules."

Rebecca pressed her lips together and followed the rest of the girls out of the room, her shoulders slumped.

Once they were left alone, Mrs. Hughes gave Georgie a disapproving look. "You would be mindful to remember that the girls are here to acquire skills to survive in this harsh world. They are not here to chit-chat and be idle."

"What kind of skills?"

"We teach them how to become scullery maids, and with any luck, they will be hired at a grand house."

"Do you not teach them how to read?"

Mrs. Hughes gave her a blank stare. "Why would they need to know how to read?"

"Surely, you cannot be in earnest," Georgie pressed.

"No one wants to hire a scullery maid that has grand notions," Mrs. Hughes said. "Besides, these girls are not smart enough to learn to read."

"That is awfully unfair of you to say."

Mrs. Hughes stepped forward and lowered her voice. "Do not give these girls false hope that they can rise above their stations," she remarked. "That would be cruel of you to do so."

"I didn't realize I was doing anything of the sort."

"Despite your reduced circumstances now, you were given opportunities that these girls can only dream about," Mrs. Hughes said. "Do you think it is fair to rub that in their faces?"

"That was never my intention."

With a haughty look, Mrs. Hughes's shoulders stiffened. "If you want to help these girls, leave them be," she asserted before spinning on her heel and departing from the room.

Georgie stared at the empty doorway. There had to be a way to help these girls without ignoring them. She had only met Rebecca, but she was confident that the girls were intelligent enough to learn how to read. Although that would explain why she saw no books in the orphanage. Did no one read to these girls? How unfortunate. Some of her fondest memories were of her parents reading to her in front of a fire.

She departed from the room and headed back towards her bedchamber. As she turned the corner, she was surprised to see Wilson approaching her with a stoic look on his face.

Her steps faltered. "Whatever are you doing here?"

The butler came to a stop in front of her. "Lord Wakefield dismissed me for helping you leave, and I thought you could use some help here."

"I am happy to see you, but I daresay that we do not have the funds to pay for a butler," she admitted dejectedly.

Wilson gave her an understanding nod. "I expected as

much," he replied. "If you are in agreement, I will work for room and board."

"I'm afraid we don't even have a room to spare for you."

"I know, but you do have a floor in the kitchen that I can sleep on. That will be sufficient enough for me, at least for now."

"Are you sure?"

"I am," Wilson replied. "I have already secured a blanket and pillow from the closet."

Georgie smiled happily. "I feel that I must warn you that there are more rats here than people."

"That doesn't surprise me. We are in the rookeries."

"I do not like rats."

"Very few people do."

She glanced over her shoulder before saying, "I should also note that the housekeeper, Mrs. Hughes, does not like me."

"I have yet to have the pleasure of meeting Mrs. Hughes."

"When did you arrive?"

"This morning," Wilson said. "Mrs. Peters let me in through the back door, and I have been trying to become familiar with the orphanage ever since."

"That would explain what I saw earlier," Georgie said, feeling great relief that the dark silhouette she had seen in the hall was, in fact, Wilson.

Wilson grew serious. "You should know that Lord Wakefield hired a Bow Street Runner to look into your disappearance."

Her heart skipped a beat. "He did?"

"He was furious when he came home and you weren't there," Wilson shared. "I have never seen him so irate before."

"How did he discover you were involved?"

Wilson winced slightly. "I admitted to it when he questioned me," he shared. "He demanded to know where you went, and even threatened to have me arrested for kidnapping you."

Georgie gasped. "Oh no!" she exclaimed, her hand flying up to her mouth.

"You do not need to worry," Wilson assured her. "Lord Wakefield thought I valued my job more than you, and he was mistaken."

"But what will you do?"

"I was hoping you would require the use of a butler once you've received your inheritance."

"Most definitely."

Wilson bobbed his head. "Then I shall get to work," he said.

"I do hope you won't be bored working here."

"There is plenty for me to do, and Mrs. Peters is preparing a list for me as we speak." Wilson tipped his head, and his eyes twinkled with mirth. "If you will excuse me, Miss Lloyd."

"I am happy that you are here."

"As am I," Wilson said before he walked past her down the hall.

Georgie continued on towards her room. She opened the door and saw Alice sitting up on her bed.

"There you are," Alice said. "Where have you been?"

"I woke up early and decided to go exploring."

Rising, Alice asked, "Shall we get you dressed for the day?"

"Yes, but first I have some news to tell you."

Alice gave her an expectant look. "Which is?"

"Wilson is here," Georgie replied. "My brother dismissed him, and he sought us out. He has agreed to work here for room and board."

"A butler working at an orphanage?" Alice giggled. "It is rather humorous to think about."

"Yes, it is."

Chapter Four

William stared out the window as his valet moved around his bedchamber. It was a new day, but he suspected that it would be just like any other day—disappointing.

He had responsibilities to see to, though, and no time to dawdle. People were depending on him, and he refused to fail them as others had failed him. He did wish that other people would take their roles more seriously. He grew tired of others' shortcomings. To succeed in life, you have to put in effort and work intelligently. But some of the people under his employ did not seem to grasp this concept, and William spent more time working to make up for that lack than he liked.

He turned away from the window and headed towards the door. As he stepped into the hall, he glanced towards his mother's bedchamber. A pang of sadness hit him, as it did every morning when he remembered again that she was no longer there. He missed her.

William needed to accept it and let it go. His mother was gone, and nothing he did would bring her back. He was trying to move forward, but it was proving to be much more difficult than he had imagined. Why did his grief have to be so encompassing? It had a hold on him that he couldn't shake.

One thing he knew, standing here wallowing in self-pity would get him nowhere. He needed to learn to live without his mother, no matter how hard it was.

He headed towards the entry hall on the first level and saw Thorne at the base of the stairs.

"Good morning, my lord," Thorne greeted with the same cheerful disposition that usually grated on his ears. "I trust that you slept well."

"I did," William replied. "I will be in my study."

"Would you care for a tray to be sent in?"

"That won't be necessary," he replied. "I am not hungry this morning."

"Very good," Thorne said.

William headed towards the rear of his townhouse, where his study was tucked away in the corner. He came around his desk and sat down. He reached for the first letter from the pile of correspondence and unfolded the paper.

He had just finished reading it and put it down when Thorne stepped into the room. "Mr. Mason would like a moment of your time."

"Send him in."

Thorne tipped his head. "Yes, my lord."

His solicitor stepped into the room only a moment later with a smile on his face. "I come bearing good news," Mr. Mason said.

"Which is?"

"I have hired a headmistress for the orphanage," Mr. Mason announced as he approached the desk.

"That is surprisingly good news."

Mr. Mason removed the satchel from his shoulder and set it down on a chair. "I thought you would be pleased."

William leaned back in his seat. "Where were you able to find her?"

"Miss Lloyd recently lost her father and fell on hard

times," Mr. Mason explained. "She came highly recommended by my sister."

"What are her qualifications?"

Mr. Mason gave him a blank stare. "She is a lady."

"Yes, but what else?"

"What else matters?"

William gave him a pointed look. "How do you know this Miss Lloyd can handle the demands of running an orphanage?"

"My sister has assured me that Miss Lloyd is clever."

"You didn't ascertain that yourself?"

Mr. Mason looked unsure. "I spoke briefly to Miss Lloyd, and she appeared to be of a sound mind."

"I shall have to determine that myself."

"I assumed as much." Mr. Mason reached into his satchel and pulled out a piece of paper. "Now that is behind us, I need your signature on this document."

William wasn't ready to move forward yet. He had a few more questions. "I wish to know more about Miss Lloyd."

Mr. Mason placed the paper in front of him on the desk. "She is a pleasant young woman, just shy of her majority."

"That is quite young," William observed. "Does she not have any other family to care for her?"

"Apparently not, my lord."

"Where does she hail from?"

"Brighton."

William picked up the paper in front of him and reviewed it. "Why are you requesting additional funds for the orphanage?"

"It is to cover the expenses for the new cook and Miss Lloyd's lady's maid," Mr. Mason explained.

"A lady's maid?" William asked. "You cannot be in earnest. Why does the headmistress of an orphanage need a lady's maid?"

"You wished for the headmistress to be a lady, and ladies

are accustomed to having a personal maid. If you are opposed, Miss Lloyd has indicated that she is willing to pay for her lady's maid out of her salary."

"That would only be fair, since I have already provided her with a generous income."

"I will notify Miss Lloyd of your decision."

William glanced down at the paper before asking, "What was wrong with the last cook?"

"Mrs. Hughes is a housekeeper, not a cook," Mr. Mason shared. "She was only filling the role until a cook could be hired."

"Where did you find this cook?"

Mr. Mason shifted uncomfortably. "It is my sister, Mrs. Peters, and she came from the same household as Miss Lloyd."

"Does Miss Lloyd intend to hire footmen, as well?" William asked dryly.

"No, my lord," Mr. Mason replied.

William extended the paper towards Mr. Mason. "If Miss Lloyd wants a cook and a lady's maid, then she can pay for them herself."

"That would leave her with very little, then."

"I have little interest in maintaining her lifestyle," William said. "She needs to accept her reduced circumstances and move forward."

"But the cook benefits the whole orphanage."

William shrugged. "Mrs. Hughes was doing a fine job until Mrs. Peters arrived. I see no reason for her not to continue."

Mr. Mason opened his mouth to no doubt object, so William continued. "My decision is final, Mr. Mason."

"I will inform Miss Lloyd of this."

"That won't be necessary," William said. "I will do so myself when I visit the orphanage today."

"Do you wish for me to accompany you?"

William shook his head. "Do not trouble yourself. I want

to speak privately to Miss Lloyd to ensure that she is a good fit for the orphanage."

Mr. Mason tipped his head. "I understand," he said. "Will there be anything else?"

"Not at this time."

After Mr. Mason departed from the room, William let out a huff. What kind of pretentious young woman would take a position at an orphanage but then insist on bringing along her cook and lady's maid? Only someone down on her luck would accept the offer in the first place. He was beginning to suspect that Miss Lloyd might not be a good fit as the headmistress. She seemed far more concerned about her own wellbeing than the welfare of the girls.

Hawthorne's voice came from the doorway. "You look more surly than usual," he said, a teasing lilt in his voice.

"My solicitor just informed me that he hired a head-mistress for the orphanage."

"That is wonderful news!"

"It is—or at least, I thought it was."

Hawthorne came to sit down on a chair in front of the desk. "What are your concerns?"

"She brought a cook and a lady's maid with her," William replied.

"That is unusual."

William nodded. "I thought so as well."

"What do you intend to do?"

"I informed my solicitor that I will not be funding her lavish lifestyle," William said. "If she wishes to employ them, she will need to pay for them out of her own income."

"That is fair."

William rose and walked over to the drink cart and picked up the decanter. "I do hope that Miss Lloyd will be reason-able. If not, I will have no choice but to dismiss her."

"You would dismiss her so easily?" Hawthorne asked. "After all, it took months to find a lady to fill the position."

"I am well aware, but I do not accept incompetence of any kind." William poured two glasses of brandy and placed the decanter down. "What brings you by this morning?"

"I was hoping to convince you to go boxing with me."

William extended Hawthorne a glass and replied, "I'm afraid I am unable to go today, but I would be happy to join you at Gentleman Jack's tomorrow."

Hawthorne tossed his drink back and placed the empty glass onto the desk. "Do not worry," he said. "I will go easy on you."

With a smile, William remarked, "I must admit that I look forward to hitting you."

"Only if you are lucky," Hawthorne joked as he rose. "If you will excuse me, I need to see to a few things before our session at the House of Lords. My father asked for me to attend in place of him since he is busy with meetings today."

"Do I even want to know what occupies your time these days?"

Hawthorne smirked. "No, you don't."

"You are a man of many secrets."

"Everyone has secrets. I'm just better at keeping them."

William took a sip of his drink. As he lowered his glass, he said, "I wish you luck, at whatever it is that you are doing."

"I don't rely on luck."

"What do you rely on?"

"Instinct," Hawthorne replied before he walked over to the door. "I shall see you at the House of Lords."

After his friend departed, William couldn't help but wonder how Hawthorne occupied his time. His actions were clouded in secrecy, but it hadn't always been that way. William may be curious, but it was none of his business. Besides, he had more important things to do, starting with putting Miss Lloyd in her place.

William was in a foul mood as his coach came to a stop in front of the orphanage. He didn't have enough hours in the day to accomplish all his tasks as it was, especially as he had to run his estate from afar in order to be in Town for the Season, and now he was forced to set everything aside to visit Miss Lloyd.

He still couldn't believe the sheer audacity of her to bring her own cook and a lady's maid. It was evident that she hadn't come to terms with her reduced circumstances yet, and he would need to remind her that she now worked for her income. More importantly, she worked for *him*.

The door opened and William stepped out of the coach. He approached the orphanage door and pounded on it.

To his surprise, the door promptly opened, and he was greeted by a tall, finely dressed older man. "May I help you, sir?" the man asked.

William stared at the man. "Who are you?"

"I am Wilson, the butler."

"The butler?" William asked, stumbling over his words. What in the blazes was Miss Lloyd thinking?

Wilson opened the door wide, ushering him in. "Would you care to have this conversation inside?" he asked. "The streets can be a dangerous place."

William stepped into the entry hall and said, "I need to speak to Miss Lloyd."

"Do you have a calling card?" Wilson asked as he closed the door.

Frowning, William pulled one out of his waistcoat pocket and extended it towards him.

Wilson glanced down at the card before saying, "If you will wait here, my lord, I will see if Miss Lloyd is available."

As the butler walked down the hall, William found himself

fuming at the utter lunacy of it all. How dare Miss Lloyd employ a butler as if this was her private residence. It was an orphanage! *His* orphanage, and he refused to let Miss Lloyd make a mockery out of it!

William wasn't going to wait around to see if she would agree to see him. No; she had no choice in the matter, and she would listen to what he had to say, whether she wanted to or not.

He had just started down the hall when Wilson emerged from a doorway. "Miss Lloyd will see you now."

William didn't say anything as he stepped into the office. He opened his mouth to start his tirade, but the words died on his lips when his eyes landed on Miss Lloyd. She was stunningly beautiful, with her dark hair piled high atop her head, blue eyes, and a fair complexion. She was not at all how he'd envisioned his new headmistress. But he was not one to be swayed by a pretty face, so he mentally shook himself and returned to the task at hand.

Miss Lloyd rose from her seat. "Lord Grenton," she said, her voice gracious. "It is a pleasure to be meeting you."

Rather than exchange pleasantries, William decided to get straight to the point. "Do you take me for a fool, Miss Lloyd?"

She held his gaze, showing no sign of fear or weakness, or even surprise at having concluded with greetings so quickly. "I do not know you well enough to decide one way or another."

"You hired a butler," William said.

"I did."

"And you brought a cook and a lady's maid."

"That is true, as well."

William walked closer to the desk. "I do not know what circumstances caused you to seek out employment, nor do I care, but I expect people who work for me to be prudent."

"I understand."

"Clearly, you don't," William remarked. "A headmistress of an orphanage does not maintain a household staff."

"There were some extenuating circumstances, and I…"

William held his hand up, stilling her words. "If you wish to keep them on, their pay will come out of your income."

"That will not pose a problem."

"I doubt your income will cover a butler, so you will need to dismiss him."

Clasping her hands in front of her, Miss Lloyd demurely shared, "You will be pleased to know that Wilson has graciously agreed to work here for only room and board."

William's brow lifted. "How did you manage that feat?"

"He offered, and I accepted."

"Can you trust him?"

Miss Lloyd nodded. "Yes, he was the butler at my previous residence," she replied. "He has always been extremely loyal to my family."

"Regardless, that is one additional mouth to feed, and I do not feel a butler will prove useful at an orphanage," he said. "You will dismiss him at once."

"I will not."

"I beg your pardon?"

Miss Lloyd tilted her chin. "I can assure you that it would be a mistake to fire him."

"And why is that?" he asked, uninterested.

"We are a school comprised of women," she said. "Do you not think it would be beneficial to have a man reside with us?"

"Do you truly think a butler could protect you from ruffians?"

"It is better than nothing."

"Your notion is ridiculous, and I don't have time for this," William said. "You will do as I say, or I will dismiss you."

"So be it."

"Surely you cannot be in earnest?" William scoffed. "You would risk your employment, your livelihood, for this butler?"

"I would, gladly."

William stared at her in astonishment. He had to admit

that his respect for her grew slightly. No one dared to stand up to him, and it was clear by the stubborn tilt of her chin that Miss Lloyd was not going to back down.

Now he had a problem.

His solicitor had searched far and wide for a lady to work at the orphanage and now he had one, albeit an obstinate one. Did he dare fire her and hope that his solicitor could find another lady to fill the position?

Botheration. He knew it would be in the orphanage's best interest to keep Miss Lloyd on as the headmistress for now, no matter how much he wanted to dismiss her.

William took a step back. "Perhaps I may have been too hasty," he relented. "You may keep Wilson on as butler, assuming he will continue to work for room and board."

"That is most generous of you," Miss Lloyd acknowledged.

"We have much to discuss," William said, gesturing towards her chair. "It might be best if you take a seat."

Miss Lloyd lowered herself on her chair, her back rigid.

William retrieved the chair in the corner and placed it in front of the desk. As he sat down, he said, "I'm afraid I know very little about you other than you are in mourning for your father." He paused, perusing her black gown. "My condolences."

Miss Lloyd gave him a weak smile. "He passed a few months ago, and I must admit that I miss him dearly."

"I understand that feeling well, since my mother died only a year ago." Why had he just shared that piece of information with someone who was practically a stranger to him?

Miss Lloyd murmured her condolences.

William leaned back in his seat and asked, "Do you not have any other family to care for you?"

Miss Lloyd's eyes grew guarded. "I do not," she replied. "I am very much alone in this world."

"But you do have staff members that are loyal to you."

"I am most fortunate for that."

"That tells me a lot about you," William said. "It informs me that you are fair in your treatment of your staff."

"My mother taught me to be kind and gracious to those around me, especially the people who serve us."

William glanced down at the ledger that was open on her desk. "Do you know anything about running an orphanage?"

"I do not." In the next breath, she added, "But I am a quick learner."

"My mother was adamant that a lady run this orphanage," William shared. "She felt that it would give the girls an advantage when they sought out employment."

"It is an interesting notion."

"Yes, it is, and I intend to follow my mother's wishes," William said. "She always had an unusual way of doing things."

Miss Lloyd moved the ledger in front of her to the side as she said, "I was hoping to request a few things for the orphanage."

"Such as?"

"We are in need of books." Miss Lloyd gestured to the bare shelves in the room. "I need to be able to read to the girls."

"That won't be a problem," William said. "Create a list of books that you require, and I will see to it."

"I should warn you that the list may be extensive."

"I can't guarantee that I will secure every book on the list, so do be mindful of that."

Miss Lloyd grew silent. "I do wish to speak to you about the funding for the school."

"I believe the funding is quite generous."

"It is, but I was hoping to hire some tutors for the girls."

William furrowed his brows. "You wish to educate them?" he asked. "For what purpose?"

"I feel that the girls could be capable of so much more

than what is expected of them," Miss Lloyd said. "If we taught them the necessary skills, including the ability to read, they could seek out employment as a lady's maid."

"That is a lofty aim for these girls."

"I disagree," Miss Lloyd said. "Do we not want to give them a better life?"

"We already are by getting them off the streets."

"We can do more to help them," Miss Lloyd insisted.

William frowned. "This is not a boarding school. It is an orphanage," he remarked. "Do you know the difference?"

"I do, but—"

He spoke over her. "I do not want to hear another word on the matter. The girls will continue being trained as scullery maids."

"I think that is a mistake."

Rising, William asked, "Do you always have to get the last word in, Miss Lloyd?"

"I do," she replied, unabashed.

"It is not very becoming."

Miss Lloyd rose. "I'm afraid I have always been too outspoken for my own good."

"That can be detrimental to you, considering you are now relying on my good graces to keep you employed."

"I do appreciate this opportunity."

William held her gaze. "Do not make me regret it," he said. "If you do your job properly, we will see very little of one another."

"Yes, my lord."

Satisfied by her response, William left, confident that he'd gotten his point across.

Chapter Five

"We need to teach the girls to read," Georgie announced as she sat at the table in the kitchen.

Mrs. Peters looked up from kneading the bread. "That is quite the undertaking."

"I know, but I do believe it would help the girls find employment," Georgie said. "Just think of the possibilities that it would open up for them."

"That it would," Mrs. Peters agreed. "But who would even teach them?"

"I would," Georgie said.

"You will teach all of the girls?"

Georgie shrugged. "It may take some time, but I have plenty of that right now."

With a pointed look, Mrs. Peters said, "I thought you were supposed to manage the orphanage."

"I can do both."

Mrs. Peters wiped her flour-coated hands on her white apron. "There are nineteen girls here, ranging from ages five to twelve," she said. "I don't even know where you would begin."

It was quite a number. Georgie had discovered at breakfast

that they couldn't all fit around their one table, so the children ate meals in shifts. She'd only met half of them, and would have to be conscious of when she ate so she could spend time with the rest. Breakfast had been a somewhat subdued affair, as only the most outspoken girls had broken the silence that descended when Georgie took a place among them. She hoped familiarity would make them more comfortable in her presence and loosen their tongues.

"Lord Grenton has agreed to supply the orphanage with books," Georgie shared.

"Yes, but for the sole purpose of you reading to the girls."

"He doesn't need to know I'm using them for something else, as well."

Mrs. Peters shook her head. "You need to be careful, dearie," she counseled. "Lord Grenton may dismiss you for your impertinence."

"He never said that *I* couldn't teach the girls how to read," she said, "just that he wouldn't be hiring tutors."

"That is a ticklish argument," Mrs. Peters remarked. "I think he made his thoughts known on the matter."

"Regardless, I do believe it would be for the best if we taught the girls how to read," Georgie said. "It just feels like the right thing to do. Does it not?"

Mrs. Peters let out a sigh. "You will discover that there is a fine line between right and wrong when you are working for your income."

Georgie rose. "I refuse to sit back and do nothing when I have the time and ability to help these girls."

"You have always been too stubborn for your own good, but I worry that this will backfire on you spectacularly."

"I won't know unless I try."

"It is a good thing you are pretty," Mrs. Peters joked. "That may work in your favor when Lord Grenton comes to dismiss you."

Georgie smiled. "I doubt Lord Grenton even pays the

orphanage any heed. Most men of his station care very little for the poor."

"You cannot be certain of that," Mrs. Peters said. "Your father lobbied Parliament to help the living conditions for the people living in the rookeries."

"And it did little good."

Mrs. Peters reached for a pan and set it next to the dough. "Be mindful that working at the orphanage is only for a short time," she advised. "You don't want to get these girls' hopes up, only for you to not make good on your promise."

"I know, but I cannot in good conscience do nothing."

Mrs. Peters sighed. "If you are insistent on doing this, I can help, as well."

"Wonderful," Georgie said. "I will start by creating a list of books for Lord Grenton."

As her words left her mouth, a lanky older girl stepped into the room with a bucket in her hand. She was dressed in a loose-fitting white frock, she had dirt on her cheeks, and her blonde hair was tousled.

With downcast eyes, the girl said in a tired voice, "I have come to clean the floor."

Georgie watched until the girl brought her gaze up before saying, "Why don't you sit down and rest for a spell?" This was a perfect opportunity to become more familiar with one of her charges.

The girl shook her head vehemently. "I don't dare," she replied. "Mrs. Hughes would be furious if I did so."

"You let me worry about Mrs. Hughes," Georgie said.

The girl put the bucket down and walked hesitantly over to the chair next to her.

Georgie gave her an encouraging smile. "I was hoping we could get acquainted."

"I know who you are," the girl remarked as she sat down. "You are the headmistress."

"I am, but I'm afraid I don't know your name."

"Sarah."

"That is a beautiful name."

Sarah bobbed her head. "I was named after my mother," she shared proudly.

"I was named after my grandmother."

"Is your grandmother dead?"

"She is."

Sarah lowered her gaze. "My mother is dead, too."

"I am sorry to hear that," Georgie said. "When did she die?"

"Six months ago," Sarah replied, dejectedly. "She died in the workhouse, as did my father. They got real sick."

Georgie felt compassion swell inside of her. "But you survived."

"I did, and so did my sister," Sarah said.

"Is your sister here, as well?"

"She is."

"I'm glad that you two have each other."

Sarah's eyes swept over the floor. "Mrs. Hughes makes her clean out the fireplaces every morning. She says that small hands are best for that chore."

"I think I met your sister," Georgie said. "Is her name Rebecca?"

"It is."

"She is a lovely girl."

Sarah fidgeted with her hands in her lap. "They tried to separate us at the workhouse after my parents died, but we ran away instead."

"You did?"

"We lived on the street for a few days, until they found us and made us go back to the workhouse."

"May I ask how you ended up in the orphanage?"

Sarah pressed her lips together. "Rebecca used to have these terrible night terrors, waking the whole workhouse, and they didn't know what to do with her," she shared. "A few months ago, we were told that we were being sent to an orphanage."

"Do you enjoy living here?"

"I do, since no one beats us here," Sarah said. "I don't mind all the chores, either. It's better than what they made us do at the workhouse."

"I know you are being trained as a scullery maid, but is that what you want to do?"

Sarah gave her a baffled look. "What else would I do?"

After exchanging a look with Mrs. Peters, Georgie asked, "What if I could teach you the skills to work as a lady's maid?"

With a shake of her head, Sarah replied, "That is much too grand for someone like me."

"Why do you say that?"

"Mrs. Hughes says if I am lucky I could one day work upstairs as a maid," Sarah said, glancing down at her calloused hands. "But she says I need to keep my head down and get to work."

"What if I taught you how to read?"

Sarah's eyes shot up. "Do you mean it?"

"I do," Georgie replied. "I want to teach all the girls here to read, assuming they want to learn."

"I want to learn!" Sarah exclaimed.

Georgie smiled at the girl's enthusiasm. "We can begin right away, but it might take some time before we acquire books."

"A lady in the workhouse had a book, and she used to read to everyone at night by the hearth," Sarah said. "She would read it over and over, but we didn't mind."

"Perhaps you will be reading your own book soon enough."

Sarah's eyes lit up. "I can't wait to tell Rebecca. She will be so excited!"

Her words had barely left her mouth when Mrs. Hughes's

critical voice came from the doorway. "What is going on here?"

Sarah jumped up from her seat with a panicked look on her face. "I was just about to clean the floor," she said, walking swiftly over to retrieve the bucket.

Mrs. Hughes frowned. "It appears as if you were dawdling, and you know the punishment for that."

"More chores," Sarah murmured.

Georgie felt compassion well up inside of her for the girl. "Do not fault Sarah. I asked her to take a break so I could become acquainted with her."

"Why would you do such a thing?" Mrs. Hughes asked. "The girls are on a tight schedule and must complete their chores before supper."

"When do the girls get to play?"

Mrs. Hughes laughed dryly. "There is no time to play."

"Even for the little children?"

"Everyone is expected to contribute to the household, no matter their age."

Georgie's eyes roamed the kitchen floor. "The orphanage is clean and orderly. Surely the girls should be rewarded for their hard work."

Mrs. Hughes lifted her brow. "Do you think these girls will get breaks when they go work at a grand house?"

"I hadn't thought about it."

"The answer is no," Mrs. Hughes responded. "These girls will work from the moment they wake up 'til they lay their heads on their pillows at night. The work will be hard, but it will keep a roof over their heads and food in their bellies."

"But they are only children," Georgie contended.

Mrs. Hughes glanced at Sarah as she cleaned the floor on her hands and knees. "These girls," she said sternly, "are old enough to take care of themselves. They must learn that the only person who cares about their welfare is themselves."

"That is a hard lesson to learn."

Mrs. Hughes's mouth was set in a grim line. "Not everyone has a lady's maid and butler to see to their every whim," she said. "I think it would be best if you don't stick your nose where it doesn't belong."

Taken aback by her harsh words, Georgie rushed out, "I meant no harm."

"You are doing harm by giving these girls hope for a different future," Mrs. Hughes said. "No one would seriously consider hiring a girl from an orphanage to act as her lady's maid. It is laughable to even think about."

"I believe you are underestimating these girls and the members of Society."

Mrs. Hughes let out a frustrated sigh. "These girls were taken from workhouses, where they were lucky to survive every single day. We have given them a second chance at life, a better life, but they are still from the rookeries. That will never change."

"I could help them by teaching them how to read," Georgie pressed.

"Read?" Mrs. Hughes huffed. "You cannot be in earnest! Most of these girls have never even seen a book."

"Lord Grenton has agreed to acquire some books for the orphanage."

Mrs. Hughes looked decidedly unimpressed by her words. "Leave the girls to me, Miss Lloyd," she ordered. "You have more important things to do with your time."

Georgie opened her mouth to respond when Mrs. Hughes turned on her heel and departed from the room.

"Insufferable woman," Georgie muttered under her breath

Mrs. Peters spoke up. "What do you intend to do?"

"I am not going to let Mrs. Hughes dictate my actions, no matter how frightening she can be," Georgie said. "If you will excuse me, I need to go make the list of books we require."

As Georgie walked out of the kitchen, she felt determined that she would help these girls, one way or another.

William put his cloth-covered fists up in front of his face and approached Hawthorne. He swung at him, but Hawthorne easily side-stepped his blow.

"What am I doing wrong?" William asked.

Hawthorne let his arms relax at his sides and replied, "Your heart isn't in it."

"How can your heart be in boxing?"

"That is the problem," Hawthorne said. "It is not enough that you want to hit me."

"I do want to hit you," William grumbled. "I have for some time now."

Hawthorne laughed. "Then let's go again."

As William advanced towards his friend, Hawthorne punched him in the side, and he doubled over.

"You left yourself open," Hawthorne said.

William brought his hand to his aching side and attempted to draw a deep breath. "I think I have had enough for today."

Hawthorne nodded. "I think that is wise."

William stepped out of the chalked area and went to sit down on a bench. As he unwrapped the cloth from around his hands, he said, "I'm afraid I do not see the appeal of boxing."

"Graylocke and I sparred nearly every morning before he married," Hawthorne shared. "I hope to keep up the tradition once he gets back from his wedding tour."

"I doubt it'll happen, now he is shackled for life."

Hawthorne sat down next to him. "Not everyone shares your disdain for marriage," he said. "I find that I am much happier with Dinah by my side."

"That is because you are blinded by love."

"So be it."

William dropped the cloth onto the ground. "I will not be foolish enough to fall for the parson's mousetrap."

"It might do you some good if you did," Hawthorne remarked.

"In what way?"

Hawthorne gave him a pointed look. "You haven't quite been yourself since your mother died, and I'm worried about you."

"There is no reason to worry about me," William said. "I can assure you that I am fine."

"You always say that, but I find it hard to believe."

"Why is that?"

Hawthorne grew solemn. "You spend nearly all of your time in meetings or tucked away in your townhouse."

"I am a busy man, and I have work that I need to see to. Surely you can understand that."

"I do, but I have never seen you so despondent before."

Shifting on the bench to face his friend, William responded, "I daresay that you are reading too much into this."

"I know you are grieving, but you must still live your life."

"How am I supposed to act?" William asked. "Should I pretend that all is well to make you feel better?"

"I am not asking that."

"No?" William asked. "Because it feels like you don't think I should properly mourn my mother."

"You misconstrue my words."

"Then what are you saying?"

Hawthorne's eyes held compassion as he replied, "You are angry, and there is no shame in that, but you must accept that your mother is gone."

"Don't you think I know that?" William asked, his voice rising. "Every morning I wake up to remember that my mother left me."

"Not by choice."

"She could have fought harder to stay with me." William abruptly rose and said, "I am tired of this interrogation."

"This is not an interrogation."

"It feels like one," William muttered.

Rising, Hawthorne said, "Join us tonight at White's for a drink."

"I'm busy."

"Doing what, precisely?" Hawthorne asked. "We both know you will be at home with a drink in your hand. You might as well drink with your friends."

William knew his friend spoke the truth, so he nodded. "I will go, but only if you promise not to annoy me."

"It is never on purpose."

"It feels like it is." William unfolded the sleeves of his white linen shirt. "How is Dinah?"

Hawthorne smiled at the mention of his wife. "She is well," he replied. "She is shopping with her sister, Evie."

"I have only been introduced to Miss Ashmore, but she strikes me as a person that balks at tradition."

"That is a good description."

"I am surprised that a woman of her beauty isn't married yet, especially since she never seems to lack for dance partners."

"Do you have your cap set for her?"

William shook his head. "I have my cap set for no one," he said. "I don't see myself ever marrying."

"That is a shame."

"Marriage isn't for everyone. Some people are just destined to be alone."

"You are not one of them."

William reached for his jacket and shrugged it on. "I have never met a woman who has piqued my interest." As he said his words, an image of Miss Lloyd came to his mind, but he quickly banished it, wondering why he had that thought in the first place.

"Perhaps you are not looking hard enough."

"I'm not looking at all."

"That is the problem," Hawthorne said. "Anything worth doing in this life takes hard work."

William stepped back from the bench. "I am happy that you married Dinah, but not everyone is as lucky as you are."

"They can be."

"No," William replied. "Most marriages are fraught with turmoil and unhappiness."

Hawthorne gave him a look that could only be construed as pity. "That doesn't mean you can't beat the odds."

"I don't gamble." William glanced at the door. "It is time that I depart. I have work that I need to do."

"I will walk you out."

As they walked towards the door, William asked, "How do you intend to occupy your day?"

"I have a few things I need to see to."

"Which are?"

Hawthorne's face remained impassive. "It would be best if you didn't know." He glanced over at him. "How is your new headmistress?"

William knew Hawthorne was intentionally changing the subject, but he let out a groan anyway. "She hired a butler."

"A butler?" Hawthorne repeated.

"Yes. Isn't it absurd?"

"It is," Hawthorne replied. "I don't believe I have ever heard of a butler at an orphanage in the rookeries."

"Miss Lloyd was adamant that Wilson remained at the orphanage and refused to back down even when I threatened to dismiss her."

"Why didn't you?"

"It took so long to find a lady to fill the position that I didn't want to do something that I might regret later."

"That is understandable."

"Besides, Wilson offered to work at the orphanage for only room and board, so it costs very little to keep him on."

Hawthorne's brow lifted. "That is generous of him."

"I thought so, as well," William said. "Frankly, I find it admirable that Miss Lloyd has inspired such loyalty in her household servants."

"Miss Lloyd sounds like a remarkable young woman."

"I wouldn't go so far as to say that. She has yet to acknowledge her reduced circumstances and still dresses in fine gowns. She looks entirely out of place there."

"Perhaps that is all she has."

"That may certainly be the case," William said. "Her father recently passed, and she is still in mourning."

Hawthorne hailed a hackney. "It sounds like you are both grieving the loss of a loved one."

"We are, but I wouldn't read anything into it," William said. "I am not entirely sure if Miss Lloyd is a good fit for the orphanage."

"You intend to fire her?"

"I haven't decided yet, but she had the ridiculous notion that we should hire tutors for the orphans."

"Why is that ridiculous?"

William knitted his brow. "The orphans are being trained to work as scullery maids, and they should be content with doing so."

"I see no harm in educating them."

"Now you are starting to sound like Miss Lloyd."

A black hackney pulled in front of Hawthorne. "Would you care for a ride back to your townhouse?"

"No, I would prefer to walk."

Hawthorne bobbed his head. "I will see you tonight," he said before shouting up an address to the driver.

William started walking down the pavement as his thoughts turned to the orphans. What if Miss Lloyd was right?

If they hired tutors, it would benefit the girls. But at what cost? The money for tutors would be minimal, but would the girls still be willing to work as scullery maids? What happened if they refused the positions they were offered? After all, he was running an orphanage, not a boarding school.

Botheration.

Why couldn't Miss Lloyd have left well enough alone? Why did she want to make changes so soon after she'd arrived?

He had a feeling that Miss Lloyd was used to getting what she wanted because she was so blasted beautiful. But that would not sway him. He was strong enough to not let his emotions dictate his actions. He had a job to do, and no one, not even Miss Lloyd would distract him from that.

A short time later, he arrived at his townhouse. The door opened and Thorne greeted him. "Good afternoon, my lord."

What was good about it? Instead of voicing the thought, William replied, "I will be in my study."

"You have a visitor," Thorne announced.

That got William's attention. "Who is this visitor?"

"A Mr. Wilson. He claims that he is the butler at the orphanage."

William frowned. "Where did you put him?"

"In your study," Thorne replied. "He was insistent that he speak to you."

With a tip of his head, William headed towards the study. He stepped into the room and saw Wilson standing near the fireplace.

"How may I help you, Wilson?"

Wilson reached into the pocket of his jacket and pulled out a few sheets of paper. "Miss Lloyd wanted me to deliver these to you personally."

"What are those?"

"The list of books that Miss Lloyd is requesting for the orphanage," Wilson said as he walked them over to him.

William accepted the papers and perused the extensive list. "There must be a hundred books on here!"

"One hundred and eight, to be exact, my lord."

William's brow shot up. "Miss Lloyd cannot be in earnest. This list would cost a small fortune to obtain."

Wilson took a step back. "Those are the books that she felt would benefit the girls, but she understands if not all of them are feasible."

"I think I would like to speak to Miss Lloyd about her list."

"Miss Lloyd thought you might want to do so," Wilson said. "She is expecting you to come to call."

William folded the papers and slipped them into his jacket pocket. "Inform Miss Lloyd that I will arrive at my convenience."

"Very good, my lord," Wilson said before he departed from the room.

William couldn't believe the audacity of Miss Lloyd. He said he would secure books for the orphanage, but he'd never intended to purchase over a hundred.

Once again, his day of endless work had been interrupted by Miss Lloyd. She was starting to make a nuisance of herself.

Chapter Six

Georgie sat in the office as she reviewed the ledgers. She was trying to find ways that she could cut expenses so she could use that money to buy the supplies needed to help the girls to read. She would have gladly parted with her salary, but that was already being used to pay for Alice and Mrs. Peters.

Wilson stepped into the room and announced, "Lord Grenton would like a moment of your time."

Georgie closed the ledger. "Please send him in."

Wilson approached the desk and lowered his voice. "I should note that he appears to be in a foul mood."

"I shall keep that in mind when I meet with him."

"Would you care for me to stay?"

"That won't be necessary," Georgie said.

With a tip of his head, Wilson stepped back. "Yes, miss."

After Wilson stepped out of the room, Georgie smoothed out her brown hair, hoping that she appeared somewhat presentable. It shouldn't matter to her that Lord Grenton was deucedly handsome, but it did. She had been around handsome men before, but none of them had affected her in such a way as he did. Perhaps that was because her interactions with the opposite sex were always during social events, and she'd never seen Lord Grenton at one of those. Regardless, he was her employer, and it would be in her best interest to not dwell on him.

Lord Grenton stepped into the room, and she took a moment to study him. He was dressed in a dark blue jacket, maroon waistcoat, and buff trousers. His blonde hair was brushed forward and his long sideburns were neatly trimmed.

Lord Grenton bowed. "Miss Lloyd," he greeted, albeit tersely.

Georgie smiled, hoping to disarm him. "It is a pleasure to see you again, my lord."

Reaching into his jacket pocket, Lord Grenton pulled out a few sheets of paper and held them up. "I have come to speak to you in regard to your list of books."

"I imagined that would be the case."

"It is ludicrous that your orphanage would require so many books, considering the girls can't even read."

"I am hoping to change that."

Lord Grenton clenched his jaw. "I thought we agreed to dismiss that ridiculous notion."

"It isn't ridiculous," Georgie countered, "and you only said that I couldn't hire tutors to teach the girls, but said nothing about me teaching the girls myself."

"You would teach the orphans?"

"I would."

Lord Grenton placed the papers onto the desk. "Have you taught anyone to read before, Miss Lloyd?"

"I have not."

"Pray tell, why do you think you are qualified to teach the girls to read?"

"If not me, then who?"

Lord Grenton reached for the empty chair and positioned it in front of the desk. "My patience is wearing thin with you," he said as he sat down. "When I give an order, I expect it to be followed."

"And I did follow it."

"No, you are trying to find ways around it, and, quite frankly, it is very aggravating. You have too much on your plate with running this orphanage to waste time with reading lessons."

"I just believe the girls are capable of so much more than we are giving them credit for."

"As I have said before, we are not a boarding school," Lord Grenton said. "We are teaching the girls a trade so they can find employment after they leave us."

"Imagine what doors would be open to them if they learned how to read."

Lord Grenton shook his head. "Or the doors that would shut for them for being overly qualified."

"I do not believe that would be the case."

"Your naïveté is on full display, Miss Lloyd," Lord Grenton said. "You were no doubt raised in a household where your every whim was indulged, but you need to understand that these orphans were raised much differently than you."

"I do understand that."

"I don't believe you do," Lord Grenton pressed. "You need to accept your lot in life, and you must accept theirs."

Georgie reached for the ledger and asked, "What if I found the funds to pay for tutors to teach the girls?"

"How would you accomplish that feat?"

"I don't rightly know, but I am sure we can trim the cost somehow."

"I doubt that," Lord Grenton said. "My solicitor has already gone through the budget, eliminating any excess."

"Lord Grenton..." Georgie started.

He put his hand up, stilling her words. "I find what you are trying to do admirable."

"You do?" She found that hard to believe, since he was fighting her on it.

"These girls are lucky to have a headmistress who cares about them as you do, but it is time to face the facts."

"I am trying to help these girls have a better life."

"Do you take issue with these girls obtaining work as a scullery maid?" Lord Grenton asked.

"I do not."

Lord Grenton gave her a curious glance. "Then what is bothering you?"

Georgie leaned forward in her chair. "I love to read. There is nothing better than escaping into a good book, and I want these girls to experience that joy."

"They were not raised like us. I doubt that any of them have ever even handled a book."

"I want to change that," Georgie said. "We have been given much. Should we not try to give back as much as we can?"

"We are, by allowing these girls to live at the orphanage."

"You must think bigger."

A line between Lord Grenton's brow appeared as he asked, "Do you always get what you want, Miss Lloyd?"

Georgie grew silent. "I used to," she replied. "My parents doted on me something fierce, but it changed after my father died."

"I am sorry to hear that." His voice sounded genuine.

Georgie forced a smile to her lips. "That is all in the past," she said. "I am here now, and I am grateful for a chance to help these girls."

"I know your reduced circumstances must be hard on you, but you must come to terms with it. You are in a life of servitude now."

"I understand, my lord."

Lord Grenton bobbed his head. "You may comb through the budget, but I doubt you will find anything that the orphanage can do without."

"I will find a way."

Rising, Lord Grenton said, "I do not approve of you teaching the girls on your own, but if you find the money, then I give my blessing for you to hire tutors for them."

"Truly?" Georgie asked. Would he really concede so easily?

"You will find that I can be reasonable when the situation warrants it," Lord Grenton remarked. "But it will not be an easy task."

Georgie perked up. "I am up to it."

Lord Grenton moved the chair back to the corner of the room. "I will see to providing some of the books on the list."

"Any books you acquire will be appreciated."

Lord Grenton returned to the desk and picked up the list. "I was surprised at some of the titles on it."

"Why was that?"

"They are books that the *ton* generally frowns upon women reading," Lord Grenton said. "Did your father know you were reading those books?"

"My father wasn't as attentive in his final years," she admitted. "His health declined until he withered away."

Lord Grenton's eyes held compassion. "It is a sad thing to watch someone we love suffer, knowing there is nothing we can do about it."

"I would agree, my lord," she replied, "but to answer your question, my father did not take issue with my reading any book on that list. He thought it was important for a young woman to be well-read."

"Your father was quite progressive."

"He was," Georgie agreed. "He told me to never hide my intellectual prowess from anyone, including the gentlemen who showed interest in me."

"Wasn't he afraid you would end up a spinster?"

Georgie arched an eyebrow. "You speak of spinsterhood as if it was an incurable disease. Some women prefer it to being controlled by a husband."

"I did not mean to insult you."

"You did no such thing," Georgie replied. "I have experienced what it feels like to have no say in one's life, and I refuse to go back to that existence."

Lord Grenton had a curious expression on his face. "You are a walking contradiction," he said. "You talk about your loving father, and in the next breath, you speak of being controlled. Which is it?"

Georgie felt her back become rigid. "I spoke out of turn, and would prefer if we spoke of something else."

Lord Grenton looked as if he had more to say, but thankfully he let the matter drop. "If you will excuse me, I have work that I need to tend to."

Georgie rose. "Thank you for allowing me to teach these girls how to read."

"You must first find the funds to do so," Lord Grenton said, walking to the door. "That was the deal."

"I am aware."

Lord Grenton held her gaze for a moment before he departed from the room.

Georgie lowered herself back onto the chair. How was she going to find the funds to hire tutors for the girls? The budget seemed fair, and she wasn't familiar enough with the orphanage to know what they could do without.

She hated to admit that Lord Grenton could have been right. Somehow she needed to come up with the funds to hire tutors. If she accomplished that feat, then Lord Grenton would allow the girls to learn how to read. But she suspected that he believed he'd sent her on a fool's errand.

As she adjusted the black sleeve on her dress, she realized that she had the perfect solution to her problem. It had been in front of her all along.

Alice stepped into the room and asked, "How did your meeting with Lord Grenton go?"

"Splendid," Georgie said, rising. "How many of my gowns did you pack?"

"Quite a few since I wasn't sure how long it would be before you were able to acquire new ones." Alice paused. "Why do you ask?"

"I want to sell them."

"Why would you wish to do that?"

Georgie came around the desk. "These gowns were made by the finest dressmaker in London, and I believe they would fetch a hefty price."

"That may be true, but what will you wear?"

"I am in mourning, so I only require a few gowns to sustain me," Georgie replied. "Everything else we can take to the market and sell."

"Why would you part with your gowns?"

"Because Lord Grenton said I could hire tutors to teach the girls how to read, assuming I found the funds to do so," Georgie explained.

Realization dawned on Alice's face. "That is generous of you."

"Besides, with my inheritance, I will buy new gowns in the latest fashion when I am out of mourning."

"But what happens when the funds from selling your gowns run out?" Alice asked. "Won't Lord Grenton make you dismiss the tutors?"

"One step at a time, Alice," Georgie said. "Perhaps with time, Lord Grenton will see the benefit of having tutors at the orphanage."

"I doubt it."

Georgie laughed. "Don't be such a naysayer. Let us go pick out the dresses that I will sell."

With a drink in his hand, William sat in his seat and listened to the ramblings of his friends. They were going on about something that he didn't have the energy or desire to listen to. He wasn't entirely sure why he'd agreed to come this evening. He wasn't in a jovial mood and hadn't been in some time. Why should he pretend all was well when his whole world was dreary?

Hawthorne's voice broke through his musings. "What do you think, Grenton?"

William glanced up at his friend. "About what?"

Hawthorne chuckled. "We are trying to convince Hugh to take a wife."

"Don't be absurd," William responded. "Why would Hugh wish to be shackled for the rest of his life to an obnoxious woman who will spend all of his money?"

"Not everyone shares that view of marriage," Hawthorne said.

"Sane men do."

Hawthorne shook his head. "I find that I prefer my life with Dinah in it."

Hugh lifted up his drink and said, "That is because you married up, brother."

"That I did," Hawthorne agreed. "Dinah makes my life have a purpose, and I would be lost without her."

"Blah, blah, blah," Hugh said, lowering his glass. "You should write sonnets and stop boring us with your declarations of love."

Haddington spoke up. "No one would read them."

"But he might stop singing praises about the joys of marriage," Hugh stated. "It is grating on my ears."

"You are all just jealous," Hawthorne remarked with a smile.

Hugh lifted his brow. "I come and go as I please. I answer to no one, especially when it comes to spending my money. I fail to see in what way I would be jealous of you."

"If you aren't careful, you'll gamble all of your money away," Hawthorne advised.

"That is impossible," Hugh responded. "I have more than enough to remove myself from London and buy an estate."

"Why don't you?" Haddington asked.

Hugh smirked. "Why would I give up a lucrative career?"

"Gambling is not a career," Hawthorne responded.

"Now you are starting to sound like Father," Hugh grumbled as he brought his drink to his lips.

"Regardless, it is time that you settle down and find a wife," Hawthorne said.

Hugh placed his glass intentionally on the table. "Why should I find a wife?" he asked. "Because you said so?"

"I just feel—" Hawthorne started.

"You don't get to have a say in my life," Hugh interrupted. "I am doing just fine without your help."

William shifted in his seat to face Hawthorne. "Leave Hugh alone. He will marry when he is good and ready."

"If at all," Hugh mumbled.

Haddington pushed his empty glass away from him and rose. "The next round is on me, gentlemen. That is, if you have the patience to await my return." He turned his attention towards Hawthorne. "I've just seen an acquaintance of mine, and I promised him some time back that I'd introduce you to him. Come, help me keep my word."

Hawthorne rose with a sigh. "If you insist. But you owe me for helping your honor remain unsullied."

After they stepped away from the table, Hugh shot William a grateful look. "Thank you for what you said."

"You would have done the same for me."

Hugh sighed. "My brother is entirely too opinionated for his own good."

"He means well, you must know that."

"Do I?" Hugh asked. "He nags me relentlessly about my

gambling, and I tire of hearing it. Surely, something else must occupy his time."

William glanced over his shoulder at Haddington and Hawthorne, their heads close together. "Do you ever wonder what they talk about?"

"No. Why should I?"

"They just seem so solemn when they speak privately."

"I wouldn't give them any heed," Hugh said. "Nathaniel's probably trying to find new ways to pester me."

"Do you know why he goes into the rookeries?"

"No. Have you asked him?"

"I do, but he just dismisses me out of hand."

Hugh shrugged. "I can't answer for my brother, but I am sure he has a good reason for it, whatever it is," he said. "If I were you, I would be more concerned that Haddington dresses like a dandy. It makes the rest of us look bad."

"He didn't always dress like that," William reflected. "That has been more of a recent development."

"Lucky us," Hugh joked.

William watched as Hawthorne and Haddington returned to their table.

"Does anyone intend to go to Lady Worton's masquerade ball?" Haddington asked. "It is to be the event of the Season."

"I don't," William replied as he reached for a glass.

"Do you have better things to do, Grenton?" Hawthorne asked.

"As a matter of fact, I do," William said.

Hawthorne sat down and encouraged, "Enlighten us."

"I have an estate that I need to see to."

"As do we," Hawthorne said. "Furthermore, you have hired a headmistress for the orphanage, so that won't take up as much of your time."

Haddington gave him a curious glance. "When did you hire a headmistress?"

"Just a couple days ago," he replied. "I am not quite sure if she is a good fit, and I might have to dismiss her."

"Why is that?" Haddington asked.

"She brought along a lady's maid, a cook, and a butler," Hawthorne interjected before William could answer.

"To the orphanage?" Haddington questioned.

William nodded. "She has also requested over a hundred books to be delivered there."

"That is no small feat," Hugh commented.

"Agreed," William responded. "She has the grand delusions that she needs to teach all the girls how to read."

Haddington gave a slight shrug of his shoulders. "Frankly, I find that admirable."

"We are training these girls to be scullery maids so they can support themselves, and there isn't enough time in the day to have reading lessons," William said.

"I would find the time," Hawthorne remarked. "I think it would benefit those girls' lives to know how to read."

"I'm not running a boarding school. I feed them, clothe them, and provide them with a skill to ensure they find employment once they leave us," William said. "I am doing precisely what is being done at other orphanages."

"But you can be better," Hawthorne urged. "How would your mother have wanted it run?"

William took a sip of his drink, then said, "She would not want me to waste money in foolish endeavors. Just keeping the orphanage open comes at a great expense."

"What if I contributed as well?" Hawthorne asked. "I have no doubt that Dinah would believe this to be a worthy cause."

"Do you think Dinah might consider being a patron?"

"I think she would greatly enjoy that."

William bobbed his head in approval. "That's a brilliant idea. She can help me with the headmistress."

"Knowing my Dinah, she will want to visit the orphanage

and meet the girls," Hawthorne said. "Do you think that will be an issue?"

"I do not, but she will need to use caution when she travels to the rookeries," William advised. "It is no place for a lady."

"I shall ensure the proper protection is in place."

William almost smiled—almost. With Dinah on his side, he was confident that Miss Lloyd would fall in line, and he wouldn't have to waste any more time arguing with her. What a vexing woman Miss Lloyd was! She kept attempting to disarm him with smiles, but he was not so weak as to be charmed by a pretty face.

He had noticed that her eyes sparkled when she smiled, and that she had a small freckle on her top lip. He shook his head. Those were things he definitely should not be noticing about his headmistress.

Hawthorne's voice drew back his attention. "Dinah will be pleased that she has found a worthy purpose to put her energy to use, especially since she is so fond of children."

"I will send word to Miss Lloyd to expect her," William said.

"I suspect that her sister, Evie, will accompany her," Hawthorne shared. "Those two are practically inseparable."

"That won't be an issue."

"I haven't seen much of Miss Ashmore as of late," Haddington said. "Is she well?"

"She is, but she is driving her aunt mad by refusing to be home when her suitors come to call," Hawthorne replied.

Haddington chuckled. "That doesn't surprise me in the least."

"Doesn't Miss Ashmore wish to settle down?" Hugh asked.

Hawthorne gave him an amused look. "I have never met a woman who was so contrary regarding marriage. Quite the match to your dislike of the institution, if I may say so."

Hugh shoved back his chair. "Gentlemen, it is time that I depart so I can get to work."

"Again, gambling is not work," Hawthorne said. "It is a game of chance, and your luck will eventually run out."

Hugh held his arms out wide. "It hasn't yet."

As Hugh walked away, Hawthorne shook his head. "When will my brother learn?"

"He is young," Haddington remarked. "Give him time."

"There is so much anger bottled up inside of him," Hawthorne said. "I worry what will happen when it finally gets released."

William tossed back his drink. "Sometimes anger is the only thing that drives a man forward." He rose. "I also have work I need to see to."

"Stay for another round," Haddington encouraged.

"I have tarried long enough," William replied. "I bid you a goodnight."

Chapter Seven

The alley blocked most of the morning sun, but enough made its way through the window as Georgie sat at her desk, reading through the newssheets. How she had missed this! Charles had banned her from reading the morning newspaper, including the Society page, because he felt she was far too opinionated for a woman. He also removed books from the library if he felt they had questionable content.

Living with Charles had been intolerable. She could finally breathe now that she wasn't under his scrutiny, or his heavy hand. She had no doubt that her parents would be saddened by Charles's ill treatment towards her. They had raised her to have her own voice, but Charles wanted to take that away from her, just as he wanted to force her to succumb to his will.

Free of his smothering ways and with a fierce determination to get to know the children, she approached mealtimes with an animated spirit. It had clearly shocked her charges at first, but Georgie crossed the space with easy conversation, and the girls soon became lively, asking questions about what her life had been like before coming to the orphanage and answering a few that she asked in return.

She smiled as she thought about some of the things they

had said. Their different personalities had become more evident as they talked, and Georgie could see that they'd all been gifted in different ways. Some of the girls lifted others up, revealing something wonderful about a quieter friend. Others gave helpful instruction in caring for themselves or completing chores. Georgie had even seen one pass the rest of her food to another, insisting that she was full when she noticed the other staring dejectedly at her empty plate.

Wilson stepped into the office, and she was brought from her memories back into the present.

"Lady Hawthorne and Miss Ashmore would like a moment of your time," he said.

Georgie's heart dropped at the unexpected news. She wasn't acquainted with Lady Hawthorne, but she had befriended a Miss Ashmore at a ball last Season. Surely it couldn't be her; that would be too great of a coincidence. Wouldn't it be?

"Will you show them in?" Georgie asked, half-hoping that they would turn on their heel and leave the orphanage.

Wilson tipped his head before he departed.

Georgie smoothed down her black gown as she tried to assure herself that Ashmore was a common name and that she had nothing to worry about.

As she watched the ladies walk into the room, the smile on her lips froze, and unease clenched her stomach like a fist.

Miss Ashmore stared at her. "Georgie?" she asked. "Whatever are you doing here?"

Georgie rose. "I…uh… am the headmistress."

"But I thought a Miss Lloyd was the headmistress," Miss Ashmore said with a baffled expression.

"She is, I mean, I am," Georgie rushed out. "But I can explain!"

"I am all ears," Miss Ashmore said.

Georgie gestured towards the chair as she hurried to close the door. "Would anyone care to sit?" When no one moved, she continued. "I know what you must be thinking…"

"I surely doubt that," Miss Ashmore stated.

"…but you must know that I truly had no choice," Georgie continued. "It was a matter of life or death for me."

Lady Hawthorne glanced between them, a bemused look on her face. "Perhaps we should start from the beginning," she encouraged. "Why don't you tell me your real name?"

Georgie sighed. "I am Georgie Holbrooke, sister of Lord Wakefield," she revealed. "My brother was trying to force my hand so I would marry the most despicable of men. When I refused, he beat me soundly. The only reason he stopped was because our butler intervened."

"Thank heavens for that," Lady Hawthorne declared.

Georgie nodded. "I have no intention of ever marrying Lord Ransdale, and I know that my brother won't allow my disobedience as long as I live in his house."

Miss Ashmore's brow lifted. "Your brother wishes for you to marry Lord Ransdale?"

"He does," Georgie confirmed.

"Lord Ransdale is beastly," Miss Ashmore said. "His mistress is heavy with child, and he walks around like a dog in heat."

"Evie," Lady Hawthorne admonished. "Don't be so crass."

"Well, it's true," Miss Ashmore said. "Lord Ransdale is a fine example of why I wish never to be wed."

"Not all men are like Lord Ransdale," Lady Hawthorne shared.

"Sadly, most amongst the *ton* are." Miss Ashmore turned her attention back to Georgie. "How did you end up at this orphanage, and using an alias?"

"The servants at my townhouse banded together and decided that I needed to escape from my brother's clutches before I ended up dead," Georgie explained. "My cook, Mrs.

Peters, is the sister of Lord Grenton's solicitor, and she knew they were looking for a lady to run the orphanage. They thought it would be for the best if I went by Miss Lloyd while I was here."

"Does Lord Grenton know the truth?" Lady Hawthorne asked.

Georgie shook her head. "No, and if he discovered it, he would dismiss me."

"You don't know that for certainty."

"I do," Georgie replied. "Lord Grenton has already threatened to dismiss me on multiple occasions for various reasons. Silly reasons, really."

"Which are?" Miss Ashmore asked.

Georgie sighed. "I refused to dismiss Wilson—"

"Who is Wilson?" Miss Ashmore asked.

"He is the butler, but he only works for room and board," Georgie said. "My brother dismissed him when Wilson confessed to helping me leave the townhouse."

Lady Hawthorne walked over to the window and looked out into the alley. "It is rather unusual for an orphanage to employ a butler."

"He had nowhere else to go," Georgie said. "I couldn't very well do nothing to help him."

"I know, but I do understand Lord Grenton's apprehension," Lady Hawthorne remarked. "My husband told me that you also employ a lady's maid and a cook."

"I do," Georgie responded, seeing no reason to deny it, "but I am paying them out of my salary."

Miss Ashmore sat down on the chair. "I am curious as to why else Lord Grenton wishes to dismiss you."

"I am lobbying to teach the girls how to read, and he is against that," Georgie shared.

"Why would he be against such a noble thing?" Miss Ashmore asked.

Georgie returned to her seat, then said, "As of now, the

girls are being trained to obtain employment as scullery maids, but I believe they are capable of so much more."

"I would agree with that sentiment," Miss Ashmore responded.

"Lord Grenton finally conceded that I could hire tutors to teach the girls, but only if I found the funds to do so," Georgie said. "I went over the books, repeatedly, but I couldn't find any expenses that we could do without. So, I decided I needed to raise some funds."

"How do you intend to accomplish that?" Lady Hawthorne asked.

"By selling my gowns," Georgie replied. "I have some dresses that I know will fetch a decent price at the market."

Miss Ashmore lifted her brow. "Have you ever been to the market before?"

"I have not, but I intend to take Wilson along with me."

"That won't be enough," Miss Ashmore said. "If you are not careful, you will be sold alongside the other goods."

Georgie's eyes grew wide. "Surely you exaggerate?"

"I'm afraid not. The market is a vile place. I have even witnessed a man selling his own wife," Miss Ashmore said.

Lady Hawthorne gasped. "Why would a man ever sell his wife?"

Georgie wondered why Miss Ashmore had been to the market in the first place.

Miss Ashmore gave a half shrug. "He claimed that he couldn't afford to keep feeding her."

"How awful," Lady Hawthorne murmured. "Did anyone buy her?"

"Yes, and the woman is in a much better place now." Miss Ashmore gave Georgie a stern look. "Promise me that you won't go to the market without me."

"Wouldn't it be safer if I went with Wilson?" Georgie asked.

"No. You must trust me," Miss Ashmore replied. "I am

familiar with the marketplace, and I can help you fetch top dollar for your gowns."

"Then I shall go with you," Georgie said.

Miss Ashmore nodded in approval. "I think it is admirable what you are trying to do to help these girls. Just think of what opportunities will be waiting for them once they learn to read!"

"Precisely! But Lord Grenton is not of the same opinion as us."

"Then we will need to change his mind. I intend to become a patron of the orphanage," Lady Hawthorne said.

"How wonderful!" Georgie gushed. "Associating your name with the orphanage gives it credence to the other members of Society."

"That was my intention," Lady Hawthorne stated.

Georgie smiled. "With you on board and the funds I collect for my gowns, we can hire tutors and begin lessons for the girls."

"How long do you believe your gowns will finance the tutors?" Lady Hawthorne asked.

"Months, perhaps," Georgie replied. "I'm hoping that Lord Grenton will see the validity of my plan and offer up additional funds."

"I do hope so, but if he doesn't, my husband and I will fund the tutors and their expenses," Lady Hawthorne said.

Georgie let out a sigh of relief. "That does please me to hear, because I want to ensure the orphanage is in good hands when I depart."

"Where would you go?" Miss Ashmore asked.

"In a few months, I will reach my majority and inherit thirty thousand pounds and a small estate in Brighton," Georgie shared.

"You are an heiress," Lady Hawthorne remarked.

"Yes, but more importantly, my brother won't be able to

force me to marry Lord Ransdale," Georgie said. "I will be free of him."

Miss Ashmore rose. "Are you sure your brother doesn't know where you are?"

"If he did, he would have already forced me to return home," Georgie replied. "He is not someone to trifle with."

"Do you carry a pistol?" Miss Ashmore asked.

Georgie gave her a blank look. "For what purpose?"

"To protect yourself," Miss Ashmore replied, removing a muff pistol from a fold within her gown. "You need to become acquainted with one."

"I have never handled a gun before," Georgie admitted.

Miss Ashmore extended it towards her. "I will teach you," she said. "But you will need to adapt to the weight of the pistol."

Georgie looked down at the muff pistol in her hand. "I don't know if I could shoot anyone."

"Let's hope it doesn't come to that, but it is best to be prepared for the unexpected," Miss Ashmore said.

Lady Hawthorne cast her sister an amused look. "You must excuse Evie. She can be quite the misanthrope."

"I merely want to keep Georgie safe from her brother, if it comes to that," Miss Ashmore asserted. "Besides, she is living in the rookeries and is surrounded by ruffians. She must learn to protect herself."

"I am safe in the orphanage," Georgie said.

Miss Ashmore walked over to the window and peered out. "You are backed up to an alley, and an assailant could easily climb through this window."

"We keep it locked at all times," Georgie shared.

"It doesn't matter," Miss Ashmore responded as she ran her fingers along the edges. "With the right tools, it would take mere moments to get in."

Georgie turned her attention more fully towards the window, aghast. "Surely it couldn't be that easy?"

"It is," Miss Ashmore said. "I have gotten into much more secure buildings than this."

Georgie's expression didn't change as she turned to her guest. "For what purpose?"

Miss Ashmore waved her hand dismissively in front of her. "Sometimes they wouldn't let me enter by way of the main door."

Georgie opened her mouth to ask another question, but Lady Hawthorne spoke first. "We should be going," she said, ushering her sister to the door. "We don't mean to occupy all of your time."

"You are always welcome," Georgie replied as she haltingly offered the muff pistol back to Miss Ashmore.

Miss Ashmore put her hand up. "I want you to keep it," she said. "Our training will begin tomorrow before our trip to the market."

"Our training?" Georgie questioned.

Lowering her hand, Miss Ashmore replied, "Good day, Georgie."

After Miss Ashmore and Lady Hawthorne had departed from the room, Georgie set the pistol down carefully on her desk. She hadn't remembered Evie being so intense, and she wasn't quite sure what to make of her.

But the thought of learning how to protect herself did have some appeal.

William sat near the fireplace in his study with a drink in his hand, his cravat hanging loosely about his neck. He had spent most of the day meeting with his man of business, who never seemed to run out of things to talk about where his estate and business interests were concerned. William was tired of the monotony of his life. It was the same thing every blasted day. He worked tirelessly, but for what purpose? He was all alone. It was a cruel twist of fate that he was even alive. If there was a God, then he would have died alongside his sister so many years ago, but instead, he was forced to go on living.

He brought the glass to his lips. He hadn't thought about Eleanor in some time, but there was something about Miss Lloyd that had brought memories of his sister to the surface. If Eleanor had still been alive, she would have been of a similar age as his headmistress. Would they have been friends?

What was it about Miss Lloyd that gave him pause? She was undeniably beautiful, but there was more to it than that, he was certain of it. But that didn't mean he would let her shirk her responsibilities. Her job was simple. If she couldn't stop setting her sights on these outlandish notions and just handle running the orphanage to his specifications, then she would be dismissed.

Perhaps he should just dismiss her and be done with it. He had spent far too much time dwelling on her as it was.

Hawthorne's voice came from the doorway. "You look like you have had better days."

"I have."

As Hawthorne walked further into the room, he said, "You were missed at the House of Lords today."

"I met all day with my man of business, but I do intend to go tomorrow for the vote."

"That's good."

William set his empty glass on the table next to him. "Not that I am complaining, but what brings you here?"

"I came to see how you are faring."

"That's a waste of time, then," William said. "I am fine."

Hawthorne claimed the seat next to him. "You always say that."

"Yet you don't seem to believe me."

"You forget that I know you."

William picked up his glass and rose. "You are worrying about nothing." He walked over to the drink cart. "Would you care for a drink?"

"I would."

"I'm afraid you came all this way for nothing," William said as he poured a pair of drinks.

"That is for me to decide."

William extended a glass to Hawthorne. "Why don't you say what you need to say and be done with it?"

"I'm worried about you." Hawthorne hesitated. "We all are."

William put his arms out as if to indicate there was no harm to his person. "There is no need."

"You hardly attend social events anymore."

"That is because they are a waste of time."

With a knowing look, Hawthorne said, "You didn't use to think so."

"I've changed."

"I know, and it has me concerned."

William returned to his seat. "You are a good friend, but it would be best if you leave it alone. This is something that I need to get through on my own."

"You are not alone," Hawthorne asserted. "You have friends that care for you, whether you want us to or not, and we can help you."

"How?"

Hawthorne placed his glass onto the table. "Dine with Dinah and me tomorrow night," he encouraged. "It would be good for you to get your mind off your mother."

"Did your wife put you up to this?"

"Perhaps, but I would have eventually thought of it," Hawthorne said cheekily.

"I doubt it."

Hawthorne looked at him expectantly. "Does this mean you will come?" he asked hopefully.

William let out a reluctant sigh. "I wouldn't dare turn down an invitation from Lady Hawthorne."

"Wonderful," Hawthorne said. "I should warn you that she visited the orphanage, and she has some ideas on how to make it better."

"I should have assumed."

Hawthorne leaned back in his chair. "Dinah found Miss Lloyd to be a delight."

"She did?" William asked.

With a nod, Hawthorne said, "She agrees that the girls should be taught to read."

"We both know that would be an expensive endeavor, and I tasked Miss Lloyd with finding the funds to do so."

"Miss Lloyd wasn't able to find additional money in the budget, but she came up with another way to raise funds."

William groaned. "Which is?"

"She is selling her gowns," Hawthorne replied. "Dinah says that she is taking her gowns to the market tomorrow."

"What woman would willingly sell her gowns to help girls she hardly knows?"

"Apparently, Miss Lloyd."

William grew quiet. His respect for the headmistress grew immensely. He had tasked her with finding additional funds and she did it, albeit not in any way he'd expected. It was truly a noble act. But now he found himself in a difficult situation. Could he allow her to sell her gowns, knowing what she was willing to sacrifice for the children?

Hawthorne picked up his glass and took a sip. "What do you intend to do?" he asked. "Are you truly going to let her sell her gowns?"

"I am debating."

"I wouldn't wait too long, since she plans to go to the market tomorrow with Evie," Hawthorne shared.

"The market is hardly a place for two ladies."

"You need not worry," Hawthorne assured him. "Evie will keep Miss Lloyd safe."

"Pardon me if I find that a little farfetched."

Hawthorne smirked. "Evie is a woman of many talents, and she carries multiple weapons on her person."

"She does? For what purpose?"

"You need not concern yourself with that," Hawthorne said. "Just know that Evie will not let anything happen to Miss Lloyd."

William furrowed his brow. "Am I to let the matter drop simply because you told me to do so?"

"I am hoping that is the case," Hawthorne replied.

"Do you ever tire of your secrets?"

Hawthorne shrugged. "I could ask you the same question."

"I don't have secrets."

"No?" Hawthorne asked. "Then, pray tell, what is bothering you?"

"Why do you think something is bothering me?"

"I can see it in your eyes," Hawthorne replied, "and eyes never lie."

William huffed. "Perhaps you are just seeing things."

"I don't believe I am." Hawthorne took a sip of his drink and lowered it to his lap. "What's troubling you?"

Experience had taught William that it was impossible to lie to his friend, so he might as well just tell him the truth. "I was thinking about Eleanor."

"Your sister?"

"Yes," William said. "I couldn't help but wonder what type of woman she would have become."

"She would have been remarkable."

William grimaced. "I believe so, but she was robbed of that opportunity because of me."

"Her death was not your fault."

"I brought influenza home from Eton," William said. "If I

hadn't come home for a holiday, then she would have never gotten sick."

"You couldn't have known that there had been an outbreak at Eton."

"I started feeling sick on the carriage ride to our country estate," William said. "I shouldn't have continued home."

"Then your mother would have worried incessantly."

William tightened his hold on his glass. "It would have been better than killing my own sister."

"You didn't kill your sister," Hawthorne said.

"Why does it feel like I did?"

Hawthorne's eyes held compassion as he said, "If I recall correctly, you barely survived, and it took you weeks to recover."

"I should have died with Eleanor."

"Then your mother would have lost everything," Hawthorne said.

William's face softened at the thought of his mother. "That would have devastated her."

"It would have devastated anyone," Hawthorne replied. "A mother is not supposed to outlive her children."

"Or her husband. My father died just a few months before Eleanor passed."

"I can't even imagine what a difficult time that must have been for her, for both of you."

William took a sip, then said, "I was more devastated by Eleanor's death than I was for my father."

"Why was that?"

"He was hardly around, so he was more of a stranger to me," William admitted. "When we did speak, it was uncomfortable and seemed contrived."

"You are not alone in that."

"I know, but he was so busy that he failed to prepare me to take over the estate," William said. "Fortunately, my mother handled the running of it until I finished university."

"Your mother was a formidable woman."

"That she was," William agreed.

A clock chimed in the corner, alerting them of the time.

Hawthorne put his glass down and rose. "I should be going," he said. "We are attending the opera this evening."

"Lucky you," William muttered.

"I would ask if you would like to join us, but I already know the answer."

Rising, William said, "I would rather chew glass than attend the Opera with you and Dinah."

Hawthorne chuckled. "A simple no would have sufficed."

"Maybe I would think differently if you two weren't so obnoxiously in love."

"I doubt it." Hawthorne walked over to the door and stopped. "Do not forget about supper tomorrow night."

"I wouldn't dare."

Hawthorne tipped his head before he departed from the room. William returned to his seat and tossed back his drink. The sound of the crackling fire was the only noise in the room.

He was alone again. It was familiar, and it was no less than he deserved.

Chapter Eight

As she stared up at the bricks, Georgie hesitantly asked, "You want me to climb this wall?"

Evie gave her an encouraging smile. "Just to the second-level window," she replied.

"For what purpose?"

"You might find yourself in a position where you need to climb out of a window to save yourself," Evie said.

"I don't think that is very likely."

"Learning how to climb walls has come in very handy for me," Evie shared, placing her hand on the wall. "Just look for bricks that are jutting out and start there."

Georgie turned to face the brick wall and stared up at the second level window. "I don't think I can do this."

"You won't know unless you try," Evie encouraged. "I should note that it is much easier to climb in trousers."

"I believe that, but I do not own a pair of trousers." Georgie shuddered at the thought, then ran her fingers along the bricks until she found one that stuck out from the others.

"That is a shame. I do believe every woman would benefit from owning a pair of trousers." Evie took a step back. "You will need to balance your weight mostly on your feet," she shared. "Your hands are mostly for support, and you will need to alternate moving your feet and hands up the wall."

Georgie put the toe of her boot on a brick that was sticking out near the ground and pulled herself up. As she looked for another brick to place her other boot on, she blew out a puff of air. "This is impossible."

"I assure you that it is not, but it is important that you check the bricks before placing weight on them," Evie advised. "If you encounter a loose brick, it could cause you to fall."

Georgie stepped back, releasing her hold on the wall. "This is pointless. I could never climb a brick wall."

"You just need practice," Evie encouraged. "I didn't get it at first either, but it has come in handy a time or two."

"So you say, but I find that unlikely."

Evie gave her an amused look. "It is true," she replied. "The buildings in the rookeries are terribly built, so it is much easier to climb them."

"Why are you climbing walls in the rookeries?"

A mischievous glint came into Evie's eye. "It passes the time."

Georgie turned her head towards Lady Hawthorne and asked, "Do you climb walls in the rookeries?"

"Heavens, no," Lady Hawthorne replied. "I don't climb walls, I rarely frequent the rookeries, and I don't carry a muff pistol on my person."

"Which I believe is a mistake," Evie said. "You need to be able to protect yourself."

"That is why I have you," Lady Hawthorne responded with a smile.

Evie turned back to Georgie and remarked, "You could use more practice with your muff pistol."

Georgie let out a groan. "We have already spent hours doing so."

"Yet you are a terrible shot."

"I am trying, but you are putting the target too far away."

Evie tsked. "You need to shoot your attacker before they are upon you," she said. "Also, I recommend you sleep with your pistol under your pillow at night."

"Why would I do that?" What an uncomfortable, hazardous idea!

"You never know what dangers are lurking around you," Evie counseled. "It is best to be prepared."

Wilson stepped out into the small square courtyard with a tray in his hand. "Mrs. Peters baked fresh biscuits and thought you might care for them."

"Thank you, Wilson," Georgie said. "Please tell Mrs. Peters that it was most considerate of her to think of us."

Wilson placed the tray down on the table and went back inside without saying another word.

Lady Hawthorne reached for a biscuit, then asked, "Have you adjusted well to the orphanage?"

"I have, but I do find sleeping on a straw mattress to be deucedly uncomfortable," Georgie replied.

"It is better than sleeping on the floor," Evie remarked.

"That it is," Georgie agreed. "But I do miss my feather mattress."

Lady Hawthorne gave her an understanding smile. "You will only be here for a few months," she said. "Once you gain your inheritance, you can sleep on a feather mattress again."

"You are right," Georgie agreed. "Furthermore, this experience has opened my eyes to realize how truly blessed I am. It makes me want to do more to help these girls."

"I find that to be admirable, and I want to help, as well," Lady Hawthorne said. "Join us for dinner this evening, and we will continue this discussion."

Georgie glanced down at her black gown. "I have nothing to wear."

"What you are wearing is just fine," Lady Hawthorne remarked. "I shall send a coach for you."

"That is most generous of you."

"Oh, and Lord Grenton will be joining us, as well," Lady Hawthorne said with a wave of her hand. "I do hope that won't be an issue."

Georgie forced a smile to her lips. "That sounds wonderful."

Evie leaned closer to her and whispered, "Liar."

Lady Hawthorne either didn't hear her sister or chose to ignore her. "I have tarried long enough," she said. "I should depart before my husband comes looking for me."

"You could join us at the market," Evie suggested.

"I think not," Lady Hawthorne said before she headed towards the door.

Evie walked over to the tray and picked up a biscuit. "Shall we depart for the market?" she asked. "I brought a coach, so we won't have to walk to the square with all of your gowns."

Georgie was only too happy to abandon wall climbing, but before she could reply, Lord Grenton stepped into the court-yard. He was dressed in a green jacket, ivory waistcoat, and buff trousers. He had the same gruff look on his face that she was accustomed to, but something about his eyes had changed. They appeared sad, withdrawn.

His eyes landed on Evie. "Miss Ashmore," he greeted with a slight bow. "It is a pleasure to see you again."

Evie dropped into a slight curtsy. "My lord," she murmured.

Lord Grenton turned his attention towards Georgie. "Miss Lloyd," he said. "I do hope I am not intruding."

"You are not," Georgie replied, relieved she hadn't made any progress up the wall next to her. What would Lord Grenton have thought if he'd arrived to find her dangling from the second-story window? "How may I help you, my lord?"

"I was hoping to speak to you in private," Lord Grenton replied.

"We can speak in my office." Georgie turned to Evie and said, "We will be back in a few moments."

Evie nodded. "Do not concern yourself with me. I will be indulging in these biscuits."

Lord Grenton gestured for Georgie to lead the way inside. As they headed into the building, neither of them spoke, and Georgie felt no desire to fill the silence with pleasantries.

Georgie stepped into the office and came around the desk. She sat down and asked, "What would you care to speak to me about?"

Lord Grenton moved the chair from the corner to sit in front of the desk. "It has come to my attention that you intend to sell your gowns to pay for the tutors."

Who had told him that? "I am," she replied, seeing no reason to deny it. "Miss Ashmore and I intend to go to the market to sell them."

"By yourself?" Lord Grenton asked.

"Is that an issue?"

Lord Grenton frowned. "Do you have no regard for your safety?" he asked. "You could be robbed, or worse."

"I do appreciate your concern, but it is unnecessary."

His brow shot up. "Why is that exactly?"

"Miss Ashmore has taught me how to use a muff pistol, and I will carry one on my person."

"You truly believe a muff pistol will protect you from ruffians?"

"I do."

"A muff pistol only has one shot," Lord Grenton pointed out. "What if you are surrounded by a group of men?"

"That is highly improbable."

Lord Grenton leaned forward in his seat. "I'm afraid it is more likely than you believe, Miss Lloyd," he said. "You are a beautiful, well-bred woman, and that will garner attention the moment you step foot into the marketplace."

Georgie couldn't pretend that Lord Grenton's remarks

didn't gratify her vanity, but it didn't sway her from her objective. "Selling my gowns will finance tutors for the foreseeable future. It is a risk that I am willing to take."

"There is no need—not anymore."

Georgie cocked her head. "Pardon?"

"I have decided to finance the tutors, albeit temporarily, so there is no reason to sell your gowns," Lord Grenton said. "You will remain here at the orphanage, where you are safe."

"I'm afraid I don't understand. You were adamant that I had to find the funds in the budget."

"But you didn't find it in the budget, did you?"

"No, but I did not think you would object to me selling my own gowns."

Lord Grenton rose. "A simple thank you would suffice."

Georgie sputtered. "But I am not thankful."

"Whyever not?"

Georgie squared her shoulders. "I do not want to be in your debt, my lord," she said. "I can take care of myself."

Lord Grenton's eyes narrowed slightly. "Why are you being so obstinate on this? I thought you would be pleased that you wouldn't have to sell your gowns."

"I want to do my part to help these girls, and selling my gowns is a minor thing."

"It isn't necessary," Lord Grenton said, his words curt. "I will pay for the tutors, and you have no reason to leave the safety of these walls."

Georgie pursed her lips together as she stared back at Lord Grenton. This was a most difficult situation. She'd vowed to never be controlled by a man again when she left her brother's house. However, she needed this job until she reached her majority, and not only for herself, but for others who were relying on her salary.

Lord Grenton took a step closer to the desk, his expression solemn. "Do we understand one another, Miss Lloyd?" he asked.

"Perfectly," she replied through gritted teeth.

With an approving nod, Lord Grenton said, "Then I shall take my leave."

Once he'd departed from the room, Georgie heard the sound of the window being opened. She turned her head and saw Evie was climbing through it.

"Dare I ask how you opened that locked window?" Georgie queried.

Evie straightened and smoothed out her pale blue gown. "It was quite easy with my dagger," she replied. "I must admit that I shamelessly eavesdropped on your conversation with Lord Grenton."

"That man vexes me."

"He does make a valid point," Evie said. "The market is no place for a lady."

"Regardless, I still intend to go and sell my gowns," Georgie announced.

"For what purpose?" Evie asked. "Lord Grenton has offered to pay for the tutors."

"That may be true, but the funds from the gowns could serve another purpose."

"Such as?"

Georgie shrugged. "I don't know, but I will not let Lord Grenton dictate my actions," she said. "I refuse to give him that control over me."

"You are playing a dangerous game," Evie advised. "Lord Grenton may dismiss you if he discovers that you went against his wishes."

"He will never find out."

"How can you be so sure?"

Georgie rose. "I can't, but it is a risk that I am willing to take."

A bright smile lit Evie's face. "Then let us depart."

Georgie sat in the coach as it slowly made its way towards the market. There was entirely too much traffic on the street, and their pace was sluggish at best.

"It would have been faster to walk," Georgie remarked.

"Perhaps, but it is far safer to travel by coach to the market," Evie said.

Georgie gave Evie a curious look. "May I ask why you frequent the market?"

"I don't go very often, but it proves useful sometimes," Evie replied. "I have met the most unusual people there."

"Do you go alone?"

"Often," Evie said. "It is safer if I only have to worry about myself."

Glancing at the pile of gowns next to her on the bench, Georgie said, "I know you must think I am mad for selling my gowns anyway."

"You don't know what I am thinking."

"How could you not?" Georgie asked. "I think a part of me just wants to sell them to defy Lord Grenton."

"Why do you suppose that is?"

Georgie clasped her hands in her lap. "I was so angry when he told me I couldn't go to the market. I could almost hear my brother's voice telling me what to do."

"But Lord Grenton isn't your brother."

"No, he is not," Georgie said. "He may be stern, but I do believe he was trying to protect me, in his own way."

"Isn't that a good thing?"

Georgie pressed her lips together before admitting, "I want to prove that I can take care of myself. My brother was so awful that I hid a part of myself away because it was safer. After a time, I forgot who I was and what I am capable of."

"It is behind you," Evie responded. "Your brother can't hurt you now."

"I know that I am in reduced circumstances, living at the orphanage, but I feel happier than I have in a long time."

Evie perused her black gown. "Were you close with your father?"

"I was," she replied. "He was a good father, and I loved him beyond words. But he became consumed with grief after my mother died and was never the same."

"How did he die?"

"The doctor said his heart gave out on him. I believe it broke when Mother passed," Georgie said. "My parents were truly devoted to one another, even to the grave."

"That is the testament of a true love story."

Georgie sighed. "My brother says that love is a weakness."

"Do you agree?"

"No," Georgie replied. "My parents' love bonded our family together, despite my brother rebelling against it."

Evie glanced over at the window, then asked, "Why did your brother rebel against it?"

"Charles never seemed to be happy with what he had," Georgie said. "He always wanted more; demanded more, really. It was a source of conflict for our family."

"Some people are never content with what they have because they are fighting a battle within themselves for what true happiness really is."

Georgie hesitated before revealing, "Charles was expelled from Eton for beating another student so severely that he almost died."

"How terrible!"

"It wasn't the first time that he had gotten into fights with his classmates," Georgie said. "He was a bully, and has a terrible temper."

"Sounds like a perfect combination for trouble."

"It was, and I was always mindful to avoid Charles when he was in a bad mood."

Evie's eyes held compassion. "Did he always hit you?"

Georgie lowered her gaze as she admitted, "He was always rough with me, but the beatings didn't start until after my father died."

"I'm sorry you were forced to endure that."

Bringing her gaze back up, Georgie said, "I will forever be in my household staff's debt for freeing me from my prison."

The coach came to a stop and dipped to the side as a footman stepped off his perch. The door opened and the footman extended his hand to offer his assistance.

As Georgie exited the coach, she kept the gowns draped over one arm and placed her hand into the footman's. She stopped on the pavement, removed her hand, and stared at the scene in front of her. Vendors were standing around with tables and carts, hawking their goods as people milled around.

Evie came to stand next to her. "Stay close to me," she said.

"I have every intention to," Georgie replied as she followed Evie through the crowded square. The vendors shouted at them as they passed by, trying to entice them to stop and look at their goods.

A tall, older man with missing front teeth stepped in front of her and smiled. "Aren't ye a pretty little thing?"

"If you will excuse me," she said as she stepped to the side to go around him.

The man did the same, blocking her path. "What are ye looking for?" he asked. "Perhaps I can help you find it."

To her relief, Evie appeared by her side. "She is with me."

The man sneered. "Two pretty little things," he said, taking a step closer to them. "It must be my lucky day."

"If you do not let us pass, you will rue the day you crossed me," Evie said as a dagger appeared in her right hand.

The man glanced down at the dagger. "Do you even know how to use that?"

"Do you really want to find out?" Evie asked.

The man hesitated before stepping to the side. "I hope you ladies find what you are looking for," he said before he disappeared back into the crowd.

Evie put a hand on Georgie's sleeve and said, "It isn't much further."

As they walked down the path, Georgie asked, "Would you really have stabbed him?"

"There are a different set of laws on the street than what we are taught in boarding school," Evie said.

Georgie noticed that Evie didn't answer her question but decided to drop the matter.

Evie led her towards a table in the corner of the square, piles of multi-colored fabric covering the surface. A woman with dark hair rose from her seat behind it as they approached.

"Evie!" she exclaimed. "How is my favorite customer?"

"I am well, Mrs. Taylor," Evie replied as she fingered the material on the table. "My friend is selling a few of her gowns. Are you interested?"

"I am, especially if they are nearly as fine as the one she is wearing." Mrs. Taylor addressed Georgie. "May I see them?"

Georgie extended the gowns towards her. "They were created by Madam Gallant."

Mrs. Taylor set the gowns atop the fabric on the table and leaned closer to study them. "The stitching is exquisite, and I do not doubt the authenticity."

Evie spoke up. "Miss Lloyd is headmistress at an orphanage and is selling her gowns to raise funds for the girls."

"What a noble cause," Mrs. Taylor replied, her eyes remaining on the gowns as she handled them. "I will take all of them." She reached into her pocket and removed a handful of bills. "This should be sufficient."

Georgie accepted the money and stared at it in disbelief. "This is far too generous."

Mrs. Taylor smiled before shifting her gaze to Evie. "I can tell that your friend is not used to how things are done at the market."

"No, she is not," Evie said. "But she is a fast learner."

The smile disappeared from Mrs. Taylor's lips. "You might want to put that money away before we both get robbed."

Georgie quickly slipped the money into her reticule.

Evie stepped closer to the table and lowered her voice. "Do you have anything new?"

"I do, but it is in the cart," Mrs. Taylor replied. "Would you care for me to show you?"

Evie nodded. "I would."

Mrs. Taylor glanced at her before asking, "Will your friend be joining us?"

"Not this time, but I was hoping Brutus would keep her company," Evie replied. "She doesn't usually frequent the market."

As if on cue, a burly man came to Mrs. Taylor's side. "I will wait with your friend," he said, his voice deeper than Georgie had been anticipating.

Evie turned to face her. "I will be right back. Don't go anywhere."

"I have nowhere to go."

With a quick nod, Evie followed Mrs. Taylor to a cart that sat a short distance away behind the table.

Georgie turned her attention back towards the fabric on the table and began to peruse it. She kept her head down, but she could feel Brutus' watchful eyes on her. She had so many questions for Evie, but she didn't think her friend would be forthcoming with her answers.

A stocky man brushed up against her, and she stumbled back.

He caught her by the arm and steadied her. "My apologies," he said. "I'm afraid I wasn't watching where I was going."

"No harm done." Georgie tried to step back, but the man hadn't released his hold on her arm.

"I'm glad to hear that, Miss Holbrooke."

Georgie's eyes widened. "How do you know my name?"

The man smirked. "Your brother is very worried about you and is eager for you to return home."

Georgie attempted to yank her arm back, but the man tightened his hold. "Let me go!" she exclaimed.

Brutus appeared by her side. "I think the lady has asked nicely for you to let her go."

The man took his other hand and removed a pistol from the waistband of his trousers, and Brutus took a step back with his hands up.

"Miss Holbrooke is coming with me," the man stated firmly.

The sound of a pistol cocking came from behind the man. "I think not," Evie said. "If you don't release Miss Holbrooke, I will kill you."

"You wouldn't dare," the man growled.

Evie's voice was low and calm. "You don't know what great lengths I would take to keep my friends safe."

Uncertainty crossed the man's face before he released his hold on Georgie and slowly tucked his pistol back into the waistband of his trousers.

"You are doing more harm than good," he said. "I am a Bow Street Runner, and Lord Wakefield hired me to find his sister because he is concerned about her. Miss Holbrooke should be home where she belongs."

Georgie huffed. "I truly doubt that."

"Tell Lord Wakefield that Miss Holbrooke has no intention of returning home," Evie said.

"Am I free to go, then?" the man asked.

Evie stepped back and lowered her pistol to her side. "You are, but if you approach Miss Holbrooke again, I will shoot you."

The man nodded his understanding before he tucked his hands in his pockets and walked off at a leisurely pace, as if he didn't have a care in the world.

Georgie watched his retreating figure. "How did my brother know where to find me?"

"I don't rightly know, but I am going to find out." Evie slipped her pistol back into the pocket hidden in the folds of her dress. "It is time for us to leave."

"I couldn't agree more."

Chapter Nine

William sat in the darkness of the coach as it made its way towards Hawthorne's townhouse. He was dreading this evening. He wasn't in the mood to converse with anyone, much less the lively Lady Hawthorne. She always had a smile on her face and a kind word on her lips, regardless of whether the situation warranted one. It was aggravating, really. What was worse was that she was genuine in her affection. How could someone be so blissfully content with their life?

The coach stopped in front of the whitewashed town-house, and William stepped out, attempting to erase all hints of irritation from his features. Why had he agreed to dine with them this evening? His time would have been much better spent working on the list of things his man of business had brought up at their last meeting or having a drink—or two.

He knew he drank entirely too much, but the numbness he received in return for his imbibing was a relief to his reality; for a brief moment of time, he didn't feel the unrelenting grief that threatened to consume him, making him more miserable in the process.

The main door opened, and the butler stood to the side to

grant him entry. William stepped inside and glanced around the expansive hall. The blue-papered walls contrasted nicely with the black and white tiles of the floor.

Once the butler closed the door, he said, "Lord and Lady Hawthorne will be down in a moment. Allow me to show you to the drawing room, Lord Grenton."

William followed the butler into the drawing room and was surprised to discover Miss Lloyd there, standing near the window and staring out into the gardens. She was dressed in a black gown, no surprise given her mourning, and her hair was piled high on top of her head with small curls framing her face. He stood for a moment watching her, reluctant at first to intrude on whatever thoughts were holding her rapt and motionless. But he eventually grew tired of waiting for her to notice him.

"Miss Lloyd," he greeted, his voice terse to his own ears. "What an unexpected surprise to see you this evening."

Miss Lloyd turned to face him, a smile tugging at her lips. "Pardon me for saying so, but you don't seem pleased to see me."

"Do not take offense where none was intended," William said. "Frankly, there are very few people that I am actually pleased to see anymore."

"May I ask why that is?"

William clasped his hands behind his back. "I have learned that people will inevitably disappoint me, and I've come to rely only on a small group of people that I trust."

"That is a sad way to live, my lord."

"I disagree," William said. "I see no issue with the way I live."

"Are you not concerned that your standards for pleasant company may be too high?"

"Why should I lower my standard of competence to satisfy another?"

Miss Lloyd studied him for a moment before saying, "It has been my experience that people will rise up when given the opportunity."

William shook his head. "Time is a limited commodity in my world, and I don't have the luxury to wait in hopes that someone has half a brain."

"That is rather crass of you to say."

"It is the truth, and I only deal in truths, Miss Lloyd." He lifted his brow, challenging her. "Don't you?"

Miss Lloyd cocked her head. "You wish for the truth, then."

Surprised by her bold assertion, he replied, "I do."

"I think you underestimate people, which is doing a great disservice to them and yourself," Miss Lloyd said.

"Perhaps you overestimate them," William countered. "I don't have time to coddle people."

Miss Lloyd stepped away from the window as she asked, "Do you ever find yourself lonely, my lord?"

"Loneliness is an old friend, a comfort."

"I don't believe you truly mean that."

William unclasped his hands. "We hardly know one another," he said. "What gives you the right to stand there and tell me what I am or am not feeling?"

"Everyone has an innate desire to be loved."

"Now you are a philosopher?" he mocked.

"No, but I can recognize someone who is hurting deeply," Miss Lloyd said.

William clenched his jaw. "You are dangerously close to being dismissed. I would proceed with caution if I were you."

"I thought you wanted the truth?" Miss Lloyd asked. "I suppose you prefer speaking the truth, rather than hearing it."

William took a step closer. "I would prefer if we waited in silence for Lord and Lady Hawthorne to join us."

"If that is your wish."

"It is," William replied.

Miss Lloyd simply turned and sat on an upholstered armchair, smoothing her gown. Her expression was unreadable as she turned her gaze towards the fire in the hearth. Why did such a beautiful woman have to be so infuriatingly opinionated? It was maddening, really.

She had no right to speak so brazenly to him. He was her employer, and she should respect him enough to hold her tongue. She'd spoken to him with no hesitation, no fear, in her voice. And the worst part was that she wasn't wrong. He was hurting; but there was nothing that could be done for him.

William walked over to the camelback settee and sat down. If he had known Miss Lloyd was invited, he wouldn't have come. She unsettled him, and he didn't like feeling that way.

Miss Lloyd spoke up. "I do apologize if I offended you with my blunt words."

He stifled the groan on his lips. What happened to the silence they had agreed upon?

She gave him a sheepish smile. "I tend to speak my mind."

"That can be a curse and a blessing."

"Which do you think it is?"

William thought about it for a moment. "A man would be praised for his bold speech, but a woman would be condemned for it."

"Is that how you feel?"

With a shake of his head, he replied, "I do not. A woman should have the right to express her opinions, whether they be right or wrong."

Relief flickered in Miss Lloyd's eyes. "Not every man feels as you do."

"I cannot speak for other men," he replied. "I can only speak for myself, and I was raised by a mother who had strong views."

"As was I."

"That is not surprising," he said lightly.

Miss Lloyd turned her attention back towards the fire, but now that the silence had been broken, he didn't want to return to it yet. There was something about the woman before him that kept drawing him back in—and it was that something that caused him to pause.

"How are you adjusting to running the orphanage?" he asked. That was a simple question, a safe question.

"Very well. The girls are a delight, but I do not think Mrs. Hughes likes me very much."

William smiled. "If it helps, I don't think she likes anyone."

"If that is the case, may I ask how she was hired on as the housekeeper?"

"She came highly recommended."

"By whom?"

"My mother," William replied. "She was a lot like you are. She saw the good in other people, which is something I didn't inherit."

"It is something that can be learned."

William shook his head. "I don't believe that to be the case."

"Although, I am curious to know what good she saw in Mrs. Hughes," Miss Lloyd joked "She told me that I was walking too loudly in the hall yesterday."

"Too loudly?"

"Apparently so," Miss Lloyd said. "Mrs. Hughes has a list of complaints that she runs through every morning."

"What else is on the list?"

"What isn't on the list?" Miss Lloyd countered, tossing her hands in the air. "She complains that my gowns are too fancy to be worn at an orphanage and insists that I dress in drab gowns."

"I see; and do you have any intention to?"

"I do not."

William nodded in approval. "I concur."

"I do feel that Mrs. Hughes is attempting to protect the girls in her own way," Miss Lloyd said. "She is not someone who accepts change very easily."

"I would give her time. Mrs. Hughes did run the orphanage until you arrived."

Miss Lloyd didn't look very convinced. As she opened her mouth to respond, Dinah stepped into the room with a broad smile on her face.

"I am sorry that we kept you waiting," Dinah said as her husband followed her into the room. "I do hope you two found something to talk about."

Rising, William replied. "That we did."

Dinah bobbed her head. "We would have been down much sooner, but Nathanial couldn't decide which cravat to wear."

"That isn't entirely true," Hawthorne replied. "My wife wasn't pleased with my original choice."

"You chose poorly the first time," Dinah said, offering him a private smile, "but your second attempt was much better."

Miss Lloyd rose from her seat. "I do thank you for inviting me this evening."

"You are always welcome in my home, Miss Lloyd," Dinah said. "Besides, we need to inform Lord Grenton of our plans for the orphanage."

"Our plans?" William asked, glancing between Dinah and Miss Lloyd.

Dinah turned towards him. "But, of course," she replied. "I am a patron now, and there are some changes that we must see to at once."

"Such as?"

Dinah tsked. "Let's not get ahead of ourselves. We must have something to discuss over dinner."

As if on cue, the butler stepped into the room and announced, "Dinner is ready to be served."

"Wonderful," Dinah said. "Shall we adjourn to the dining room?"

"Splendid idea, my love," Hawthorne replied as he offered his arm.

As they walked out of the room, William knew he had no choice but to accompany Miss Lloyd into the dining room for propriety's sake. He approached her and put his gloved hand out. "May I escort you to the dining room?"

Miss Lloyd glanced down at his hand, indecision on her features. "That isn't truly necessary, my lord."

"But it is my privilege," he forced out.

She tentatively slipped her hand into his and he tucked it into the crook of his arm. "Thank you," she murmured.

William led her out of the drawing room, and he couldn't help but notice her rigid posture. "Are you all right, Miss Lloyd?"

"I am."

He could tell that she was lying, but decided to let the matter drop. He had more important things to deal with than trying to convince an obstinate woman to confide in him.

Georgie sat in the dining room as she listened to everyone converse, but she was reeling from the fact that she had felt something when she touched Lord Grenton. An undeniable spark—which was preposterous! That boorish man had shown her no favor, nor did she want him to. So why had she reacted in such a fashion?

It would be in her best interest to stay far away from Lord Grenton. She was sure of that. If he knew the truth, she had no doubt that he would dismiss her without a second thought.

Lady Hawthorne's voice broke through her musings. "Do you agree, Miss Lloyd?"

Georgie brought her gaze up and was forced to give an apologetic smile. "I apologize, but I'm afraid I was wool-gathering."

"That is what I supposed." Lady Hawthorne returned her smile. "I was just discussing with Lord Grenton about our vision for the orphanage."

Lord Grenton wiped the sides of his mouth with his napkin. "I do worry that your vision is much too progressive for these girls."

"I disagree," Lady Hawthorne said. "These girls need to be educated, giving them ample opportunities."

Lord Grenton huffed. "I only agreed to hire tutors to help the girls learn how to read. I have no intention of educating them."

"But you must!" Lady Hawthorne pressed. "It wouldn't cost much more to educate them."

"It is an orphanage, not a boarding school," Lord Grenton pressed.

"It could be both."

Shifting his attention towards Lord Hawthorne, Lord Grenton asked, "What are your thoughts on this matter?"

Lord Hawthorne reached for his wife's hand. "I am a smart enough man to side with my wife on this issue."

Lord Grenton frowned. "What if the girls hope to rise above their stations?" he asked. "Are we not doing a disservice to them?"

Georgie spoke up. "Educating one's mind is never a mistake, since it inspires them to hope for a better future."

"A future that may never come to pass," Lord Grenton said.

"At least we tried," Georgie countered.

Lord Grenton sighed. "This endeavor sounds like it will cost me a great deal of money."

"It won't," Lady Hawthorne said. "We will help fund the girls' education, and I will personally oversee it."

Lord Grenton shifted in his seat to face her. "Will that be an issue, Miss Lloyd?"

"Not at all," Georgie replied. "I welcome Lady Hawthorne's assistance."

Lord Grenton hesitated for only a moment before saying, "Very well. I see that I am outnumbered; but I do hope you two know what you are getting yourselves into."

"We do," Lady Hawthorne responded.

Lord Hawthorne chuckled. "My wife is rather confident in her abilities."

Lord Grenton glanced at Georgie. "Now that is all worked out, you will have the funds at your disposal to hire tutors," he said.

"Thank you, my lord," Georgie said.

As Lord Grenton leaned to the side to allow the footman to collect his bowl, he remarked, "It must be a relief that you didn't sell your gowns to fund the tutors."

Georgie's eyes shot over to Lady Hawthorne, who in turn gave her a quizzical look. "It is," she murmured.

"Although it was a kind gesture on your part to offer, I daresay that you wouldn't have been able to raise enough funds to cover the tutors' expenses."

An uncomfortable silence descended upon them as Georgie tried to formulate her next words carefully. She didn't want to lie to him, but she was hesitant to reveal the truth. Would he dismiss her for disobeying him?

Lord Grenton continued. "A lady has no place at a market."

"Quite right," Lord Hawthorne said, raising his glass.

Anger flashed through her at their words. Georgie would not be controlled by any man ever again, and felt as if she had to prove it to Lord Grenton.

As she reached for her glass, she remarked, "Frankly, it

wasn't as terrible as I thought it would be." She hoped her words sounded much more confident than she felt at the moment.

Lord Grenton clenched his jaw. "Did you visit the market?"

"I did." Georgie took a sip of her drink. "I was able to sell my dresses for a fair price."

"For what purpose?" Lord Grenton asked, his voice curt. "I had already informed you that I would cover the expense of the tutors."

"That was most generous of you, but I noticed that the girls could use new dresses and boots," Georgie replied as she returned her glass to the table. One of the girls had mentioned her feet being soaked when she stepped in a puddle, prompting Georgie to take visual stock of their attire. "My gowns will more than cover that additional expense."

"Why didn't you inform me of your decision?"

"Because I knew you would disapprove," Georgie said.

Lord Grenton tossed his napkin onto the table and shoved back his chair. "May I speak to you for a moment, Miss Lloyd?" he asked, rising.

Georgie rose. "Yes, my lord."

As she followed Lord Grenton out of the room, Lady Hawthorne gave her an encouraging smile. She was fortunate to have an ally in her.

They had just departed from the dining room when Lord Grenton turned back to face her with an irritated look on his face. "Do you intend to disobey me on every directive that I give?"

"Only the ones that I disagree with."

Lord Grenton's eyes narrowed. "I agreed to pay for the tutors so you wouldn't have to go to the market," he said. "That is no place for a lady."

"And I believe I informed you that I can take care of myself."

"Surely, you cannot be that naïve?" Lord Grenton asked. "You are lucky that you weren't abducted or robbed!"

"For your information, someone did attempt to abduct me, but Miss Ashmore was able to convince him otherwise."

Even as the words left her mouth, Georgie knew that she had made a terrible mistake.

Lord Grenton's eyes grew wide. "Someone attempted to abduct you?"

"They did, but it was of little consequence."

That was the wrong thing to say.

"It was of little consequence?" Lord Grenton growled. "Are you mad?"

"I assure you that I am not."

Lord Grenton took a step closer to her. "Do you have any idea of what would have happened to you if you had been abducted?"

"I have a fairly good idea," she replied.

"You cannot fathom the depravity of men," he said. "You could have been made to do unspeakable things."

Georgie tilted her chin. "You need not concern yourself with me."

"Pray tell, what would have happened to the orphanage if you had been abducted?" Lord Grenton asked. "Who would run it?"

"Nothing will happen to me."

Lord Grenton huffed. "Why? Because you carry a muff pistol on your person?"

"That is one reason."

"You are a fool, Miss Lloyd, and I don't employ fools."

Georgie stared back at him, unsure of his meaning. "What are you saying?"

"You are dismissed."

"Because I went to the market?"

Lord Grenton's expression was stern. "You deliberately disobeyed me."

"You hired me only to run your orphanage," Georgie said. "You do not get to dictate my every action."

"Those go hand in hand, I'm afraid."

"You are wrong."

"Whether I am right or wrong doesn't matter now," Lord Grenton remarked. "I have made my decision, and we both must live with it."

Georgie shook her head. "You are a stubborn jackanapes."

"There is no need for name calling."

"Your mother wanted a lady to run the orphanage for a specific reason," she said. "Why do you suppose that was?"

A frown of displeasure crossed his features. "You will leave my mother out of this."

"Your mother wanted to give the orphans a chance to succeed in this life, and I was helping them to do so."

"Lady Hawthorne will carry on with your work."

Georgie took a step closer to him, and she had to tilt her head to look up at him. "You were looking for a reason to dismiss me from the moment you met me," she said. "Do not insult me by pretending otherwise."

"It is true," Lord Grenton responded. "You are not the type of headmistress that I imagined for my mother's orphanage."

"What did you envision?"

"Someone who followed my dictates."

"You mean someone that you could control."

Lord Grenton leaned closer. "If you had only listened to me, you wouldn't find yourself in this position."

"My position is less than ideal, but it matters not," Georgie said. "I will survive this, and I will come out stronger because of it."

Lord Grenton hesitated before asking, "What will you do now?"

"I don't know, but it isn't your concern." Georgie took a

step back and tried to pretend that she wasn't angry or hurt by this maddening lord. "I will inform the girls of your decision and depart tomorrow."

Reaching into his pocket, Lord Grenton pulled out a few pounds and extended them towards her. "This should help you until you secure your next position."

Georgie put her hand up. "No, thank you," she said firmly. "I will be just fine without your assistance."

"Just take the money."

"I do not require or want it, my lord."

"But it would make me feel better knowing you weren't destitute."

Georgie could hear the concern in his voice, and her posture softened slightly. "I can assure you that I am not destitute," she said. "You know very little about me and my circumstances."

Lord Grenton lowered his hand to his side. "That is a true statement. You haven't seemed inclined to be very forthcoming."

"Why should I trust you when you have only tried to control me?"

"I am trying to protect you," he replied. "You are a lady who is living in the rookeries. That is a harsh place to live, much less survive."

"I don't need a protector."

"I think you do."

Georgie didn't take offense at his words because she knew he believed them. "I do believe, deep down, that you are a good man, but I refuse to be controlled. Not anymore. I want to be in control of my own destiny."

"But you are a woman."

"Thank you for noticing."

Lord Grenton ignored her attempt at humor and continued. "Your prospects are limited."

"That may be true, but I am not under anyone's rule," Georgie said, "and that is a wonderful feeling."

Lady Hawthorne stepped into the doorway and glanced between them. "Is everything all right?"

Georgie turned towards her. "I'm afraid I have developed a headache. I think it might be best if I depart for the evening."

"That is most unfortunate," Lady Hawthorne said, a frown appearing on her lips. "I will see to the coach being brought out front."

As Lady Hawthorne walked away, Lord Grenton said, "It will ease my conscience if you accept the money."

"I don't want your money."

"Then what do you want?"

Georgie softened her tone a little. "Nothing that you can give me."

"It has been my experience that people always want something from me."

"Then you are associating with the wrong people, my lord."

Lord Grenton returned the money to his waistcoat pocket. "I wish you luck with your endeavors, Miss Lloyd," he said.

"Thank you," she murmured. "I hope you find a headmistress who will love those girls as much as I do."

"That is a tall feat."

Georgie looked at him furtively, trying to read his eyes, but they were guarded, revealing nothing. "Enjoy the rest of your meal, my lord." She didn't wait for his response before she brushed past him and headed towards the entry hall. She could feel tears welling up in her eyes, but she didn't dare cry in front of Lord Grenton.

She may have only been at the orphanage for a short time, but she had grown to love those girls. They had been her responsibility, and she believed in them. She knew they were capable of great things, and they needed to be given the chance to prove it. Would the next headmistress share her same vision? She certainly hoped so.

Georgie came to a stop in the entry hall and swiped at a tear that had escaped and was rolling down her cheek. She would be just fine. She would have to sell some of her mother's jewelry, but she would survive this. It would be all right.

Chapter Ten

William watched as Miss Lloyd walked away, working hard to ignore the twinge of guilt that he felt. He'd had no choice but to dismiss her. She had deliberately disobeyed him, and he couldn't overlook that. Why did she have to be so obstinate?

He had made the right choice. Miss Lloyd was entirely too headstrong to be a headmistress. She would fill the girls' heads with a sense of grandeur, and he couldn't allow that. He needed to find a headmistress who would be practical and more submissive to his requests.

He stifled the groan on his lips. It had been so difficult to find a lady to fill the position of headmistress in the first place. Finding a replacement wouldn't be an easy task, but he couldn't stand by and let Miss Lloyd continue to run the orphanage. She would turn all of the girls into bluestockings.

A part of him knew that he was just looking for a reason to justify his actions.

As he turned back towards the dining room, Lady Hawthorne approached him with a frown.

"You dismissed her?" she asked.

"I did."

"Are you mad?"

It was William's turn to frown. "I am not."

Lady Hawthorne rested a hand on her hip. "Miss Lloyd was the best thing that happened to that orphanage. She breathed fresh life into it."

"She was insubordinate."

"In what way?"

"I told her not to go to the market, and she defied me."

Lady Hawthorne arched an eyebrow. "Is she your prisoner?"

"She is not."

"Then why should you dictate her every action?"

"Miss Lloyd is my employee." He stopped and corrected himself. "She *was* my employee, and I expected her to behave accordingly."

"Why is going to the market so terrible?"

"It isn't safe for a lady."

"Why should that matter to you?" Lady Hawthorne asked. "Did she ask you to accompany her to the market?"

"She did not."

"Then why did you take issue with it?"

William tensed, tired of being forced to justify his actions. "I told her not to go. That should have been sufficient."

"Miss Lloyd was selling her gowns to help the orphans," Lady Hawthorne said. "Her intentions were far from nefarious."

"I had already informed her that I would pay for the tutors, so there was no need for her to sell her gowns."

"You did, which is why she plans to use the money to buy the girls new frocks and boots."

"I never asked her to do that."

"You didn't have to," Lady Hawthorne said. "Miss Lloyd is a kindhearted person who only wants the best for those girls."

"*I* want the best for those girls," William argued.

"Clearly not, because you fired the one person who could enact real change in that place."

William huffed. "I daresay that you are giving her far too much credit."

"Perhaps you are not giving her enough."

Hawthorne stepped into the doorway. "Is something amiss?" he asked.

His wife turned towards him and replied, "William dismissed Miss Lloyd."

"You did?" Hawthorne asked.

"It was the only logical thing to do," William defended. "I told her not to go to the market, and she defied me."

"I see," Hawthorne muttered. "And you think that warranted termination?"

"I do," William said. "Do not forget that she employs a butler, a lady's maid, and a cook at the orphanage."

"Do the girls not benefit from the cook?" Lady Hawthorne asked.

"They do, but it is an extravagance."

"Does Miss Lloyd not pay for the cook's salary out of her own income?" Lady Hawthorne pressed.

"Yes, but—"

Lady Hawthorne spoke over him. "Then I see no reason for you to take issue with it." She brought a hand up to her head. "I feel a headache coming on. I have no doubt that it is caused by the sheer stupidity of this conversation."

Hawthorne walked over to his wife. "Would you care for me to escort you to your bedchamber?"

"That won't be necessary," she answered. "Why don't you try to talk some sense into Grenton?"

As Lady Hawthorne headed towards the stairs, her husband's eyes remained on her retreating figure. "I haven't seen her this worked up in quite some time."

"I do not understand why she is so upset, especially since it doesn't affect her."

"But it does," Hawthorne said. "She is now a patron of the orphanage, and she had great plans for the girls."

"She can still proceed with her vision."

"Not without Miss Lloyd," Hawthorne replied. "She was the driving force behind their plans."

"I will strive to hire a new headmistress who shares your wife's passion."

Hawthorne gave him a knowing look. "Do you think that is likely?" he asked. "I recall how difficult it was for you to find a headmistress in the first place."

William shifted uncomfortably in his stance. "Do you think I made a mistake?"

"I can't say, but I can say for certainty that Dinah thinks you did." Hawthorne gestured towards the dining room. "Shall we finish our dinner?"

"I'm afraid I am not hungry."

Hawthorne gave him an understanding look. "A drink, perhaps?"

"That would be splendid."

William followed Hawthorne to his study and stopped near the settee. He watched as his friend picked up the decanter and poured two drinks.

As Hawthorne picked up the glasses, he asked, "What do you think your mother's vision was for the orphanage?"

"I don't rightly know."

"She wanted a lady to run it," Hawthorne said as he extended him a glass. "Why do you suppose that was?"

"To exhaust me."

"I doubt that. Your mother always had a specific way of doing things. She was purposeful in her thoughts and actions."

"That she was," William agreed.

Hawthorne took a sip of his drink. "If she wanted a lady to run the orphanage, there had to be a reason behind it."

"My mother was progressive," William said. "I know she would approve of what Miss Lloyd was trying to do."

"But you don't?"

William brought the glass up to his lips. "I am just worried that the orphans will not be content with their lot in life afterwards."

"Isn't that for them to decide?"

After William took a sip, he lowered the glass to his side. "What Miss Lloyd proposed will require a lot of time and effort."

"Which she was willing to provide."

"She cannot understand the intricacies of those orphans' lives."

"But you do?" Hawthorne asked.

William sat down on the settee. "What am I to do?" he asked. "Allow Miss Lloyd to do as she pleases in running the orphanage?"

"That sounds like a solid plan."

William shot his friend an annoyed look. "Do be serious."

"I am," Hawthorne replied. "Miss Lloyd appears to be, by all accounts, a clever woman, and Dinah seems to like her."

"There must be another lady who will run the orphanage and do precisely as I say."

"Is that what you want?"

"Pardon?"

Hawthorne came to sit across from him. "I have discovered that women who challenge us make us better men."

"I am not looking for a challenge."

"No?" Hawthorne asked. "Because I can't help but notice that you act impulsively around Miss Lloyd."

"I do no such thing."

Hawthorne placed his glass down onto the table. "Do you want to know what I think?"

"Not particularly."

"You have developed feelings for Miss Lloyd."

William scoffed. "You think I developed feelings for that stubborn, vexing woman?"

"I do, and I think it has clouded your judgement."

"You couldn't be more wrong." William tossed back his drink. "I feel nothing for Miss Lloyd."

"Then why did you fire her?"

"Because she defied me," William said, his voice rising.

Hawthorne reached for his glass and took a sip. As he lowered it to his lap, he asked, "Why does it bother you so much that she defied you?"

Rising, William replied, "I am done with this line of questioning."

"She unnerves you, and that scares you."

William slowly returned to his seat. "Miss Lloyd is infuriating, and she doesn't seem to be intimidated by me."

"Do you want her to be intimidated by you?"

"Yes… no…" He stopped. "I don't know."

Hawthorne moved to sit on the edge of his seat. "I don't believe that Miss Lloyd is the problem. I think it is you."

"Me?"

"You can't dictate everyone's actions," Hawthorne said. "If Miss Lloyd wants to go to the market, then you can't stop her."

"But she could be hurt, or worse!"

"I'm sure she understands the risk."

William placed his empty glass onto the table. "If she gets herself killed, then I am out a headmistress."

"Aren't you already out one?" Hawthorne pointed out.

William leaned back in his seat and thought for a moment. "I blundered this, didn't I?"

"It's not too late to fix it."

"Do I want to fix it?"

Hawthorne shrugged. "What is more important to you—your pride, or your mother's orphanage?"

William let out a sigh, knowing his friend had made a valid point. "I suppose when you put it like that." He rose. "Now I am in the uncomfortable position of having to hire Miss Lloyd back."

"I wish you luck."

"I don't need luck. I just hope that she will be sensible about it." William walked over to the door and stopped. "Will you please inform Dinah that I intend to rehire Miss Lloyd?"

"I will."

"I do hope that will appease her."

"I have no doubt that it will."

William tipped his head. "I bid you good night," he said before he departed from the room.

As he walked towards the main door, he couldn't believe how the evening had unfolded. He had fired his headmistress only to realize that he had been too hasty in his decision. But it had nothing to do with having feelings for her; that was ludicrous. He felt nothing for Miss Lloyd. Why would Hawthorne even suggest such a thing?

He would offer Miss Lloyd her job back, and if she refused, then he would drop the matter. He had no intention of groveling. He had never groveled before, and he refused to start now.

***

As Georgie exited the coach, the main door to the orphanage opened and Wilson stood to the side to let her enter.

"Good evening, miss," Wilson greeted as he closed the door. "You are home much earlier than expected."

"Yes, well, it is because Lord Grenton dismissed me as headmistress."

Wilson's brow lifted. "He dismissed you?"

"He did," Georgie confirmed. "He took issue with me going to the market."

"Even though you did so to help the girls?"

"He didn't seem to care about that."

"That is a shame."

Georgie bobbed her head. "It is, but I have a plan."

Wilson gave her an amused look. "That doesn't surprise me."

"We will sell a few pieces of my mother's jewelry and use that money to rent rooms at a boarding house," Georgie explained. "We only need to bide our time until I reach my majority."

"What of the money that you earned from selling your gowns?"

"That money is allocated for the girls' new dresses and boots," Georgie said. "I wouldn't dare deprive the girls of new clothing."

"That is most gracious of you."

Georgie waved her hand dismissively in front of her. "It is a small thing."

"To you, perhaps."

She had just opened her mouth to respond when she saw Sarah walking towards her with a questioning look.

"Do you still intend to teach us how to read?" Sarah asked as she came to a stop in front of her.

"I do," Georgie confirmed. "I am in the process of hiring tutors to do so."

A bright smile came to Sarah's face. "Wonderful! I've dreamed of learning to read for so long, but I didn't think I'd ever have the chance."

"I am pleased that you have a desire to learn."

"Oh, yes!" Sarah gushed. "And I know Rebecca will be thrilled, too."

Georgie smiled. "I just want…"

Her voice trailed off as Mrs. Hughes's sharp voice came from the top of the stairs. "Sarah!" she shouted. "What on earth are you doing?"

Sarah gave Georgie a rueful look. "I was just talking to Miss Lloyd."

"Your chores won't get done if you are dawdling," Mrs. Hughes stated as she descended the stairs.

"Yes, Mrs. Hughes," Sarah murmured, lowering her gaze.

Mrs. Hughes stopped at the bottom of the stairs. "Go along, then," she said. "You know how I feel about shirking your responsibilities."

Sarah turned on her heel and hurried down the hall without so much as a glance behind her.

Mrs. Hughes turned to Georgie, her chin lifted. "I would appreciate it if you did not distract the girls from doing their chores."

"I was merely speaking to Sarah," Georgie defended.

"The girls are on a strict schedule, and you need to be mindful of that." Mrs. Hughes frowned. "The whole orphanage is buzzing about how you intend to teach them how to read."

"It is wonderful news, isn't it?"

"Is it?" Mrs. Hughes asked. "After all, the girls will still have to complete their chores, so they will need to wake up even earlier to do so."

"Do the girls take issue with that?"

Mrs. Hughes huffed. "I take issue with that," she declared. "What you are doing is sheer foolishness, and I fear that you are doing more harm than good."

"I disagree."

"You were raised in privilege, but these girls were lucky to be born," Mrs. Hughes said. "Educating them will not help them."

"It will give them more opportunities."

"And what is wrong with becoming a scullery maid?" Mrs. Hughes demanded. "It is an honest profession for a young woman."

"That may be true, but educating the girls will allow them

to apply as housekeepers or lady's maids."

Mrs. Hughes eyed her critically. "What type of lady would hire a young woman from the rookeries to act as their lady's maid?"

"One who sees value in what we are attempting to do here."

"You are only fooling yourself," Mrs. Hughes said. "The orphanage was doing just fine before you arrived."

"I am only trying to help."

"If you truly cared about these girls, you'd accept the fact that they were born nothing and won't amount to anything in this life."

"I refuse to accept that."

"Then you are doing them a disservice."

A knock came at the door, interrupting their conversation.

Wilson stepped over to the door and opened it, revealing Lord Grenton. He stepped into the entry hall, holding his top hat in his hands, and met Georgie's gaze.

"I do apologize for calling on you at this late hour, but I was hoping for a moment of your time," Lord Grenton said.

Georgie schooled her features into what she hoped was politeness. "Of course, my lord," she said. "We may speak freely in the office."

Mrs. Hughes stepped forward, her face softening. "It is a pleasure to see you again, Lord Grenton."

Lord Grenton tipped his head. "Mrs. Hughes," he acknowledged.

A faint blush came to the housekeeper's cheeks. "Would you care for some refreshment?" she asked.

"That won't be necessary. I do not intend to stay long." Lord Grenton gestured towards the hall, indicating Georgie should go first. "Shall we, Miss Lloyd?"

Georgie headed down the hall and stepped into the office, turning as Lord Grenton ducked into the room. Her gaze remained fixed on him, but she felt no need to speak first. She wasn't quite sure why he was even here. He had already fired her; what else needed to be said between them?

Lord Grenton attempted to smile, but it looked more like a grimace. "How are you this evening?"

"Not well," she replied. "I would appreciate if you would skip the pleasantries and just say what needs to be said."

Lord Grenton's eyes held approval. "After you left, I realized that I may have been hasty in my decision to dismiss you."

"You did?"

"Yes, and I have come to correct my mistake."

Georgie had not been expecting that. She hadn't thought it possible for a man like Lord Grenton to admit that he made a mistake.

Lord Grenton continued. "If you are in agreement, you may stay on as the headmistress, and we can put this unfortunate situation behind us."

"May I ask why you changed your mind?"

"Does it matter?"

"It does to me."

Lord Grenton shifted uncomfortably. "Lady Hawthorne appears to be quite fond of you, and she took issue with my dismissing you," he said. "Furthermore, I came to realize that my mother would have appreciated all that you are doing for the orphans."

"I do hope that is the case."

"May I speak freely?"

Georgie's lips twitched. "I thought you were."

"I am not quite sure what to make of you," Lord Grenton said. "Your stubborn nature is maddening, and you refuse to listen to reason."

Georgie remained silent, unsure of how to respond.

Lord Grenton glanced over at the darkened window before continuing, "But you love these orphans, and I do credit your feelings."

"It is easy to love these girls, my lord."

"I believe that is what my mother would have wanted," Lord Grenton said. "You are bringing her vision for this orphanage to fruition."

"Out of curiosity, why did your mother want a lady to run the orphanage?"

Lord Grenton shrugged one shoulder. "She never said why," he replied, "but my guess is that she wanted someone who would advocate for the girls."

Georgie could hear the love in Lord Grenton's voice as he spoke about his mother. "Your mother sounds like a good woman."

"She was the best of women," Lord Grenton responded. "I have never met a more formidable person than her. When she set her mind on something, she would do everything in her power to make it happen."

"My mother was similar in that regard," Georgie admitted.

Lord Grenton grew silent. "After my sister died, my mother turned her sights to opening an orphanage. She was determined to save as many girls as she was able to."

"That is a noble pursuit."

"It took her much longer than she intended, and she passed before it opened," Lord Grenton shared. "She made me promise that I would continue her life's work."

"And you are fulfilling that promise."

Lord Grenton's eyes grew guarded. "It is the least I can do," he said. "I know how important this orphanage was to her."

"I can see how important it is to you, as well." Georgie unclasped her hands, then said, "I will stay on, but I have one condition."

"You should know that I do not respond to ultimatums, but I find myself curious as to what you are foolish enough to demand of me."

Georgie held his gaze as she replied, "You will spend time here and become acquainted with the girls."

"For what purpose?"

"I think it is important that the girls know their benefactor," she said. "Don't you?"

Indecision crossed Lord Grenton's face, and she feared that he would call her bluff. If he refused her request, she still intended to stay on as the headmistress, assuming he would let her. She knew she was being brazen, but she suspected that Lord Grenton would benefit from spending time at the orphanage. She certainly had, and was hopeful that the girls' vibrant energy would help the intractable lord as well.

After a long moment, Lord Grenton said, "I agree to your condition, but you should know that I am a very busy man. I will spend only as much time as I am able to."

"That is all I can ask for, my lord."

Lord Grenton frowned. "Can I hope that you won't be frequenting the market anymore?"

"There is no need, since I have already sold my gowns," Georgie replied. "Those funds will go to clothing the girls."

"You could have asked me for additional funds."

"I could have, but you are already doing so much for them."

Lord Grenton turned his attention towards the empty bookshelves. "I have rounded up many of the books on your list, and I will see that they are delivered tomorrow."

"That is wonderful news!" Georgie gushed. "I can't wait to start reading to the girls."

Lord Grenton brought his gaze back to meet hers. "May I ask you a question?"

"You may."

"Why do you care so much about them?"

Georgie gave him a baffled look. "Why wouldn't I care about them?"

"I just find it odd that a lady of your station would

embrace these girls so lovingly. After all, they are nothing to you."

"I have never met someone who isn't important," Georgie replied. "I've been using every opportunity I can to get to know the girls here, and they are no different. They have had a rough go of it and deserve to be loved. Furthermore, they need someone to advocate for them, no matter their status in society."

Lord Grenton studied her for a moment, as if gauging her sincerity. "I have never met someone quite like you before, Miss Lloyd."

Georgie smiled. "I shall take that as a compliment."

"You should, because it was meant as one."

He was staring at her so intensely that she felt a betraying blush creep up onto her cheeks, but she refused to drop his gaze. She found solace in his eyes. It was a feeling that she hadn't had since her father was still alive.

Lord Grenton blinked and stepped back. "It is late, and I should depart before I wear out my welcome."

"This is your orphanage, my lord," Georgie responded graciously. "You are welcome to come and go as you please."

"I intend to." Lord Grenton walked over to the door and stopped. "Thank you for staying on as headmistress. I know it will mean a lot to the girls."

"It is my privilege."

Lord Grenton tipped his head. "Good evening, Miss Lloyd," he said before departing from the room.

Georgie walked around the desk and sat down. Good heavens, what had just transpired? Lord Grenton had opened up to her, and now appeared less standoffish. Her job was not to help him, but she could hear the pain in his voice. He was hurting, and she couldn't in good conscience ignore that. With any luck, the more time he spent at the orphanage, the more it would soothe the ache in his heart.

Chapter Eleven

With the morning sun streaming into their room through the window, Alice sat on her mattress and stared up at Georgie in disbelief. "He dismissed you, but then he hired you back?"

"That he did," Georgie said.

"Why?"

Georgie shrugged. "He said that he regretted his hasty decision."

Alice leaned back against the wall, then said, "I didn't think it was capable for Lord Grenton to feel anything."

"He isn't an ogre."

"No, but he has fought you on everything you have attempted to do here," Alice pointed out.

"That he has, but it is different now."

"How?"

Georgie rose from her bed and walked to the window to feel the warmth of the sun on her skin. "Lord Grenton has agreed to visit the orphanage more often and get to know the girls."

Alice lifted her brow. "Why would you want him around more?" she asked. "Aren't you afraid he will continue to criticize every decision you make?"

"I think it would benefit the girls to know their benefactor." Georgie didn't dare mention that she also thought it would benefit Lord Grenton, as well.

"Lord Grenton might scare them," Alice said. "He doesn't exactly invoke a calming presence about him."

"No, he does not, but I do believe he has a good heart."

"Are we speaking about the same lord?"

Georgie laughed. "You are being much too hard on someone that you haven't even met."

"I've just heard him yelling at you from a distance."

"He hasn't yelled at me, per se," Georgie contended. "He is just… loud, sometimes."

Rising, Alice said, "I think you might be blinded by his handsome face."

"I can assure you that is not it."

Alice didn't look convinced. "We should go down to the kitchen before our breakfast gets cold," she encouraged.

A knock came at the door.

Georgie walked over to the door and opened it, revealing a blonde-haired girl. "Mr. Wilson wanted me to inform you that Miss Ashmore has come to call, and she is waiting for you in the study."

"Thank you," Georgie replied. "I will be down shortly."

Alice's voice came from behind her. "Miss Ashmore has been coming around more frequently."

"That she has, but she is teaching me how to protect myself."

"From what?"

Georgie turned around to face her lady's maid. "With luck, I will learn to protect myself from my brother."

"You do not need to fear him, not anymore," Alice said. "He has no idea that you are here, and even if he did, he couldn't get to you."

"I'm not entirely convinced of that."

Alice walked over to the door. "Would you mind if I went

to visit my mother this afternoon?" she asked. "I will be back before supper."

"I take no issue with that."

"Thank you," Alice said. "I need to buy some medicine at the apothecary before I see her."

"Do you have the money to do so?"

"I do," Alice replied. "I've been saving up."

Georgie nodded. "If you need additional funds, I can sell a piece of my jewelry."

"That is kind of you to offer, but I have sufficient for my needs."

"How is your mother faring?"

A sad look came to Alice's face. "Her health is deteriorating, and the apothecary is at a loss for what to do."

"Has she seen a doctor?"

"There is no need," Alice said. "Our apothecary is just as competent as any quack that we could afford to see."

Georgie opened her mouth, but Alice spoke first. "I do not need your money," she said, putting her hand up. "With any luck, the medicine will help with her cough."

"If you change your mind, I am more than happy to help."

Alice smiled. "You are too kind," she said. "You best not keep Miss Ashmore waiting any longer."

As Georgie started walking down the hall, Alice met her stride and asked, "Do you miss your grand townhouse?"

Georgie shook her head. "I do not," she replied. "I am not under my brother's rule anymore, and that is a wonderful feeling." She glanced at her lady's maid. "Do you miss it?"

"I do, actually. I grow tired of hearing the rats scurrying inside of the walls."

Georgie shuddered. "That is a sound that I could do without, as well."

"Mostly I miss the other staff," Alice said in a dejected

voice. "I was close with a few of them, and I am saddened that I didn't get to say goodbye."

The way Alice spoke made Georgie wonder if there was more to the story. So, she decided to prod a little. "Was there someone in particular that you miss more than the others?"

Alice lowered her gaze to the worn floorboards. "There was someone," she said softly.

"May I ask who it is?"

"Thomas," Alice said, bringing her gaze back up. "He was training to become a footman, and I think he was sweet on me."

"I hadn't realized."

Alice waved her hand in front of her. "I know consorting with the opposite sex is looked down upon, but Thomas was always kind to me. He made me feel special."

"There is no shame in that," Georgie said. "I am glad you found someone who makes you happy."

"Do you mean that?"

"I do," Georgie replied. "Hopefully we can convince him to come work at my estate once this is all over with."

Alice bobbed her head. "That would be grand!"

After they descended the stairs, Georgie said, "Please inform Mrs. Peters that I will be along shortly for my breakfast."

"Yes, miss."

Georgie headed down the hall towards her study and stepped into the small room. She saw that Evie was pacing back and forth with a solemn look on her face.

"Whatever is the matter?" Georgie asked.

Evie stopped pacing and said, "I was thinking about your attempted abduction, and I have to ask something." She paused. "How well do you know the staff that came with you?"

"Very well."

"Would any of them betray you?"

Georgie shook her head vehemently. "Absolutely not."

Evie walked over to the door and closed it. "It would be best if this conversation remained private."

"There is no need for secrecy," Georgie insisted. "None of my staff betrayed me to my brother."

"If it wasn't any of them, then how did that Bow Street Runner know where to find you at the market?"

"That must have been a coincidence."

Evie walked over to the window and ran her gloved hand over the latch. "I don't believe in coincidences, and neither should you."

"If my brother knew I was here, why hasn't he retrieved me himself?" Georgie asked.

"Because he doesn't want to show his hand yet."

"I doubt that. He is not known for his patience."

"No, he is not," Evie agreed. "He has quite the temper."

Georgie gave her a curious look. "He does, but how did you know that?"

"I made some inquiries."

"To whom?"

Evie gave her a complacent smile. "You need not worry about that," she said. "I discovered that your brother has made some enemies with some disreputable people."

"I'm afraid I don't understand."

"Did you know your brother was a gambler?" Evie asked.

"That doesn't surprise me."

"He owes people a large sum of money."

Georgie furrowed her brow. "That can't be right," she said. "My brother has the funds to pay his debts."

"Are you sure about that?"

"I am," Georgie said. "My father left my brother a thriving estate."

"Then why hasn't he paid his debts?"

"I can't answer that."

Evie stepped away from the window and remarked, "You

were wise to disassociate yourself from Lord Wakefield. He is not a good man."

Georgie forced her hand to remain at her side instead of rising up to her cheek as she remembered the last time she'd seen him. "I know that all too well."

"I think it would be best if you remained at the orphanage until I can throw the Bow Street Runner off your scent."

"How will you do that?"

"A few well-placed lies should do the trick," Evie said. "I know people who will help fabricate and spread the story."

"May I ask how you are associated with these people?"

Evie gave her an amused look. "It would be best if you didn't know." She glanced at the closed door before asking, "What of Mrs. Hughes?"

"What about her?"

"Do you think she might have discovered the truth about who you are and tipped off your brother?"

"I wouldn't put it past her, but I have been careful about concealing my true identity," Georgie said.

Evie's eyes grew wary. "I would be cautious around Mrs. Hughes if I were you. There is something about her that I don't fully trust."

"Just something?" Georgie asked. "I don't trust her whole person."

"Good point." Evie went to open the door. "Shall we practice your shooting in the courtyard?"

"I think I have fairly good aim."

Evie laughed. "Perhaps for a drunken bear."

"Surely I cannot be that bad."

"You are better than my sister," Evie conceded. "She doesn't like the loud noise of the discharge."

"It does take some time to get accustomed to it."

"That it does, but perfecting your aim could mean the difference between life and death," Evie said before departing from the study.

Georgie sat in her chair as she reviewed the ledger. She took a deep breath and listened to the quiet around her. In the distance, she could hear the smallest hint of the girls' going about their chores.

Wilson stepped into the room and announced, "A Miss Francis Walter is here to see you."

"Please send her in," Georgie instructed as she closed the ledger and placed it to the side.

A moment later, a tall, thin woman, wearing a brown, unassuming dress, stepped into the room. She had her hair pulled back into a tight chignon, emphasizing her dainty nose.

"Good morning," Miss Walter greeted. "I do hope I did not arrive too early."

"There is no such thing at an orphanage." Georgie pointed towards the chair that was facing the desk, indicating that she should sit.

Miss Walter sat down, her back rigid. "I am responding to your advertisement for a tutor."

"I assumed as much."

Reaching into her bag, Miss Walter pulled out a folded sheet of paper. "I do have a letter from Lord Matthew. He was most insistent on providing me with a reference."

Georgie leaned forward and accepted the letter. After she'd perused it, she said, "It says here that you worked for Lord Matthew for six years as a governess to his daughter, Isabella."

"That I did."

Folding the letter, Georgie extended it back to Miss Walters. "Lord Matthew heaped praises upon you."

"He was a most generous employer."

"If you worked as a governess," Georgie asked, "why are you not trying to secure another position as one?"

Miss Walters shifted in her seat, appearing uncomfortable. "I'm afraid there are no positions available."

"I see," Georgie said. There was more to the story, but she wouldn't pry. "This position does not come with room and board. We don't have enough room as it is."

"That won't be an issue. I am renting a room at a respectable boarding house, and I do not mind walking to work every morning."

Georgie nodded with approval. "I have already hired a tutor to work with the older girls," she explained. "You would be tasked with teaching the younger girls how to read."

Miss Walters perked up. "I can do that."

"Some of the girls haven't even held a book before, so you'll have your work cut out for you," Georgie said.

"I understand, and I do thank you for this opportunity."

Georgie smiled. "After reading Lord Matthew's letter, it would be foolish of me not to hire you," she stated. "The younger girls will begin their studies immediately after breakfast. You may join us for breakfast if you are so inclined.

"I believe I shall," Miss Walters said. "It would give me a good opportunity to become acquainted with the girls."

"I've been making use of mealtimes for exactly that purpose," Georgie said, nodding in approval. "The older girls will begin their lessons after the mid-day meal, and that is when the younger girls will go about their chores."

Miss Walters bobbed her head. "I think what you are doing here is a really fine thing. These girls will greatly benefit from learning to read."

"I agree, and I hope we can do more for them. Just think of the advantages they will have if we can educate them even further."

Wilson stepped into the room and said, "My apologies, but Lord Grenton has arrived, and he would like a moment of your time."

"Do send him in," Georgie said.

After Wilson departed, Miss Walters rose abruptly. "I should be going. I do not wish to trouble you any longer."

"Nonsense," Georgie declared. "I would like you to meet Lord Grenton."

Miss Walters glanced at the door nervously. "Yes, miss."

As she uttered her words, Lord Grenton stepped into the room, looking quite dapperly dressed in a blue jacket, ivory waistcoat, and buff trousers. His eyes landed on her, and a hint of a smile came to his lips. Or had she just imagined that?

Georgie rose. "Lord Grenton, please allow me the privilege of introducing you to our new tutor, Miss Walters."

Lord Grenton tipped his head at Miss Walters.

Miss Walters dropped into a curtsy. "My lord," she murmured.

"I have hired Miss Walters to be the tutor for the younger girls," Georgie shared. "I decided it would be most prudent if I divided the girls into two groups."

"I do agree." Lord Grenton turned his gaze towards Miss Walters. "May I ask what experience you have?"

"I was a governess for Lord Matthew's daughter," Miss Walters said.

"That is very good," Lord Grenton responded. "The girls will be lucky to have you as their tutor."

Miss Walters started moving towards the door. "When would you like me to start, Miss Lloyd?"

"Tomorrow morning would be fine," Georgie replied. "We eat our morning meal when the sun comes up."

Miss Walters acknowledged her words before she hurried out of the room.

Georgie shifted her gaze towards Lord Grenton. "I am most curious as to why Miss Walters was so eager to leave when you arrived."

"It could be the fact that Lord Matthew and I despise one another."

"Why is that?"

"Lord Matthew is a philanderer and a despicable rakehell. He was a few years older than me when we were at Eton, but a leopard does not change his spots. The mothers in the nearby village had to hide their daughters when Lord Matthew would visit."

"Sadly, that is not uncommon for Society men."

"It doesn't make it right," Lord Grenton said. "Our animosity towards one another has continued over the years, and his wife gave me the cut direct last Season."

"That is awful."

Lord Grenton shrugged. "I only feel pity for his wife," he admitted. "It is rumored that Lord Matthew has fathered many illegitimate sons with his mistresses, but has only had one daughter with his wife."

"Many people would not be as gracious as you if they were given the cut direct."

"Words only have power if you let them," Lord Grenton said, "and I refuse to give the gossips' words any heed."

"That is very insightful of you, my lord."

"I have stopped caring what people thought about me. There is a true power that comes with that."

"That there is..." Her words trailed off when she saw Rebecca standing in the doorway, a downcast, withdrawn look on her face.

Georgie came around her desk and asked, "Whatever is wrong?"

Rebecca looked up at Lord Grenton with hesitancy in her eyes before saying, "I can't find Sarah." Her voice was so quiet Georgie had to strain to hear her.

"What do you mean you can't find her?" Georgie asked as she came to a stop in front of the girl. "This orphanage isn't that big."

"We had breakfast, and then Mrs. Hughes asked to see her."

"I am sure she is just completing a chore for Mrs. Hughes, and will be along shortly," Georgie attempted.

Rebecca shook her head. "I saw her get into the coach."

"What coach?"

"It was a black coach, and the woman who came to get her looked mean," Rebecca said. "I don't want her to be gone like all the others."

"This has happened before?"

Rebecca nodded with tears in her eyes. "Whenever this happens, they are gone forever. We don't even get to say goodbye."

Georgie needed answers, and she knew there was only one person who could help her. She stepped into the hall and shouted, "Wilson!"

The butler promptly appeared and asked, "Yes, miss?"

"Can you inform Mrs. Hughes that I would like to speak to her at once?" she asked urgently.

Wilson spun on his heel to do her bidding.

Georgie stepped back into the room and crouched down in front of Rebecca. "I am sure this is all just a terrible misunderstanding. We will get your sister back."

Rebecca didn't look convinced, but she didn't say anything. Instead, she just wiped at the tear that slipped out of her eye.

Rising, Georgie gestured towards Lord Grenton. "Rebecca, allow me to introduce you to Lord Grenton. This is his orphanage."

Rebecca brought her gaze up and murmured, "Hello, Lord Grenton."

To her surprise, a smile came to Lord Grenton's lips. Not a forced smile, but a genuine one. "It is a pleasure to meet you, Rebecca." His tone was gentle, soft.

Rebecca's small frame visibly relaxed, but it became rigid again when Mrs. Hughes tromped into the room.

Mrs. Hughes came to a stop next to Rebecca and demanded, "Why are you not working on your chores?"

Without saying a word, Rebecca ran off down the hall.

Georgie arched an eyebrow. "That was poorly done." She stepped back and said, "Do come in."

Mrs. Hughes frowned. "As I have said before, you can't coddle the girls," she said, stepping into the room. "You must be firm with them."

"That is not what I wish to discuss with you," Georgie responded as she stepped behind her desk.

"Then what do you wish to discuss?" Mrs. Hughes asked with a glance at Lord Grenton.

Georgie pressed her lips together, then said, "Rebecca informed me that Sarah got into a coach this morning."

"Is that what this is about?" Mrs. Hughes asked brusquely.

"Pray tell, where did Sarah go?"

Mrs. Hughes gave her a look of indignation. "Sarah was hired on as a scullery maid, and her employer retrieved her this morning."

"Yet you failed to mention that to me?"

"Why would I?" Mrs. Hughes asked. "Sarah is eleven years old and is entirely too old to be at an orphanage. She needs to be working to earn her keep."

"Shouldn't I have made that decision?" Georgie questioned.

The frown lines around Mrs. Hughes's lips tightened. "It was decided on before you even arrived," she said. "Sarah was lucky that her employer was willing to overlook her pedigree."

"Who is her employer?"

"It hardly matters, now does it?" Mrs. Hughes asked.

Georgie squared her shoulders and repeated her question. "Who is her employer?" she demanded.

Mrs. Hughes let out a frustrated sigh. "Mr. and Mrs. Willis," she replied. "They reside in Cheapside."

"Do you have their address?"

"I do," Mrs. Hughes replied, looking unsure. "Why do you ask?"

"Because I am going to retrieve Sarah and bring her back where she belongs."

Mrs. Hughes's eyes widened. "You cannot do that!" she cried. "It's foolish! If you do, no one will want to hire these urchins."

"These girls are not urchins, and I would ask that you refrain from calling them such."

Mrs. Hughes turned towards Lord Grenton. "Surely you cannot be in agreement with this madness, my lord?"

Lord Grenton met Georgie's gaze. "I have hired Miss Lloyd as the headmistress, and I will respect her decision."

Mrs. Hughes tossed up her hands and declared, "You are going to ruin this orphanage with all of your grand notions."

"I disagree," Georgie said. "You will not send any girl away from this orphanage without my permission."

"But…"

"No arguments," Georgie declared. "Now, go retrieve the Willis' address."

With a huff, Mrs. Hughes departed from the room, not bothering to say another word.

Lord Grenton looked at her with questions in his eyes. "May I ask why you are retrieving Sarah?" he asked.

"I made her a promise," she replied. "You should have seen the way Sarah's eyes lit up when she learned that she was going to learn to read. I can't just abandon her now."

"But she is employed."

"There will be other jobs."

"How can you be so sure?"

"Once she learns how to read, she will have greater opportunities than becoming a scullery maid," Georgie insisted. "You must trust that I am doing right by these girls."

Lord Grenton watched her for a moment before saying, "I

do, but my patience does have its limits. Eventually, these girls will need to get jobs and leave the orphanage."

"We are of the same mind, but today won't be that day for Sarah." Georgie came around the desk and asked, "Did you come by way of coach?"

"I did."

"That is good," Georgie said. "We should be on our way."

Chapter Twelve

William saw the determined look in Miss Lloyd's eyes, and he knew that she was in earnest, but what she was implying was preposterous.

Putting his hand up, he said, "I will go and retrieve Sarah."

"Without me?" Georgie asked. "I think not."

"It is entirely inappropriate for us to ride in the same coach," William pointed out.

"Then I shall take a hackney."

William lowered his hand. "Hackneys do not operate in this part of town. Furthermore, no hackney drivers would be foolish enough to pick up a woman as a fare."

"There must be a way for me to accompany you."

"I'm afraid not," William replied. "You may not care a whit about your reputation, but I must think of mine."

Miss Lloyd's shoulders slumped slightly. "How do I know you will do everything in your power to retrieve Sarah?"

"You must trust me. I will explain the situation to Mr. Willis, and I have no doubt he will release Sarah to me."

"And if he doesn't?"

"Sarah is not their prisoner. Although I would be remiss to inform you that I will not force Sarah to return to the orphanage, either. If she would rather stay, then so be it."

"Why would she?"

"It is a job, and those can be hard to come by."

Miss Lloyd didn't look convinced. "I am sure she will return to the orphanage straightaway."

"We shall see," William said as he started for the door.

As he was about to depart, Miss Lloyd said, "Thank you, my lord."

He stopped and turned to face her. "I do not fully understand your reasons, but I hope you know what you are doing."

"I do."

"Then that is all I can ask."

Miss Lloyd took a step closer to him. "I know you must think me foolish."

His lips twitched. "You cannot possibly know what I am thinking."

"I just know that there is more to Sarah than becoming a scullery maid," Miss Lloyd said. "We just need to give her the opportunity to prove it."

"Why is it that you have so much faith in other people, Miss Lloyd?"

"I suppose I just want to believe the best in others."

"And what if you are wrong?"

A sad look shadowed Miss Lloyd's face. "I have been wrong before," she admitted. "It took me a long time to accept that there was no good inside of my brother."

"I hadn't realized you had a brother. Does he know where you are?"

Miss Lloyd shook her head. "Heavens, no," she replied, "and I hope he will never find out."

"Why is that?"

"He was trying to force me into an arranged marriage

with an awful man," Miss Lloyd shared. "He beat me when I refused."

William felt a surge of protectiveness wash over him. "He beat you?"

"Most soundly, and more and more often," Miss Lloyd murmured. "I daresay that he would have eventually killed me if I hadn't left when I did."

William stared at her, shock and awe blending in his heart. Miss Lloyd had always seemed a pillar, standing up to him without a hint of fear. To learn she had been subjected to such cruelty—and still retained such strength—was amazing and humbling at the same time.

"Why didn't you say anything before?" William asked.

Miss Lloyd gave him a weak smile. "I didn't think it was prudent."

William lifted his brow. "Whyever not?"

"I am your headmistress, your employee," she started, "and I have no desire to become a burden to you, and it is not your responsibility."

"I am, first and foremost, a gentleman, and am duty-bound to help a woman in need."

"I am not in need."

"That is not how I perceive it." William crossed his arms over his chest. "Do you suppose your brother is looking for you?"

Miss Lloyd pursed her lips, hesitated for a moment, then said, "I know he is."

"How?"

"The man who attacked me at the market said he was there to take me home, that he'd been hired by my brother," Miss Lloyd replied.

"How did you escape?"

"Evie pointed a pistol at the man and made him release me."

Uncrossing his arms, William asked, "What would have

happened if he'd tried to take you while you were here? Do you not suppose that your actions put this orphanage at risk?"

"That was never my intention. I was just trying to get as far away from my brother as I could," Miss Lloyd said. "That's why I accepted this position."

William let out a frustrated huff. "I'm sorry your brother is a scoundrel, and as a gentleman, I feel it is my duty to help you. But how can I do that if you are not honest with me? You lied to me. How can I ever trust you?"

"I never lied to you," she said. "I just didn't tell you the full truth of the matter."

"Is that supposed to make me feel better?" he demanded. "Did my solicitor know, or did you withhold the truth from him, as well?"

Her eyes grew downcast. "He knew."

"I shall deal with him later," William said. "As for you, I don't know what I am to do. You are not the person I thought you were."

"I am the same person."

A clearing of the throat came next to the door before Wilson stepped into the room with a piece of paper in his hand. "Pardon the interruption, but Mrs. Hughes provided the address for Mr. and Mrs. Willis."

William waited until Miss Lloyd met his gaze before saying, "We shall continue this conversation when I return."

"Yes, my lord," Miss Lloyd replied.

William turned towards the butler and held his hand out. "The address, please."

As Wilson placed it in his awaiting hand, he asked, "Would you care for me to accompany you, my lord?"

"I will see to this myself."

William departed the orphanage and headed towards his coach, handing the address to the driver before he stepped inside. The vehicle merged into traffic, and William found himself growing increasingly annoyed. Miss Lloyd had lied to him, deceived him. How could she have not told him the truth?

She put the orphanage at risk, and that was unacceptable. The orphanage, his mother's wish, was all that mattered to him. He would need to dismiss Miss Lloyd—again. But could he turn a blind eye and ignore Miss Lloyd's plight? He meant what he'd said about being a gentleman. That meant something to him.

Blasted woman. He could no more turn her out than he could go on pretending that he didn't hold her in some regard. What was he to do? Pretend that her lying did not affect him? He would need to have a frank conversation with her and root out the truth. He wouldn't make a decision until he was presented with all of the facts.

The coach came to a stop in front of a townhouse. As he approached the main door, it opened, and he was greeted by a short, balding man.

"Good morning," the butler said. "How may I help you?"

"Is Mr. Willis home?" William asked, extending his card.

The butler accepted it and replied, "I will see if he is available for callers, my lord." He opened the door wide to let him enter.

William waited patiently in the modest entry hall as the butler disappeared into an adjacent room. He appeared a moment later and said, "Mr. and Mrs. Willis will see you now."

William tipped his head in acknowledgement and headed into the drawing room. Mr. Willis was sitting near his wife, and they both wore bemused expressions.

The white-haired Mr. Willis rose and said, "To what do I owe the great honor of your visit, my lord?"

William stopped near an upholstered armchair. "I have come in regard to your new scullery maid, Sarah."

Mrs. Willis frowned. "What did she do?" she asked,

turning towards her husband. "I knew we should never have hired someone from an orphanage."

Putting his hand up, William said, "I'm afraid you misunderstood me. I would like to collect her so I may return her to the orphanage."

"Why would you do such a thing?" Mrs. Willis asked, aghast. "Are we not suitable employment for her?"

"I assure you that has nothing to do with it. The new headmistress I hired would like to teach Sarah how to read first."

Mrs. Willis laughed. "What a funny notion," she said. "Why would a girl like that need to learn how to read?"

"Be that as it may, I would like to speak to Sarah and see if she is willing to return with me."

"That will not be an issue." Mrs. Willis picked up a bell from the table and rang it. A moment later, the butler appeared in the doorway.

"Will you inform Mrs. Johns that I require Sarah's presence in the drawing room?" Mrs. Willis asked as she set the bell back down on the table.

After the butler departed, William said, "I do hope for your discretion on the matter."

"But of course," Mrs. Willis responded. "I just find it odd that an orphanage is wasting its resources on teaching these urchins how to read. It is a skill that is completely wasted on them."

"The headmistress only has the girls' best interest at heart, and she believes it will benefit them."

"Are those girls even capable of being taught?" Mr. Willis asked.

"They are," William replied.

Mrs. Willis smiled and gestured towards a teapot. "Forgive me, but I have yet to offer you refreshment," she said. "Would you care for a cup of tea while we wait?"

"No, but I thank you kindly for the offer."

An uncomfortable silence descended over them as they waited for Sarah to arrive. Fortunately, he didn't have to wait long.

A thin girl stepped into the room wearing an ill-fitting maid's uniform. She had black soot on her cheeks and hands, and her eyes were downcast.

Mrs. Willis gestured towards the girl. "Is this the girl you are seeking?"

William turned to address the girl. "Do you know who I am?"

The girl nodded but didn't raise her gaze. She must have seen him during one of his visits to the orphanage, then.

"Miss Lloyd sent me," he said.

At the mention of his headmistress, the girl looked up at him. "She did?"

"Am I to assume you are Sarah?"

She nodded. "I am."

"Your sister is very worried about you," William said, "and I am hoping you will accompany me back to the orphanage."

Sarah's eyes shot towards Mrs. Willis. "But I work for them now."

"Not if you don't want to. Miss Lloyd is hoping you will return so she can fulfill her promise of teaching you how to read."

Sarah's voice grew sad. "But she sent me away."

"No, that was not her doing, and she wants to rectify that mistake right now by sending me to retrieve you," William explained.

Sarah slowly bobbed her head. "I would like to go back."

William allowed himself to smile. "So be it."

Mr. Willis's voice met his ears, drawing back his attention. "There is still some unfortunate business that we must discuss."

"Which is?" William asked.

"What we are out by taking in this," Mr. Willis hesitated, "girl."

William removed his coin purse from his jacket pocket. "What is owed to you?"

"We had little choice but to rent a coach to pick her up from the rookeries," Mr. Willis said. "We couldn't very well have picked her up in a hackney."

Removing a few coins, William placed them onto the table and asked, "Will this be sufficient?"

Mrs. Willis glanced down at the coins as she replied, "That would be if she had been given proper clothes to wear at the orphanage. We require all of our staff to pay for their own clothing, and we couldn't let her wear the frock that she arrived in. It was in such a state that we had to burn it."

William removed two more coins and placed them onto the table. "Are we done here?"

Mr. Willis interjected, "We were also forced to bear the expense of buying her a new mattress and bedding to sleep in the attic."

Not wanting to remain in their presence for a moment longer, William dropped a few more coins on the table with a meaningful glare. "Which bedding you will use for the next maid you hire. This concludes our business." If they still weren't satisfied, so be it. He turned towards Sarah. "Let us depart."

Georgie sat in the kitchen as she watched Mrs. Peters stir the contents of the pot hanging over the hearth. She was in a terrible mood. Why had she been so intolerably stupid, telling Lord Grenton the truth? Well, part of it. She hadn't revealed everything about her situation, and she refused to do so.

What was it about Lord Grenton that had made it so easy

to confide in him? When he had offered to retrieve Sarah, she had found herself so touched by his thoughtfulness that she let her guard down. But it would not happen again. His handsome face would not beguile her.

Drat. She knew that was a lie. Lord Grenton had a gruff exterior, but she'd seen past that. There had been glimpses of a kind heart, but she had a suspicion it hadn't been used in quite some time. What had caused him to lock it away?

Now that Lord Grenton knew what circumstances led her to the orphanage, would he send her away? She hoped not. She had grown fond of the girls, and she didn't want to leave yet. There was still too much to do to help them.

Mrs. Peters stopped stirring and turned around to face her. "Are you done feeling sorry for yourself, dearie?"

"I am not."

Mrs. Peters gave her an understanding smile. "All is not lost," she said. "If he dismisses you, we will make do until you reach your majority."

"But what will happen to the girls?" Georgie asked. "If Mrs. Hughes is left in charge, she will dismiss the tutors and return the orphanage to the way it was before I arrived, spiriting girls away at whim."

"That is true, but you don't know what Lord Grenton will do. He may surprise you."

"I doubt it," Georgie muttered.

Mrs. Peters placed a hand on her hip. "You are being quite the naysayer," she chided lightly.

Leaning back in her chair, Georgie said, "I'm sorry. I am just frustrated at myself for telling Lord Grenton about my brother."

"What's done is done," Mrs. Peters advised. "There is no good that will come out of sulking. That won't change anything."

The back door opened, and Alice stepped into the room.

She glanced between them and asked, "Am I interrupting something?"

Georgie knew it would be best to tell her the truth and be done with it. "I let it slip to Lord Grenton about my brother and the circumstances of how I arrived at the orphanage."

Alice's eye shone with disapproval. "Why would you do such a thing?"

Mrs. Peters interjected, "I suspect it has something to do with her having feelings for the boorish lord."

Georgie shook her head. "I do not have feelings for Lord Grenton."

"Then why did you take him into your confidence?" Mrs. Peters asked knowingly.

"I was touched by his thoughtfulness when he offered to go retrieve Sarah," Georgie admitted.

Alice looked at her curiously. "Where did Sarah go?"

"Mrs. Hughes sent her off to be a scullery maid without consulting me," Georgie explained. "Lord Grenton should return shortly with her."

Pulling out a chair, Alice sat down and asked, "What did you reveal to Lord Grenton?"

"Only that I fled to escape an unwanted marriage and my brother's heavy hand," Georgie said. "I did stop short of telling him my real name."

"Does he know that you are an heiress?" Alice asked.

"No, and I have no intention of telling him."

Alice didn't look convinced, but she thankfully didn't argue with her. "I must say that I missed a lot when I visited with my mother this morning."

Mrs. Peters placed a cup of tea in front of each of them and asked, "How is your mother's health?"

Alice sobered as she reached for the cup. "Not well."

"Is the medicine not helping?" Georgie asked.

"Nothing seems to help," Alice replied as she brought the

cup up to her lips. "I worry that she will grow tired of fighting her sickness."

"You must not give up hope," Georgie encouraged.

Alice lowered the cup to the table. "That is easier said than done," she muttered.

Someone cleared their throat from the doorway, and Georgie turned her head to see Sarah, looking terribly disheveled, and Lord Grenton standing there.

"Sarah!" Georgie shouted as she jumped up from her seat. "You've returned." She hurried over to the girl and embraced her.

Sarah returned her embrace before stepping back. "Thank you for sending Lord Grenton to retrieve me."

"You are welcome," Georgie said. "We couldn't have you leave us before you learned how to read, now, could we?"

A smile came to Sarah's lips. "I would like that very much."

"Were Mr. and Mrs. Willis kind to you while you were in their care?" Georgie asked.

Sarah's smile slipped. "I didn't meet them until they called for me, but the other servants weren't nice," she revealed. "They yelled at me."

With compassion in her voice, Georgie said, "You are back where you belong now, and you won't ever have to go back there again."

Sarah looked relieved by her words. "May I go see Rebecca now?" she asked.

"You may," Georgie said.

In a swift motion, Sarah turned around and threw her arms around Lord Grenton's waist. "Thank you," she murmured before she dropped her arms and hurried down the hall.

Lord Grenton looked stunned, but his eyes softened as he watched Sarah's retreating figure.

Georgie spoke up. "I do believe Sarah was most grateful for your help, my lord."

"It would appear so," Lord Grenton said, bringing his gaze to meet hers. "A word, Miss Lloyd?"

Georgie gestured towards the back door. "We can speak freely in the courtyard."

"Very good."

No one in the room spoke as they exited the kitchen. Georgie walked towards the middle of the small courtyard and turned around.

Lord Grenton came to a stop, a short distance away from her. His eyes were guarded, and she realized that didn't bode well for her.

"You lied to me," Lord Grenton said.

"I did."

Lord Grenton clasped his hands behind his back. "I have every reason to dismiss you, but something is holding me back."

Georgie remained quiet.

"This orphanage was very important to my mother. She wanted it to succeed more than anything else," Lord Grenton said, "and she was adamant that a lady should run it, causing many people to wonder if her designs were too lofty."

Lord Grenton continued. "But here you stand. Proof that my mother knew precisely what she was doing. It takes a lady to stand up to injustice, to question the way things have always been done."

"I just want to give these girls a better life."

Dropping his arms to his side, Lord Grenton said, "Most women wouldn't have given Sarah a second thought. Yet you were willing to drive across town to collect her, risking your reputation and mine."

"No one should be forgotten."

"How is it possible for a woman of your station to show

such compassion?" Lord Grenton asked, his eyes searching hers.

"You flatter me, sir, but I am nothing special."

Lord Grenton took a step closer to her. "You are wrong," he said. "I daresay that you are not giving yourself enough credit."

"I am doing my job, nothing more."

"I want full honesty between us."

Georgie held his gaze as she admitted, "That is one thing I cannot give you, my lord."

"And why is that?" he asked, his voice holding a hint of indignation.

"There are some things that I dare not reveal."

"Even at the risk of being dismissed?"

She slowly bobbed her head. "Even then."

Lord Grenton stared at her for a long moment before taking a step back. "What is so important that you would risk your livelihood over?"

"Safety, my lord."

Lord Grenton ran a hand through his hair. "You have put me in an impossible situation. I cannot employ people I do not trust."

"You can trust me."

"How can you in good faith say that to me?" Lord Grenton asked, his voice rising. "You, by your own admission, are keeping things from me."

"I must protect myself," Georgie said.

"From me?"

"I never said that."

"You didn't have to."

Georgie clasped her hands in front of her to keep her from fidgeting. "I do not mean to insult you, but I must be careful who I trust right now," she said. "If my brother learned of my location, I would be at his mercy, and I cannot go back to living in fear."

"Let me help you."

"You already are by allowing me to work here," Georgie said.

"That is not what I meant."

"I know, but I do not want to be in anyone's debt."

Lord Grenton turned his back to her and muttered something incoherent under his breath. After a long moment, he turned back around.

"You are a stubborn young woman."

"So you have told me on multiple occasions."

"I should dismiss you."

"That is your right."

Lord Grenton let out a frustrated sigh. "But I won't. Not yet."

Georgie let out the breath she hadn't even realized she had been holding. "You won't regret this."

"I have a feeling that I will." Lord Grenton glanced at the orphanage. "Truth be told, I do not trust Mrs. Hughes to run the orphanage in your stead, especially after today."

"Mrs. Hughes is…" Her words trailed off as she tried to think of the right words. "Frankly, I don't know how to properly describe her."

"I do not condone her sending Sarah to work for Mr. and Mrs. Willis," Lord Grenton said. "They were both very unpleasant people, and I was forced to pay a substantial sum for Sarah's release."

"She wasn't a prisoner."

"No, but they claimed to have accrued expenses in her name," Lord Grenton shared. "I could have returned with the magistrate, but it wasn't worth my time to do so."

"You did a good thing today."

"I am just grateful that I was in a position to help," Lord Grenton said. "Although, you must accept that there will be a time when the girls do need to seek out employment."

"I am well aware, but with any luck, they will obtain positions better than a scullery maid if they wish it."

Lord Grenton nodded in agreement. "Now, if you will excuse me, I have tarried long enough, and I have work that I must see to."

"Of course, my lord."

Lord Grenton hesitated for a moment before he offered his arm. "May I escort you inside?"

"Thank you." As she placed her hand on his sleeve, a thrill coursed through her, causing her to wonder what her fickle heart was about.

Chapter Thirteen

William sat in the corner of White's as he sipped his drink. He was in a surly mood, and he knew the source of his discontent—Miss Lloyd. He kept replaying their previous conversation in his head, wondering if he could have said or done something different that would have convinced Miss Lloyd to confide in him.

It greatly bothered him that she didn't fully trust him. She had confessed some details of her past, but she was still keeping secrets from him. Why did he care? Miss Lloyd should mean nothing to him, but she did. There was something about her that intrigued him. She had the ability to draw him in, beguiling him in the process, and he was powerless to stop it.

Blasted woman! He had wasted entirely too much time dwelling on his headmistress. Why couldn't he just dismiss the woman for good and be done with it, ending this loop of torment? But he already knew the answer. Miss Lloyd was precisely where she needed to be. She was bringing his mother's vision of the orphanage to fruition—which he had to admit both pleased and aggravated him.

His mother would have liked Miss Lloyd. She had a fierceness about her that very few women of Society possessed, but she also lacked restraint. She'd proven it by going to the market, despite him ordering her not to. Miss Lloyd had been most fortunate that Miss Ashmore was able to save her from her attacker.

What if Miss Lloyd had been abducted and he'd never seen her again? William tightened his hold on his glass at the unpleasant thought. Miss Lloyd may have disrupted his life, but that didn't mean he wanted her gone. Frankly, she was the only thing lately that gave him a reason to smile.

Hawthorne's voice broke through his musings. "I didn't expect to find you here this evening," he said as he sat across from him.

"I wanted a drink," he replied, bringing the glass up to his lips.

Haddington pulled out a chair and sat down. "We can see that, but it doesn't explain why you appear to be in a churlish mood."

William placed his empty glass onto the table. "If you must know, I was thinking about Miss Lloyd."

"Ah, the lovely headmistress," Haddington said.

"How do you know she is lovely?" William asked.

Haddington shrugged. "I just assumed, considering the amount of time you have dedicated towards her."

"I have done no such thing," William responded. "I am just ensuring the orphanage is running efficiently."

With a smirk on his lips, Haddington said, "You are in denial, my friend."

Hawthorne motioned towards a server passing by, indicating they needed drinks. "What did Miss Lloyd do this time?"

William frowned. "She doesn't trust me."

"That doesn't surprise me, since you did dismiss her as the headmistress," Haddington said.

"But I promptly hired her back," William contended.

Haddington chuckled. "My apologies. I don't understand why Miss Lloyd isn't falling at your feet."

"I don't want her falling at my feet." William glanced at the empty tables around him before he said, "What I am about to reveal must stay in the strictest confidence."

Haddington and Hawthorne both nodded their heads, their expressions solemn.

William leaned forward in his chair. "Miss Lloyd revealed that she ran away from her brother to escape an arranged marriage and his heavy hand."

"I find that brave," Haddington said.

"As do I," Hawthorne agreed, "but I thought you said Miss Lloyd didn't trust you. Why would she take you into her confidence?"

William shrugged, then sighed. "I know there is more to the story, but Miss Lloyd remains secretive about it," he said. "It is very aggravating."

"What else could she be hiding?" Haddington asked.

"It could be a myriad of things," William replied, "but I do suspect that Miss Lloyd isn't her real name."

"It's not," Hawthorne said.

William turned on his friend. "How do you know that?"

"When Dinah went to the orphanage with her sister, Evie recognized Miss Lloyd from last Season," Hawthorne revealed.

"And you didn't think that was important for me to know?" William growled.

"It was not my secret to share," Hawthorne said.

William clenched his jaw. "I suppose you won't reveal her name to me."

Hawthorne shook his head. "I'm afraid not, but she isn't lying about her brother. He was trying to force her into marriage with a scoundrel."

"How did you discover that?" William asked.

"I made some inquiries."

William lifted his brow, but Hawthorne merely returned his stare.

A server approached the table and put three glasses down in the center, then walked off with William's empty one.

As William reached for another glass, he said, "I suppose I do feel some relief that Miss Lloyd is telling at least the partial truth."

"Did you doubt her?" Haddington asked.

"I did not," William replied. "I could hear pain in her voice, and it seemed her admission cost her greatly."

Hawthorne nodded in approval. "That is a good start."

"To what?" William asked.

"Proving to her that you can be trusted," Hawthorne said. "She has had a rough go of it since her father died."

William huffed. "Haven't we all suffered from the loss of loved ones?"

Hawthorne took a sip of his drink before saying, "Some people feel more deeply than others, and they hold onto the grief too tightly, causing them to lose focus on what is most important."

"I don't suppose we are still talking about Miss Lloyd anymore," William muttered.

Hawthorne placed his glass onto the table. "It is time for you to move on with your life. Your mother wouldn't have wanted you to put your life on hold."

"How would you know what my mother would've wanted?" William grumbled.

"She wouldn't have wanted this," Hawthorne said, pointing at his glass. "She'd want you to be out living your life, not sequestered behind work and alcohol."

William tossed back his drink and slammed the glass down. "You do not get to lecture me about what my mother would have wanted!"

Haddington interjected, "We are just worried about you. I can't recall the last time you attended a social event."

"They are pointless," William stated.

"Agreed, but they are an important part of Society," Haddington said. "How else do you intend to find a bride?"

"I don't," William said.

"Surely you don't mean that," Haddington responded.

William met his gaze and asked, "Pray tell, where is your wife?"

A pained look came to Haddington's eyes, but he blinked, and it disappeared, making William wonder if he had imagined it in the first place.

Hawthorne spoke up, drawing William's attention. "What is your plan to convince Miss Lloyd to trust you?" He hesitated. "At least, I assume that is what you intend to do."

Reluctantly, William admitted, "I don't have a plan. Not yet."

"Then we must help you with one." Hawthorne shifted his gaze towards Haddington. "Do you have any ideas?"

Haddington bobbed his head. "You could bring her flowers."

"That is a terrible idea. I'm not trying to court her," William said. "Flowers would give her the wrong impression."

"Because you have no intention of pursuing Miss Lloyd, none whatsoever?" Haddington pressed.

"That would be correct," William replied.

Haddington's lips twitched. "Then I must pose the question, why do you care if she trusts you?"

William grew silent. Why did it bother him so greatly that she didn't trust him? He wanted her—no, he needed her—to trust him. He was unable to help her if she refused to confide in him, and he wanted to help her.

Fortunately, before he could answer, Hugh approached the table and held up a hand in greeting. "Good evening," he said before he pulled a chair out.

Hawthorne turned his attention towards his brother. "Are you not gambling this evening?"

"The night is still young," Hugh said with a smirk. "I stopped by White's in hopes that one of you would accompany me."

"I would rather spend time with my wife," Hawthorne responded.

"You are no fun," Hugh said. "You have become even more boring since you married."

Hawthorne shrugged. "Married life agrees with me."

Hugh turned his attention towards William. "Grenton?" he asked. "Are you in?"

With a shake of his head, William replied, "I have no desire to attend a gambling hall and lose money at cards."

"Nor I," Haddington said.

Hugh didn't appear offended by their refusals, but instead seemed to find it amusing. "Your loss," he said, "but I shall think of you all when I have a winning hand."

A server placed a glass down in front of Hugh and collected the empty glasses before departing.

Hugh picked up the glass and glanced between them, a curious look on his features. "Did I interrupt something?"

"No," William said. "You came at the perfect time."

Haddington smiled. "Grenton was just sharing how enjoyable it has been to work with his headmistress."

"That doesn't sound like Grenton," Hugh remarked.

William shoved back his chair and rose. "On that note, I shall bid you a good night. I have work that I need to see to, and it is of upmost importance."

Holding up his glass, Hugh encouraged, "Stay for one more round."

"I'm afraid not," William said as he pushed his chair in. "Good evening, gentlemen."

Georgie awoke to a calloused hand covering her mouth. Her eyes flew open, and immediately recognized the stocky Bow Street Runner from the market in the moonlight. His face was just inches from hers, and as he spoke, she could feel his hot, foul breath on her cheeks.

"If you scream, I will have no choice but to hurt you," the man whispered harshly. "Do you understand?"

She slowly nodded.

This seemed to appease the man, and he removed his hand from her mouth. "I want you to follow my directions precisely." When she didn't object, he continued. "Get out of bed."

Georgie waited until he took a step back before she put her legs over the side of the bed and rose. She glanced over at the mattress in the corner and saw that Alice was not there. Where was her lady's maid at this hour?

The Bow Street Runner followed her gaze and asked, "Where is your companion?"

"I don't know."

"It is a good thing that she wasn't here, or else I would have had no choice but to tie her up."

Georgie met the Runner's gaze and asked, "Why are you doing this?"

"I already told you at the market," he said. "Your brother is paying for me to return you home."

"I will double what he is paying," she attempted.

The man huffed. "With what money?" he asked. "You are living like a pauper in an orphanage."

"Once I reach my majority, I will have the funds to pay you."

"I'm not interested."

Georgie glanced back at her pillow, and she knew she needed a distraction to retrieve her muff pistol. She was grateful that she had taken Evie's advice and slept with it under her pillow.

"Come along," the Bow Street Runner ordered.

She feigned outrage. "I can't possibly go out in public in my nightgown," she said. "It is entirely inappropriate to do so."

"You will have no choice but to do so. Besides, a coach is waiting out front to take us to your townhouse."

"May I put my wrapper on?" she asked.

"Make it quick," he snapped.

Georgie reached for the wrapper, which rested on a hook by the bed. She turned her back to the Bow Street Runner and slowly put the wrapper on, bending lower as she tied the sash. Once she was done, she slid her hand under her pillow until she found the cold metal of her muff pistol.

"We don't have all night," the Runner complained.

In a swift motion, Georgie straightened, turned around, and pointed her weapon at the man. "I am going nowhere."

Shock, then surprise, registered on the man's face. "Where did you get a pistol?"

"I sleep with one under my pillow."

"Isn't that uncomfortable?"

"I don't mind it, especially since I was told that it might come in handy."

The man furrowed his brows. "What is with you women and your guns? I bet you don't even know how to use it."

"I assure you that I do, and I won't hesitate to shoot you."

With a frown on his lips, the Bow Street Runner said, "It would appear that we are at a standstill, then."

"How did you find me?"

"It was rather an easy feat, considering you brought a household staff with you to the rookeries," he said. "If you wanted to blend in, you might have wanted to forego the butler."

Fair enough. "I want you to inform my brother that I have no intention of going home."

"He won't be pleased by that."

"I don't care," Georgie said. "He shouldn't have arranged a marriage for me to a despicable man."

"Listen, lady, I was just hired to do a job, and I will see it done," the Runner said, clearly exasperated. "It is time to end this and get you home, where you belong."

"This is where I belong."

The Bow Street Runner chuckled dryly. "You don't belong in an orphanage," he remarked. "You are the daughter of a viscount."

"This is my home for now, and no one is going to take it away from me."

All humor left the man's face and he reached behind him, retrieving a pistol. "It would appear that you aren't the only one armed."

Georgie's eyes fixated on his pistol. "It would appear so."

"Have you ever shot anyone before, Miss Holbrooke?"

"I have not."

The Bow Street Runner nodded. "I thought not," he said. "There is nothing worse than watching the life draining out of someone's eyes. No matter the reason you pulled the trigger, you lose a part of yourself in that moment."

He gave her a look and continued, "Are you prepared to kill me?"

"I do not want to kill you," she replied. "I just don't want to go home to my brother."

"That didn't answer my question."

Georgie kept her firearm unwaveringly aimed at the man before her. "Frankly, I don't know what I am capable of."

"Ah, an honest answer," he said. "I can see it in your eyes. You are no killer."

"You don't know me."

The Bow Street Runner smirked. "I know more about you than you realize." He aimed his weapon at her. "Your brother requested that you were returned alive, but he never specified if you were to be unharmed."

Georgie felt dread in the pit of her stomach at his words, mainly because she was afraid of what he might do to her. She wanted to believe that she could save herself by shooting him, but she wasn't sure if she was strong enough to do what needed to be done.

In a voice that was far more confident that she felt, she said, "If you shoot me, then you will alert the whole orphanage to your presence."

"I am hoping it won't have to come to that." He lowered his aim towards her leg. "It is a terrible thing to be shot. The pain is so intense that you will pray for death."

Georgie knew what he was trying to do. He was trying to scare her into lowering her weapon, but she wasn't about to give up so easily.

The Bow Street Runner brought his gaze up. "I chipped a tooth when the doctor removed a bullet," he said. "I was given a stick to bite down on when he dug it out."

"I know you are trying to scare me, but it won't work. I would rather be shot tenfold than be returned to my brother."

His eyes turned hard. "I thought you were a reasonable chit," he growled. "I was wrong, and you will suffer for it."

As he took a commanding step towards her, the door opened, and Alice stepped into the room with a glass in her hand. She let out a loud gasp as the glass slipped from her hand, shattering onto the floor.

The Bow Street Runner let out a groan. "Until next time." He spun on his heel and shoved past Alice in haste.

Alice stood at the door, frozen in fear.

Georgie lowered her pistol and laid it on the bed. "Alice," she encouraged. "Are you all right?"

Her lady's maid blinked. "Why were you pointing guns at one another?"

"My brother hired a Bow Street Runner to bring me home," she explained, "but he was caught off-guard when I retrieved my pistol from under my pillow."

"You sleep with a muff pistol?"

"I do," Georgie replied. "Evie recommended that I start doing so."

"That was most fortunate." Alice glanced down at the ground. "Look at the mess that I made. Don't move, or else you might step on glass."

The sound of pounding footsteps could be heard coming down the hall. A moment later, Wilson stepped into the room, his hair tousled.

"Is everyone all right?" he asked in between breaths.

Georgie bobbed her head. "A man attempted to abduct me, but Alice thwarted his plan by dropping her glass, alerting everyone to his presence."

Wilson's eyes grew wide. "Why would someone try to abduct you?"

"My brother hired a Bow Street Runner to bring me home," she explained. "This isn't the first time I have seen him. He tried to take me from the market, as well."

"Why didn't you say anything before?" Wilson asked.

Georgie shrugged, trying for a nonchalance she didn't feel. "I didn't think he would find me here at the orphanage. I thought I was safe."

Wilson frowned. "How can I keep you safe if you are keeping things from me?"

"I should have told you, and I am sorry," Georgie said.

Wilson glanced down at the floor. "Wait here," he encouraged. "I will go ensure the man is truly gone, and then I will go to the kitchen to retrieve a broom."

As the butler hurried off, Alice shook her head. "I didn't think your brother would go to such great lengths to bring you home."

"Neither did I," Georgie responded. "I didn't think he cared that much about me."

"You could have been killed."

"The Runner said that my brother wants me alive."

"Thank heavens for that," Alice said.

Georgie sat on her bed. She'd begun to quake and wanted something sturdy beneath her. "Why do you suppose my brother wants me to return home so badly?"

"I'm afraid I can't answer that."

"Neither can I, and it is infuriating," Georgie remarked. "Perhaps his pride took a hit when I left home?"

"Possibly, but you shouldn't underestimate him again."

"I won't."

Mrs. Peters stepped into the room with a broom. "I spoke to Wilson in the hallway, and he instructed me to bring a broom."

Alice held her hand out and accepted the broom.

As Alice started sweeping up the glass, Mrs. Peters leaned her shoulder against the doorway and met Georgie's gaze. "Are you all right?" she asked, her voice full of concern.

"I am."

Mrs. Peters watched her for a moment before saying, "You should try to get some sleep before the sun rises."

"I doubt I could sleep now."

"I suspected you might say that." Mrs. Peters straightened from the doorway. "How does a cup of tea sound?"

"That sounds heavenly."

Chapter Fourteen

From behind her desk, Georgie watched as Evie paced back and forth across her small office, a look of contemplation on her face. It had been hours since her attempted abduction, and she was still trying to make sense of it all.

Evie stopped, turning to face her. "How did this man gain access to the orphanage?"

Georgie motioned towards the window. "This window was found ajar, so it is reasonable to assume he climbed through."

"I think not," Evie said. "That window is barely large enough to let me crawl through it. I doubt a grown man would be able to."

"Then how do you think he got in?"

Evie was silent for a moment. "I think someone might have let him in."

Georgie's lips parted in disbelief. "Pardon?"

"I believe he departed the same way he came in," Evie said, "through the main door."

"Based upon what?"

"I know it sounds farfetched, but it is the only thing that makes sense."

Georgie raised her brow over the implication. "Does it?

Because you are asking me to believe that someone in the orphanage allowed my attacker to enter."

"You mentioned before that Mrs. Hughes hates you," Evie said. "What if she discovered the truth about you and decided to work with the Bow Street Runner to get rid of you?"

"I don't know…" Georgie said hesitantly. It wasn't entirely unplausible. Mrs. Hughes had made no secret of her dislike for her. But would she go to such great lengths?

Evie sat down on the chair. "Did Mrs. Hughes come to see you after the attempted abduction?"

"She did not."

"It is just something you might want to consider." Evie smoothed down her pale green gown. "I am glad that you took my advice and slept with a muff pistol under your pillow."

"As am I," Georgie said. "Although, the man was taunting me."

"In what way?"

"He said that he knew I wouldn't shoot him and threatened to shoot me before returning me to my brother."

"He was trying to make you doubt yourself."

"It worked," Georgie admitted. "I don't think I would have pulled that trigger, no matter the reason."

Evie gave her an understanding look. "The time will come when you have to decide what kind of person you are," she said. "Are you going to save yourself, or hope that someone else will come along to save you?"

"I want to believe I will save myself."

"Then be that person."

"It isn't that easy," Georgie insisted. "What if I kill someone?"

"Killing is not something that should be done lightly, mind you, but if I had the choice of killing or be killed, I would not hesitate to pull that trigger," Evie paused, "and neither should you."

Georgie's hand went into the folds of her gown, and she retrieved her pistol from her pocket. As she placed it on the desk, she said, "I need to practice more."

"Practice is always a good thing."

"Yes, but I have only shot at targets."

Evie opened her mouth to respond when Lord Grenton stepped into the room, his green eyes holding an intensity she hadn't seen before.

"*You were attacked last night?!*" he shouted.

Georgie rose and smiled. "Good morning, Lord Grenton," she greeted. Maybe she could disarm him with pleasantries.

It did not work.

He approached the desk, giving Evie a small nod as he passed her. "Wilson informed me of the news. What happened?" he demanded.

"Last night, someone broke in and tried to abduct me," she said, "but he ran off into the night like the coward that he was."

"How did you stop him?"

"With a pistol," Georgie replied. "I sleep with a muff pistol under my pillow."

If Lord Grenton was surprised by her admission, he didn't show it. Instead, he asked, "Was this person sent by your brother?"

She bit her lower lip before admitting, "He was."

Lord Grenton looked displeased. "Your actions have put this orphanage at risk. I cannot in good conscience let you continue to remain here."

"You wish to fire me?"

"I don't know," Lord Grenton said in an exasperated voice. "What if this man comes back and tries to hurt the girls to get to you?"

"He wouldn't do that."

"How can you be so sure?" Lord Grenton asked.

"Because he is a Bow Street Runner, and he upholds the law."

Lord Grenton's brow shot up. "The man that tried to abduct you was a Bow Street Runner?" he asked. "Perhaps you might want to start from the beginning."

Lowering herself onto her seat, Georgie said, "My brother hired a Bow Street Runner to find me and bring me home. The same man tried to abduct me from the marketplace."

"I see," Lord Grenton muttered.

"I didn't think he would discover my whereabouts, but I was wrong," Georgie shared. "He found me, and I don't think he will quit so easily."

Georgie could see the muscles in Lord Grenton's jaw clench. "You can't remain here, not if he knows you are here," he declared.

"Where would I go?"

"You can come stay with me," Evie interjected. "I have more than enough room at my townhouse, and I know that my aunt would love the company."

"What about the girls?" Georgie asked. "The tutors have already arrived for the day."

"You can travel to the orphanage by day and reside with me at night," Evie said. "No one would dare try to abduct you from my townhouse."

"I suppose that could work."

Evie jumped up from her seat. "Wonderful," she said. "I will send a coach for you this evening. We shall have such fun!"

Lord Grenton glanced between them, a look of skepticism marring his features. "Do I not get a say in the matter?" he asked gruffly. "After all, this is *my* orphanage, and Miss Lloyd is still under my employ."

"I do apologize, my lord," Evie drawled. "We shall defer to you and your infinite wisdom."

Lord Grenton narrowed his eyes slightly. "I do not like your tone."

Evie's lips twitched. "And I do not like your cravat. It is crooked." She dropped into a curtsy. "If you will excuse me, I need to be anywhere but here."

Georgie brought her hand up to cover the smile on her lips. She couldn't believe Evie had been so brazen as to say those things to Lord Grenton.

After Evie had departed, Lord Grenton adjusted his cravat as he turned to face her. "Do you intend to stay with Miss Ashmore in the evenings?"

"That appears to be the plan."

"I do hope you will not develop her sharp tongue."

"There is nothing wrong with her tongue," Georgie said. "I find it admirable that she speaks her mind."

Lord Grenton huffed. "To a fault." He moved to sit on the chair. "Why do you suppose your brother hired a Bow Street Runner to bring you home?"

"I have been asking myself that same question. He never really showed any interest in me unless he found some reason to discipline me."

"You must be worth something to him."

Georgie shook her head. "When I was younger, I idolized my brother. I thought he could do no wrong until I realized that he didn't care for me."

"That is a sad lesson to learn."

"When I was thirteen, I received my first commissioned dress from the dressmaker in town. I adored that dress and felt like I was a princess," Georgie shared. "My brother thought it would be amusing to trip me, and I fell into a mud puddle. No matter how hard my lady's maid tried, she couldn't get the stains out."

"Perhaps he didn't do it on purpose."

Georgie gave him a sad smile. "It wasn't the only time he did it. My brother has never shown me any consideration."

"I am sorry to hear that," Lord Grenton said. "I was most fortunate that my sister and I were close."

"How I envy you."

Lord Grenton grew visibly tense. "She was many years younger than me, but I doted on her. She always wore a bright smile on her face. I didn't know a happier child."

"She sounds like a wonderful person."

Lord Grenton cleared his throat. "She was," he said as he appeared to be blinking back tears. "She passed away many years ago."

"My condolences."

Rising, Lord Grenton walked over to the window and announced, "I will send men over to put more secure locks on the doors and windows."

"That isn't necessary—"

"It is the least I can do, at least until you trust me enough to tell me your real name."

How had he known she was going by a false one? "Why would that make a difference?"

"I could go to your brother and demand that he leave you alone," Lord Grenton said. "I could even bring in the magistrate."

"I'm afraid that will do little good, since my brother is my guardian," Georgie explained. "I haven't reached my majority, which is why we can't involve the magistrate. They will just force me to return home to him."

"So what is your plan? I assume you have one."

Georgie bobbed her head. "I reach my majority in a few months, and then I receive my inheritance."

"May I ask how much your inheritance is?"

"Thirty thousand pounds."

He stared at her for a moment. "You are an heiress."

"I am," she replied, seeing no reason to deny it.

Lord Grenton frowned. "I tire of this game. Why won't you just tell me the truth, all of it, rather than piece by piece?"

"Because this is no game; this is my life."

Her words seemed to appease Lord Grenton somewhat. "I will let your charade continue, for now," he said, "but I will discover the truth eventually."

Lord Grenton walked over to the door but stopped. She waited for a further rebuke, but when he spun back around, she noticed the unusual softening in his face. "I am relieved beyond words that you were not taken last night."

"Thank you, my lord."

He shifted in his stance, looking uncomfortable. "I… uh… was wondering if I could call on you at Miss Ashmore's townhouse, to ensure you are all settled in."

"I would like that very much."

"Very good, then." He held her gaze for a moment longer than necessary before saying, "Good day, Miss Lloyd."

Georgie kept her gaze on the empty doorway, wondering what had just transpired. Lord Grenton must hold her in some regard if he wanted to call on her at Miss Ashmore's townhouse. Or perhaps she was reading too much into his kind gesture?

***

William sat at his desk as he read through his correspondence. He had many hours of work ahead of him, but he found his thoughts kept straying towards Miss Lloyd. He couldn't believe he had spoken to her about his sister. He rarely spoke about Eleanor; it was much easier that way.

So why had he brought her up to Miss Lloyd, someone who didn't even trust him with her real name?

He knew he could be standoffish, but that didn't mean he wouldn't help a lady in need. The fact that he hadn't fired Miss Lloyd proved just that. He had every reason to, yet he couldn't bring himself to do so. He didn't want her gone. He enjoyed her company. She was lively, stubborn, and quick to smile. Furthermore, she cared deeply for the girls at the orphanage, and she advocated for them. He had never met a young woman like her before.

Although, he meant what he had said before. He was not a patient man. He refused to sit back and wait for Miss Lloyd to tell him the truth. He would root it out on his own.

His butler stepped into the room and announced, "Mr. Mason has arrived, my lord."

"Send him in."

A moment later, Mr. Mason stepped into his room with a satchel over his arm. "Good afternoon, my lord. I received word that you wished to see me."

"Yes," William said, motioning towards the chair in front of his desk. "Please have a seat."

Mr. Mason sat down and set his satchel near his feet. "I brought the documents that you need to sign."

"We will get to that, but first I need to speak to you about something important."

"Which is?"

William leaned forward in his seat. "Do you know Miss Lloyd's real identity?"

Mr. Mason's face blanched. "I do."

"Will you kindly tell me her name so we can end this ruse?" William asked.

"I cannot do that."

William lifted his brow. "I beg your pardon?" he asked. "Do I need to remind you that you work for me, Mr. Mason?"

"I know, and I am grateful for this job, but I can't betray Miss Lloyd's confidence."

William knew he needed to switch tactics to get Mr. Mason to reveal the truth. "Pray tell, did your sister tell you about the ill treatment that Miss Lloyd received at the hand of her brother?"

Mr. Mason nodded. "She did. She was convinced that Miss Lloyd's brother would kill her if we didn't intercede."

"I understand that she also left to avoid an arranged marriage."

"You seem remarkably informed."

"Miss Lloyd has confided some things to me, but she won't tell me her real name," William said. "I want to help her, but I am unable to do so without knowing the whole truth."

"It might be best if you left things the way they are."

"I'm afraid I can't do that because her brother wants her back. He has hired a Bow Street Runner to bring her home, by any means necessary."

"I hadn't realized."

"The Runner broke into the orphanage last night and tried to abduct her," William shared. "She was able to scare him off with her muff pistol."

"How fortunate!"

"But this isn't the first time that he has attempted to abduct her. His first try was at the market."

Mr. Mason frowned. "I hadn't realized that Miss Lloyd's brother would be so persistent in bringing her home."

"It is only a matter of time before the Runner or her brother is successful," William paused, "unless you let me help her."

"How would you help her?"

"If I knew her real name, I could speak to her brother and convince him to leave her be," William said.

"Miss Lloyd's brother is a powerful man."

"As am I."

"That you are, but her brother is not a good man. He would just as easily dismiss you as he would hear you out."

"I won't know unless I try."

Mr. Mason looked unsure. "What if your actions put Miss Lloyd in more danger?"

"How would that be possible?" William asked. "Her brother already knows she is residing at the orphanage."

"May I ask why you are willing to help Miss Lloyd?"

William leaned back in his seat. "I would like to think that Miss Lloyd and I have become friends."

"Does she consider you a friend?"

"I can't speak for her, but I want to help her," William said. "I cannot in good conscience just sit back and do nothing, knowing her plight."

Mr. Mason let out a reluctant sigh. "I hope I don't regret this, my lord, but I know my sister. She would want me to do anything I could to protect Miss Lloyd."

"I swear to you that I will not reveal your part in this. My only intention in learning the truth is to help Miss Lloyd."

"I believe you." Mr. Mason reached for a handkerchief from his pocket and wiped the sweat that had formed on his brow. "Miss Lloyd is, in fact, Miss Georgie Holbrooke, sister to Lord Wakefield."

"She is the daughter of a viscount?"

"Yes," Mr. Mason said. "Now do you see the need for secrecy? If someone discovered that Miss Holbrooke ran away to work at an orphanage, she would be ruined."

"I understand."

"It is only for a few months, and then she will reach her majority," Mr. Mason said. "I have already agreed to help her if the need arises."

William nodded approvingly. "That is good of you."

"I think it is fair to say that we all have a vested interest in ensuring Miss Holbrooke remains safely away from her brother."

"That we do," William agreed.

Mr. Mason reached into his satchel and removed some papers. "Now that we have resolved that issue, will you sign these documents?"

As William accepted the papers, he said, "I can respect the

need for secrecy, but if you deceive me again, you will be dismissed."

To his surprise, Mr. Mason challenged him by saying, "I may lose your confidence for saying so, but I would do it again if it meant helping a woman in need."

William's hand stilled on the quill. "I do believe my respect for you just rose a little."

"Thank you."

Once William finished signing the documents, he handed them back to his solicitor. "Does anything else require my attention?"

Mr. Mason returned the documents into his satchel before saying, "Not at this time." He rose and looped the satchel's strap over his shoulder. "I hope I did the right thing by telling you the truth of Miss Holbrooke's identity."

"You most assuredly did. I will do right by Miss Holbrooke; I promise you that."

His response seemed to appease Mr. Mason, who tipped his head. "I bid you a good day, my lord."

After his solicitor left, William rose from his chair and walked over to the drink cart, where he poured himself a drink. Now that he knew the truth about Miss Holbrooke, he felt oddly relieved. He needed to find a way to help her.

Lord Hawthorne stepped into his study. "I have come to see if you would like to join us at White's this evening."

"I could be persuaded to do so." William held up his glass. "Would you care for one?"

"No, thank you."

William took a sip, then walked over to the settee and sat down. "I just had an informative meeting with my solicitor."

Hawthorne came to sit across from him. "May I ask what you discussed?"

"Miss Holbrooke."

His friend's face remained expressionless, giving nothing away. "Interesting," he said. "What did you learn?"

"Except for her real identity, I learned very little, since Miss Holbrooke has already told me quite a bit about her perilous circumstance."

"Now that you know the truth, what do you intend to do with it?"

"I want to find a way to help her."

"That is what we all wish."

William took a sip of his drink, then said, "I could go speak to Lord Wakefield."

Hawthorne shook his head. "That is a terrible idea."

"I disagree."

"Could you imagine if Eleanor had run away to work at an orphanage and another lord came to speak to you about leaving her be?" Hawthorne asked. "What would your response be?"

"It wouldn't be favorable. I see your point."

"Precisely."

Leaning forward, William set his drink on the table. "I have to do something to help Miss Holbrooke," he insisted. "I can't just ignore her plight and hope it goes away."

"Which it won't. Bow Street Runners aren't known for giving up so easily."

William nodded. "I am not sure if you are aware, but Miss Ashmore invited Miss Holbrooke to reside with her in the evenings," he shared.

"That's good. Evie will keep her safe."

"How can you be so sure?"

"You must trust me," Hawthorne replied. "Evie is no simpering miss, and she has special skills that will benefit Miss Holbrooke."

"May I ask how Miss Ashmore learned these special skills?"

"It is best if you don't know."

William furrowed his brow. "More secrets? How do you live with so many?"

"Everyone has secrets. I have just managed to have more than most." Hawthorne rose. "I must depart. I have work I need to see to."

"You have mentioned before that you have contacts around London," William said as he reached for his glass.

"I do."

"Will you see what you can find out about Lord Wakefield?"

Hawthorne bobbed his head. "I will make some inquiries."

"Thank you." William took a sip of his drink. "I don't pretend to understand how you spend your time, or why you sometimes dress like a man down on his luck, but I suppose it can be useful at times like this."

"Will I see you at White's this evening?"

"I'll be there, but I have an errand I need to see to first."

Hawthorne gave him a knowing look. "I assume you will be visiting Miss Holbrooke at Evie's townhouse."

"Am I so obvious?"

"Just to me."

"I am only going to ensure Miss Holbrooke has settled in nicely and is protected."

Hawthorne gave him an amused look. "If you say so."

"For what other reason would I go?"

"It is all right if you admit that you enjoy her company," Hawthorne said knowingly. "There is no shame in that."

William watched as Hawthorne departed from his study. Why did it matter so much to him, that he needed to see for himself that Miss Holbrooke was safe? It shouldn't, but it did.

Heaven help him, but he did enjoy Miss Holbrooke's company.

Chapter Fifteen

Georgie rode in the coach as it slowly made its way down the street. Alice sat across from her and stared out the window, a pensive look on her face.

"What's the matter?" Georgie asked.

"Nothing."

Georgie gave her a look. "I know you better than that."

Alice gave her a weak smile. "I was just thinking about my mother," she revealed. "She wasn't very lucid this morning."

"I am sorry to hear that."

"I just don't know what I will do without her," Alice whispered. "She binds our family together. Without her, I imagine that my sisters and I will all go our different ways."

"You don't know that."

"I do," Alice said. "My youngest sister, Elizabeth, works across Town at a dressmaker's shop, and my oldest sister is busy raising her five children."

"Five children?" Georgie asked. "Good heavens! She must be busy all the time."

"Well, right now she is also tending to our mother," Alice said. "She holds some resentment towards us for not sharing that burden, but neither Elizabeth nor I are in a position to."

"I know you are doing all that you can."

"Thank you, but the truth of the matter is that I wish I could do more," Alice admitted. "I have enjoyed seeing Mother so frequently these past few days."

"Then you must continue to do so."

"It won't be so easy when we leave the orphanage," Alice said. "If we go to your estate in Brighton, I may never see my mother again."

"I won't let that happen."

"You are kind, but we don't know what the future brings. My mother might succumb to her illness, or she might rally like the doctor believes."

"It is most fortunate that you were able to afford a doctor to see to your mother."

Alice's eyes grew downcast. "He says that she has a weak heart."

"But he believes that she might rally?"

"With the right medication, he believes she could live a few more years."

"That is better than nothing, don't you think?"

"I suppose," Alice murmured.

"You mustn't give up hope," Georgie encouraged. "Without it, life is meaningless. For what is the point of all our pain and suffering if we don't yearn for something greater?"

"I would do anything to save my mother," Alice said.

"As well as you should. You don't want to have any regrets when the time comes to say goodbye."

Alice looked at her curiously. "Did you have any regrets when your mother died?"

"Only that I didn't spend enough time with her."

They arrived at their destination, and once her feet were on the pavement, Georgie admired the lovely townhouse.

The main door opened, and she was greeted by a tall, bald butler with kind eyes. "You must be Miss Lloyd."

"I am."

"Very good," he replied, closing the door behind her. "Miss Ashmore is expecting you in the drawing room. If you will follow me."

As soon as the butler announced her, Evie jumped up from the settee. "You have arrived!"

"I have," Georgie replied. "I do thank you for the use of your coach."

"It is my cousin's coach, and he has allowed us to use it while we are in Town."

"That was thoughtful of him."

Evie gestured towards an older woman with dark hair streaked with grey. "Miss Lloyd, allow me to introduce you to my aunt, Mrs. Carter."

Mrs. Carter smiled from her seat. "It is a pleasure to meet you, Miss Lloyd."

Georgie dropped into a slight curtsy. "Thank you for allowing me to reside with you."

"I hope you don't mind, but Evie told me why you can't reside at the orphanage anymore," Mrs. Carter said.

"She did?"

"Yes; I wouldn't want to live with rats, either." Mrs. Carter shuddered. "I can't imagine the feeling of them crawling over me at night."

Evie gave her a pointed look. "I told my aunt all about your rat infestation at the orphanage."

"Yes, we do have rats," Georgie replied honestly.

Mrs. Carter reached for her teacup on the table. "It must be a relief that the rats remain on the first level so as not to bother the girls."

"It is most fortunate," Georgie murmured. It was a ridiculous notion, but she decided it would be best to remain silent on the matter.

Evie pointed towards the teapot on the tray. "Would you care for a cup of tea?"

"I would love one," Georgie said eagerly. "I haven't had a good cup of tea since I arrived at the orphanage."

Mrs. Carter gestured towards a chair. "Why don't you have a seat so we may become more acquainted?"

"I would like that," Georgie said as she accepted the proffered seat.

Evie poured a cup of tea and extended the cup and saucer to her.

Georgie took a long, lingering drink, and let out a sigh when she brought her cup down to the saucer. "I have missed this."

Mrs. Carter gave her an amused look. "Evie was rather cryptic on how you became the headmistress at an orphanage."

Georgie decided that it would be best to be honest with Mrs. Carter. "I found it preferable to marrying a man of my brother's choosing."

"Your brother being Lord Wakefield?" Mrs. Carter asked.

Georgie's eyes grew wide, and she found that she was at a loss for words.

Mrs. Carter placed her teacup down onto the table. "I should explain that you are quite the likeness of your mother, Lady Wakefield. She was my dear friend."

Evie shifted in her chair to face her aunt. "I can explain," she rushed out.

Mrs. Carter shook her head. "I am not a simpleton, dear. I may not be a rat expert, but even I know that rats go wherever they want. They don't just remain on the lower levels." She arched an eyebrow. "Something else is going on here, and I would prefer the truth."

"It is not my story to tell," Evie said.

"But it is mine, and I believe your aunt deserves to know the truth." Georgie took a sip of her tea before saying, "I left my home because my brother wanted to force me into a marriage with Lord Ransdale. When I refused, he beat me, and it wasn't the first time."

"But you are clearly in mourning," Mrs. Carter said, perusing her black gown.

"That matters very little to my brother."

"Do you have no other family you could go to for help?"

"I'm afraid not. They would all turn me over to my brother," Georgie replied. "In a few months, I will reach my majority and receive my inheritance."

Mrs. Carter nodded her understanding. "So you are hiding from your brother until you can gain access to your own funds."

"Precisely; but he has been rather determined to bring me home," Georgie said. "He was able to discover my whereabouts."

"I invited Georgie to reside here at night so I can keep her safe," Evie interjected. "Lord Wakefield wouldn't dare send his ruffians to our townhouse."

"What if he brings the magistrate and demands that we turn his sister over to him?" Mrs. Carter asked. "We will have little choice in the matter."

"That is why no one knows that Miss Holbrooke is here. The household staff will only know her as Miss Lloyd so they won't have to lie," Evie said.

Mrs. Carter looked unsure. "This isn't one of your best plans."

"I know, but it will keep Georgie safe," Evie asserted.

Shifting her gaze towards their guest, Mrs. Carter said, "You are always welcome in our home, Miss Holbrooke."

"Please, you must call me Georgie."

"I would like that," Mrs. Carter responded. "Evie did mention that you are doing some remarkable things at the orphanage."

Georgie nodded her head. "We hired tutors to teach the girls how to read. They started today."

"How did the girls respond?" Mrs. Carter asked.

"They were quite enthused by the prospect," Georgie replied. "It is very encouraging."

"How did Mrs. Hughes handle it?" Evie asked.

"Who is Mrs. Hughes?" Mrs. Carter questioned.

"She is the housekeeper at the orphanage, and she has fought me on every change I have made there," Georgie explained.

"Doesn't she want the girls to learn to read?" Mrs. Carter asked.

"No, she just wants the girls to complete their chores and do precisely what they are told," Georgie said.

The butler stepped into the room and announced, "Lord Grenton has requested a moment of Miss Lloyd's time. Are you taking callers, miss?"

"I am," Georgie replied as she reached up and smoothed back her hair, hoping that she looked presentable for Lord Grenton.

"Give us a moment before you send in Lord Grenton," Mrs. Carter commanded.

The butler tipped his head before he departed the drawing room.

With a twinkle in her eye, Mrs. Carter asked, "Is Lord Grenton your suitor?"

"Heavens, no!" Georgie exclaimed. "I am the head-mistress at his orphanage. He is my employer, nothing more."

"Am I to assume that Lord Grenton knows the truth about you?" Mrs. Carter asked.

With a shake of her head, Georgie said, "Only some of it. I have yet to reveal my true identity to him."

"Then I shall not say a word," Mrs. Carter said.

"Thank you," Georgie replied.

"Although, I have heard that Lord Grenton is one of the most eligible bachelors," Mrs. Carter remarked. "He would make a fine catch for any young woman."

Georgie reached for her teacup and took a sip, hoping no one would notice the blush on her cheeks.

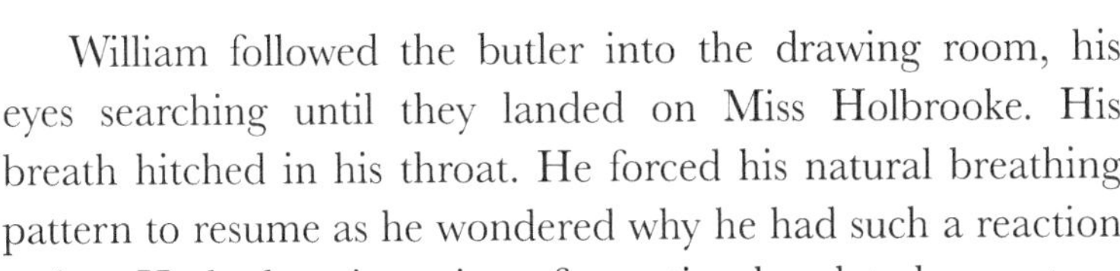

William followed the butler into the drawing room, his eyes searching until they landed on Miss Holbrooke. His breath hitched in his throat. He forced his natural breathing pattern to resume as he wondered why he had such a reaction to her. He had no intention of courting her, let alone act on his feelings. But here she was, affecting him in ways he hadn't even thought was possible.

Georgie rose from her seat and addressed him. "Good evening, Lord Grenton."

He bowed. "Good evening, Miss Lloyd." It was not the time to reveal that he knew her real name. He would continue to play along for now.

Shifting his gaze toward Miss Ashmore, he tipped his head in acknowledgement. "Miss Ashmore."

Miss Ashmore smiled graciously. "Lord Grenton, allow me the privilege of introducing you to my aunt, Mrs. Carter."

"I am honored," William said with a slight bow to the matron.

Miss Ashmore reached for the teapot on the tray. "May I offer you some tea, my lord?"

"No, thank you," William replied. "I do not intend to stay long."

"That is a shame," Miss Ashmore responded as she released the teapot.

William turned his attention towards Miss Holbrooke. "I came to ensure that you have settled in."

"I only just arrived a short time ago," Miss Holbrooke said, "and I have been getting acquainted with Mrs. Carter."

"I'm sure it's been a pleasurable use of your time." Lord

Grenton took a step closer to her. "Will you be at the orphanage tomorrow?"

"I intend to," Miss Holbrooke confirmed.

"Wonderful." Why was he feeling nervous? There was no need, yet he felt like a blubbering idiot.

Miss Holbrooke looked expectantly at him. "Can I expect you at the orphanage tomorrow?"

"I will be there."

"I shall have something to look forward to." He doubted she had meant to say those words out loud, because a flush formed on her cheeks.

William didn't want to embarrass her, so he decided it would be best to change topics. "How did the girls respond to the tutors?"

"Very well, my lord."

He bobbed his head in approval. "I shall have to witness this for myself when I visit."

"I would expect nothing less from you."

William's eyes briefly roamed her beautiful face, and he noticed a wayward piece of hair had slipped out of her tight chignon. He had the errant desire to step forward and tuck it behind her ear, to see if the skin of her cheek was as soft as it looked, but thankfully sanity prevailed. "Well, I have business I need to see to. I shall bid you a goodnight."

"Allow me to walk you to the main door," Miss Holbrooke offered.

"I would appreciate that." He tipped his head at Miss Ashmore and Mrs. Carter as Miss Holbrooke approached. He offered his arm to her and was pleased when she placed her hand on his sleeve.

They walked out of the drawing room in silence, and William knew he only had a few minutes alone with Miss Holbrooke. He needed to use the time to his advantage.

Leaning closer, he said, "I know your secret."

Her gaze remained straight ahead. "Which is?"

"I discovered your name."

Miss Holbrooke withdrew her hand and turned to face him. "May I ask how you did so?"

"It doesn't matter, now, does it?"

"I suppose not." In a voice barely above a whisper, she asked, "Now that you know the truth, what do you intend to do with it?"

"I haven't decided yet."

She pressed her lips together. "You must promise me that you won't go anywhere near my brother. He is a bad man, and he will use you to get to me."

"I am sure that your brother can be reasoned with, Miss Holbrooke."

"No. He once killed his own horse because it reared up and upended him," Miss Holbrooke fervently shared. "He was so furious that he took out his pistol and shot it."

"That is terrible!"

"You don't know all of the things he has done over the years. He is not an honorable man."

"You do not need to concern yourself with me," William said.

Miss Holbrooke appeared displeased at this. "You are right," she said brusquely. "Do as you please."

"I only want to help you."

"If that is true, you will leave things be."

"I'm afraid I can't do that."

"Why not?"

William took a step closer to her, and she tilted her chin to maintain eye contact. "I can't forsake you," he said.

"This isn't your fight."

"You made it my fight when you came to work for me."

Miss Holbrooke lowered her gaze. "I should have never come and put you or the girls in this position."

William lifted her chin with his finger to meet her eyes with a solemn gaze. "I'm glad that you did come into my life."

"But look at all the trouble I have caused."

A smile tugged at his lips. "You did upend my life, but in a good way. It was far too boring and predictable."

Her eyes searched his. "Do you mean that?"

"I do, but you must let me handle this for you," William said. "I'll go speak to your brother, and…"

She took a step back and shook her head, and William's hand dropped to his side. "I can assure you that it will do more harm than good," she stated. It was clear she firmly believed it.

"But I have to try to do something—for your sake."

Miss Holbrooke was about to reply when Miss Ashmore's voice interrupted their interlude. William took a step back.

"I have come on my aunt's behest," Miss Ashmore said. "She was worried that Georgie might have gotten lost on the way back to the drawing room."

William cleared his throat. "I was just saying my goodbyes."

"Apparently, your goodbyes are rather lengthy," Miss Ashmore teased. "You might want to consider shortening them, my lord."

"I shall take that into consideration." He brought his gaze back to meet Miss Holbrooke's. "Do avoid taking any unnecessary risks. I shall see you tomorrow."

Miss Holbrooke bobbed her head. "You need not fear. I am safe here with Evie."

William wasn't fully convinced of that, but he could see that Miss Holbrooke was. "Then I shall bid you goodnight."

Miss Holbrooke rewarded him with a tremulous smile. "Good evening, Lord Grenton."

He left and stepped into his coach, only to find it already occupied.

"What are you doing here?" William asked Hawthorne as he sat across from him.

"I was on my way to White's, and I saw your coach in front of Miss Ashmore's townhouse."

"Why didn't you join us inside?"

Hawthorne shrugged as the coach jerked forward. "I thought it would be best if I waited here."

"Where is your coach?"

"I felt like walking."

"To White's?" William asked.

"Seeing your coach was just the thing to change my mind." Hawthorne adjusted his cravat. "I made some inquiries into Lord Wakefield, and have some troubling news."

"Which is?"

"According to my sources, Lord Wakefield has long since gambled away his fortune, and his creditors are getting restless."

"That doesn't explain why he's so determined to bring his sister home."

"No, but it does go to his state of mind," Hawthorne said. "He is losing control. He first lost his fortune and now his sister. It might be too much for him."

"We need to keep Miss Holbrooke away from him, at all costs."

"I agree, especially since there is chatter about her marrying Lord Ransdale."

William's brow shot up. "I knew Miss Holbrooke had run away to avoid an unwanted marriage, but I had no idea it was to Ransdale. He is a despicable man, in no way worthy of her."

"He is most likely only marrying her for a legitimate heir."

The thought didn't sit well.

"As long as Lord Wakefield is her guardian, Miss Holbrooke is in danger," Hawthorne continued. "He could force her into that marriage with Ransdale."

"She would never agree to it."

"There are ways around that," Hawthorne said. "Lord

Wakefield is known to be unscrupulous in his business dealings and would think nothing of paying people to look the other way."

William reached over and opened the window, allowing the cool night air to circulate in the stuffy coach. "Do you believe she is truly safe at Miss Ashmore's townhouse?"

"I do," Hawthorne replied without any sign of hesitation.

"How are you so confident in Miss Ashmore's abilities?"

"Did she not already save Miss Holbrooke once at the market?" Hawthorne pointed out.

"She did," William conceded.

Hawthorne gave him a knowing look. "Besides, there is nowhere else Miss Holbrooke could go that the Runner couldn't gain access to her. Family members might side with her brother, and inns are out of the question."

"What if the Runner tries to abduct Miss Holbrooke from Miss Ashmore's house?" William asked.

"You need not worry," Hawthorne reassured him. "Evie will keep her safe."

"All right," William said with a resigned sigh. "I shall take your word for it."

Hawthorne gave him a curious look. "You seem to be very protective of a woman whom you claim you do not hold in high regard."

William tensed. "Miss Holbrooke is my headmistress, and I am responsible for her."

"Interesting choice of words," Hawthorne said, amused. "Wouldn't she be the orphanage's headmistress, not yours?"

"I misspoke."

"I don't think you did."

William didn't like Hawthorne's bothersome questions, so it was most fortunate that the coach came to a stop in front of White's, effectively ending their conversation.

Chapter Sixteen

The following morning, William stood on the pavement and stared at Lord Wakefield's townhouse. He had tossed and turned last night as he wrestled with what he should do to help Miss Holbrooke, and the only thing that made sense was to reason with her brother. It may be a fool's errand, but he had to try.

He had just taken a step forward when he heard his name being called. He turned in surprise as he saw Hawthorne approaching him in high dudgeon.

"What in the blazes are you doing?" Hawthorne demanded, stopping in front of him.

"I am going to speak to Lord Wakefield."

"That is evident, but it is madness."

William shook his head. "Surely Lord Wakefield can be reasoned with."

"Haven't you been listening to anything that I have said?" Hawthorne asked. "Lord Wakefield is not a man that you can trust."

"I daresay that you exaggerate. He cannot be as bad as you perceive him to be."

Hawthorne frowned. "He will not do your bidding, no matter how nicely you ask."

"I can be rather convincing."

"I know you want to help Miss Holbrooke, but I can assure you that this is not the right course of action."

"I thank you for your concern, but I know what I am doing." William cocked his head. "Why are you here? How did you know I would try to meet with Lord Wakefield?"

"I listened to what you weren't saying, and I knew you would do something foolhardy in an attempt to help Miss Holbrooke."

"I have to do something," William pressed. "I can't stand back and let her be abducted."

Hawthorne let out a frustrated sigh. "Then I shall accompany you."

"There is no need—"

"Trust me," Hawthorne asserted. "You do not want to go in there without me."

Gesturing towards the door, William said, "After you, then."

William followed Hawthorne towards the door and removed his calling card from his waistcoat pocket. As Hawthorne lifted his hand, the door was opened and a large, white-haired man answered the door.

"How may I help you?" the butler asked in a dry tone.

William extended his calling card. "Will you inform Lord Wakefield that I would like a moment of his time?"

The butler glanced down at the card and opened the door wide, ushering them inside. "Lord Wakefield has been expecting you, my lord."

"He has?" William asked as he came to a stop in the expansive entry hall.

"For many days now." The butler turned his attention towards Hawthorne. "Do you have a card, sir?"

Hawthorne removed a card from his jacket pocket and handed it to the butler.

The butler accepted the card and said, "Remain here, and I will announce you."

Once the butler had walked away, Hawthorne's eyes roamed the room and remarked, "Do you hear that?"

"Hear what?"

"Exactly. It is too quiet," Hawthorne said. "Where are the servants?"

William lifted his brow. "They might just be going about their chores," he replied.

"And the footmen?" Hawthorne asked.

Before William could answer his question, the butler returned and said, "Lord Wakefield will see you now. If you will follow me to his study."

The butler spun on his heel and headed down a narrow hall to the rear of the townhouse. He stopped outside of the door and indicated that they should enter.

Once William and Hawthorne stepped inside of the room, the door was closed behind them. Lord Wakefield was standing near the drink cart.

The man held up a glass. "Would you care for something to drink?"

"No, we would not," Hawthorne said gruffly.

Lord Wakefield walked over to an upholstered armchair and sat down. "I knew you would come, Grenton, but I did not expect you to bring along Hawthorne to act as your muscle."

"I did no such thing," William said. "We are here to speak to you about your sister."

"Yes, we have much to discuss." Lord Wakefield gestured towards the chair across from him. "Perhaps it might be best if we all had a seat."

William walked over and sat down but Hawthorne remained standing.

Lord Wakefield took a sip of his drink before saying, "I want you to return my sister, or there will be dire consequences for you."

"Pardon?" Had Lord Wakefield just threatened him?

"I don't know how I could have been clearer." Lord Wakefield paused. "I want my sister home."

"I'm afraid she has no intention of returning."

"I don't care what she wants!" Lord Wakefield exclaimed. "She has a duty to this family, and she will fulfill it."

This was not going well. "Miss Holbrooke does not wish to marry Lord Ransdale."

"Bah. She doesn't know what she wants," Lord Wakefield said. "She would be a countess if she married Lord Ransdale."

"Your sister does not appear to be the type of woman to be tempted by a title."

"Then she is more foolish than I thought." Lord Wakefield sipped his drink. "I blame all the books that she's been allowed to read. If my parents hadn't indulged her every fancy, then she would be more grateful for what she has."

"Regardless, I do believe that Miss Holbrooke knows her own mind."

Lord Wakefield chuckled dryly. "Did you have your fun with her?"

"I am unsure of what you are implying."

"Did you lift her skirts?" Lord Wakefield asked. "I wouldn't blame you if you did. But I do hope you know that she does not belong to you. She belongs to me."

William felt his hands ball into tight fists. "I did not touch your sister, and I do not appreciate your insinuation."

"That is surprising, considering she ran off to your orphanage. I had it on good authority that you visited her quite frequently."

"She is the headmistress of the orphanage, and I did have

meetings with her there," William said, "but nothing unto-ward happened."

"Lord Ransdale won't mind if you had her first, as long as you remain discreet."

William jumped up in outrage. "How dare you speak about your own sister in such a fashion?"

"How am I supposed to speak about her?" Lord Wakefield demanded. "My sister, a lady, ran off to the rookeries to obtain employment. She has defiled herself."

Hawthorne stepped forward and asked, "How did you learn where Miss Holbrooke was?"

Lord Wakefield smirked. "Georgie is not as loved as she thought."

"What do you mean by that?" Hawthorne pressed.

"Georgie convinced the household staff that she was horribly mistreated, and they fell for her lies," Lord Wakefield said, "just as you did."

"Did you dismiss them?" Hawthorne asked.

Lord Wakefield rose. "I did. I got rid of the whole worth-less lot, and I refused to give any of them references." He walked over to the drink cart and picked up the decanter. "I will not have insubordination in my own home."

Lord Wakefield refilled his drink, then picked up the glass and continued. "I wanted to be civil about this, but you have left me little choice."

William scoffed. "We are far past civil, as you threatened me early on."

"Yes, I did, and you did not have the good sense to believe me," Lord Wakefield said. "I know how much this little orphanage means to you and Georgie, which leads me to believe that you will do whatever it takes to keep those filthy urchins safe."

"You will leave the girls out of this," William growled.

"Or what? You will go to the magistrate and report me?" Lord Wakefield asked. "No one would believe you, and even if they did, they wouldn't care. We are talking about abandoned children in the rookeries. They are nothing."

"You are wrong," William declared.

"I'm not, and it is pathetic that you care so much." Lord Wakefield put his glass down on the tray. "If you do not return Georgie to me by tomorrow, I will kill one urchin for every day you do not deliver her."

William's eyes narrowed. "You wouldn't dare."

"Do not test me!" Lord Wakefield snapped. "You will lose."

Hawthorne's voice held a hardness to it as he asked, "You would kill innocent children to achieve your purposes?"

"You do not know what I am capable of," Lord Wakefield said, his eyes sparking with fury. "I want my sister home, where she belongs."

"Where you can force her to do your will?" William asked with a shake of his head. "I think not."

"Then those girls' deaths are on your hands," Lord Wakefield stated.

William advanced towards Lord Wakefield, but he stopped when the hector retrieved a pistol from his waistband.

Lord Wakefield pointed the weapon at William. "Did you think I wouldn't come prepared for this meeting?" he asked. "You lose, Grenton. Bring me my sister, or I might just kill you, too."

"I will never bring her to you. I don't care what you do to me," William said, staring into the barrel of the gun unflinchingly.

"You are a fool, and I don't have time for this," Lord Wakefield stated.

William heard a pistol cock behind him and realized Hawthorne must have come armed. The man deserved a drink for his foresight.

"Put the pistol down, Wakefield, or I will shoot you," Hawthorne commanded.

"This doesn't concern you, Hawthorne," Lord Wakefield said. "Just be a good lord and walk away before you are in a position where you can't."

"I do not take kindly to being threatened," Hawthorne declared, "and I can promise that this will not end well for you." He spoke his words in such a way that there was no question as to whether he would deliver on his promise.

Lord Wakefield's eyes flashed with uncertainty before he lowered the pistol to his side. "If I am killed, I have instructed my men to kill all the worthless orphans."

"This isn't over," Hawthorne said. "We will find a way to stop you."

"Promises, promises," Lord Wakefield responded. "You know what you need to do to end this. I hope you make the right choice."

William found himself rooted in place as anger welled up inside of him. He wanted to end this now, but he knew he wasn't in a position to do so.

"Grenton," Hawthorne said. "It is time for us to depart."

"But—"

"Don't worry; we will be back," Hawthorne asserted.

William stepped back until he stood next to Hawthorne, maintaining his gaze on Lord Wakefield. He had no intention of turning his back on the man.

Hawthorne's eyes were intense as he kept his pistol trained on Lord Wakefield. "You have crossed the wrong man, Wakefield."

Lord Wakefield sneered. "What can a pretentious lord do to me?" he mocked. "I bet you don't even know how to use that pistol."

A shot rang out, and Lord Wakefield screeched as his pistol clattered to the floor.

"You shot me!" Lord Wakefield exclaimed, clutching his arm.

Hawthorne lowered his gun. "You are lucky; it shouldn't

kill you," he said. "Next time, don't ask me if I know how to use a pistol."

The door flew open, and the butler ran into the room. His mouth dropped open as he stared at Lord Wakefield's bloody arm.

Without saying a word, Hawthorne turned and departed from the study, and William followed close behind. They didn't speak until they'd let themselves out and stepped into the coach.

William heaved a heavy sigh. "That is not at all how I thought it would go."

"Frankly, that is precisely what I was expecting," Hawthorne said. "I'm glad I shot him."

"As am I."

As the coach merged into traffic, William asked, "What are we to do? We can't turn Miss Holbrooke over to him."

"No, we can't," Hawthorne said, "but I have friends who can help us. We will find a way to stop Lord Wakefield."

"I'm sorry I brought you into this."

Hawthorne gave him a pointed look. "There is no place I would rather be than helping a friend in need."

"Thank you."

"But you get to be the one who tells Miss Holbrooke the bad news."

William winced. "I was afraid you were going to say that."

***

Georgie was reviewing the ledger when Mrs. Hughes stepped into the room with an annoyed expression.

"I hope you are pleased with yourself," Mrs. Hughes declared. "You have managed to ruin this orphanage."

Georgie closed the ledger. "How exactly did I accomplish that?"

"The girls should be doing their chores, but instead they are getting instructed on how to read," Mrs. Hughes said. "This whole orphanage will fall apart now. You will see."

"I am confident that these changes will only enhance the orphanage."

Mrs. Hughes approached the desk, coming to a stop in front of it. "I know your secret."

Georgie met her gaze, feeling dread in her stomach. "Which is?"

"You have beguiled Lord Grenton, using your status and beauty," Mrs. Hughes said, "but he will not be fooled for long."

"Mrs. Hughes…" Georgie started.

The housekeeper stepped back. "These girls will have misplaced grandeur and won't be satisfied with the jobs that are available to them," she said. "Learning to read is not the only way to determine their worth."

Something in Mrs. Hughes' manner didn't fit with the animosity of her words. Georgie considered her for a moment, then quietly asked, "Do you know how to read?"

Mrs. Hughes visibly tensed. "I never saw a need for it."

"Would you like to learn how?" Georgie asked.

"For what purpose? I have done just fine without it."

"I agree; but I would be happy to teach you."

Mrs. Hughes gave her a look of disbelief. "You would be willing to teach me, even after everything that has transpired between us?"

"I would, gladly."

Mrs. Hughes hesitated before admitting, "I did try when I was younger, but I was unable to."

"You are older now. It might be a different experience."

"I had a problem recalling my letters, and my mother declared me a lost cause. I stopped trying and I accepted my lot in life."

Georgie gave her an encouraging smile. "There is no

shame in that. You have made something of yourself, and you should be proud of everything that you have accomplished."

Mrs. Hughes held her head high. "I am."

"These girls would be fortunate to hold a position such as yours," Georgie said, "but if they start off as a scullery maid, there would be little chance of that."

"There is no shame in being a scullery maid."

"There isn't, but don't you want more for these girls?"

To Georgie's surprise, Mrs. Hughes's face softened. "I suppose I see your point. I have grown rather fond of them. But that doesn't mean I will let them shirk on their chores."

"I expect nothing less."

Mrs. Hughes looked at her as if seeing her for the first time. "I may have misjudged you, Miss Lloyd," she said. "I just assumed a lady, such as yourself, would look down on someone like me."

"I assure you that I have never thought less of you, nor would I," Georgie responded. "After all, my own circumstances have been reduced."

"But you have still experienced a world that I will never be privy to."

"A cage is a cage, no matter how gilded it is." Georgie leaned back in her seat as she admitted, "It wasn't always that way, but it all changed when my father died. I was forced to accept that my life would never be as it was again, and it was terrifying."

Georgie had just uttered her words when Lord Grenton stepped into the room and said, "That is most unfortunate. No one should be in that position." He gave her a sheepish smile. "I hope you don't mind, but I told Wilson I didn't need to be announced."

"Not at all. This is your orphanage, after all," Georgie said, holding his gaze.

Mrs. Hughes glanced between them. "If you will excuse me, I need to ensure the girls are on task."

After the housekeeper left the room, Lord Grenton removed his top hat and held it in front of him. "I apologize, but I couldn't help but overhear your last comment. It resonated with me, deeply." He paused, looking unsure for a brief moment. "I have felt trapped in a cage of my making for so long that I can scarcely believe that I will ever be free of it." His words were sad, resigned.

Georgie's heart lurched at the vulnerability she saw in his eyes, and she rose from her seat. "What is keeping you there, my lord?" she asked as she came around her desk.

"I'm afraid it is my penance for what I have done."

"What could you have done that was so horrible?"

Lord Grenton's expression grew solemn, and his eyes filled with anguish. "I killed my sister."

"Why do you believe you killed your sister?" Georgie asked. There had to be more to the story.

"I was infected with influenza when I traveled home from Eton for a holiday, and I gave it to Eleanor," he said. "I should have been the one who died that day, not her."

Georgie stepped closer and placed a hand on his arm. "That sounds more like a tragic accident to me. I do not see how you were at fault."

"I should never have come home." He glanced down at her hand. "If I hadn't, my sister would still be alive, and I wouldn't be burdened with knowing that I took my sister away from my mother."

"Did your mother blame you for your sister's death?"

"No, but the light dimmed in her eyes after Eleanor died. She was never quite the same." Lord Grenton blinked back his tears that were forming in his eyes. "Pardon me. This is not why I came here today. I shouldn't burden you with this."

"I'm glad that you did, especially since you have been punishing yourself for far too long for something that wasn't your fault."

"Didn't you hear me?" he asked, his voice rising. "I infected Eleanor. I killed her!"

"Did you know you were infected when you left Eton?"

"No, but it doesn't matter, now does it?" he asked. "My mother sent a coach for me so we could spend Christmas together."

"Do you not think that perhaps your mother blamed herself for Eleanor's death since she sent for you?"

"But she did nothing wrong."

"Neither did you," Georgie pressed. "You were just a boy and could have just as easily died."

"I wish I had."

Georgie held his gaze and asked, "Then who would have carried on your mother's work?"

Lord Grenton grew silent. "I want to believe your words, but I don't think I am capable of it. I will always know that I was responsible for my sister's death."

"That is faulty logic," Georgie said. "Influenza killed your sister, not you." She paused. "Would your sister want you to blame yourself?"

"No, she wouldn't," Lord Grenton said after a moment's reflection.

"Then it is time for you to stop blaming yourself and grieve your sister properly," Georgie encouraged. "It is time to step out of your cage."

Georgie watched a range of emotions race over Lord Grenton's face, and she couldn't even begin to know what he was thinking. Finally, he spoke.

"Do you think I am capable of such a thing?"

"I believe you can do anything you put your mind to."

"Why do you have so much faith in me?" he asked.

"Because I believe you to be an honorable man," Georgie said.

Lord Grenton's eyes roamed over her face. "I do not like most people, but I do like you, Miss Holbrooke."

Georgie felt her breath catch in her throat. What did that mean?

"I don't know why I feel as if I should confide in you, but it feels right," Lord Grenton murmured. "Your voice soothes me, and you make me rethink everything I have believed to be true."

He slowly leaned close, and she realized that he was going to kiss her.

And she was going to let him.

Just as she felt his warm breath on her lips, Wilson's voice came from the doorway, startling her. "Miss Ashmore's coach has arrived."

Lord Grenton took a step back and cleared his throat, looking deucedly uncomfortable.

Wilson remained by the door, regarding Lord Grenton with disapproval. "Would you like me to escort you outside now?"

After she had taken a moment to recover, Georgie said, "Will you notify the driver I will be just a moment?"

"Yes, miss," Wilson responded, but he made no effort to move, nor did he remove his gaze from Lord Grenton.

Georgie gave Wilson an understanding look. "I will be fine. You need not worry about me."

Wilson's eyes shifted towards her before he tipped his head.

Once Wilson had departed, Lord Grenton sighed. "I would like to apologize for my untoward behavior."

"That is not necessary." She didn't want Lord Grenton to admit that it had been a mistake, because she had wanted to kiss him.

A frown tugged at Lord Grenton's lips. "I did wish to speak to you about something disconcerting, but I'm afraid I got distracted."

Georgie clasped her hands in front of her. "What do you wish to discuss?"

"I went to see your brother this morning."

She could feel the color draining from her face. "Why would you do such a thing?" she demanded. "I told you that no good would come out of speaking to him."

"You did, but I wanted to see if I could reason with him."

"There is no reasoning with my brother," Georgie said.

"I am aware of that now," Lord Grenton said with a nod. "He was expecting me. He even threatened me with a pistol."

She gasped. "You could have been killed!"

"I was fortunate that Hawthorne accompanied me. He was able to diffuse the situation and even got a shot off at your brother."

"Did he kill him?"

"No, he only grazed his arm."

Georgie processed this, then put a hand on her hip. "What were you thinking?"

"I was thinking that I wanted to help you."

"And did you?"

He shook his head. "I'm afraid I made it worse."

"How is that possible?"

A line appeared between Lord Grenton's brows. "He says if I don't turn you over to him by tomorrow, he will kill one of the girls for every day that you aren't home."

Georgie's legs wobbled and she wavered. Lord Grenton rushed to steady her.

"Perhaps you should sit?" he asked.

"I think that is wise." Lord Grenton assisted her to the chair, and she sat down.

"What are we to do?" she asked, looking up at him.

"I refuse to hand you over to your brother."

"If I don't go, then he will make good on his threat," Georgie said.

Lord Grenton crouched down next to her and reached for her gloved hand. "We will find a way to stop him."

"How?" Georgie asked, glancing down at their hands. "He

always finds a way to win. It has been that way since we were little."

"Not this time," Lord Grenton asserted. "Besides, you are not alone in this. I will not abandon you, nor will my friends. We are working to protect the orphanage, as well."

"But what if he comes after you?" Georgie asked.

Lord Grenton smiled complacently. "Do not worry about me. I can take care of myself."

Wilson stepped back into the room and said, "I apologize for interrupting, but the driver is insistent that you depart before the sun goes down."

"I understand," Georgie said.

Lord Grenton rose and assisted her in rising. "You will be safe at Miss Ashmore's townhouse. I will call upon you tomorrow with a plan on how to stop your brother."

Georgie gave him the briefest of smiles. "Thank you."

"Be strong, and don't lose hope," he encouraged.

"I shall try."

Lord Grenton offered his arm. "Allow me to escort you to the coach."

Chapter Seventeen

The ledgers laid out on his desk, with their straight lines and careful figures, seemed to mock him, but it was pointless. He couldn't focus on any of it. All he could think about was Miss Holbrooke and her plight. He would rather die than hand her over to her brother. He had to find a way to help her, but how?

Despite his best efforts, he had developed feelings for Miss Holbrooke, and he could deny it no longer. He didn't want to, either. She had come into his life like a whirlwind, disrupting everything, but when the dust settled, he realized that she had brought a purpose back into his life. He could no longer remain as he once was or else he would risk losing her.

He rose and walked over to the drink cart. He picked up the decanter, but his hand stilled. Hawthorne had sent word over that he would be there shortly, and he no doubt would need a clear head.

As he replaced the decanter, Hawthorne stepped into the room as if William's thought had summoned him, with Haddington and a stocky man in tow.

"It is about time you showed up," William grumbled.

Hawthorne seemed unperturbed. "I have been a little

busy." He gestured towards the stocky man. "Allow me to introduce you to Mr. James Wycoff. He is the Bow Street Runner that was hired to abduct Miss Holbrooke."

William narrowed his eyes. "What is this man doing in my home?" he roared. "You should know that he is not welcome."

"You must trust me," Hawthorne said.

"I do, but that doesn't mean I trust him," William said, motioning towards Mr. Wycoff. "He has tried to abduct Miss Holbrooke twice."

"But he failed," Haddington pointed out.

"Thank you for that reminder," Mr. Wycoff muttered.

Hawthorne put a placating hand up. "You must hear him out."

"Why is that precisely?" William demanded.

"Because we want to help Miss Holbrooke," Hawthorne replied, "and hearing him out would be beneficial to that cause."

Some of William's anger dissipated at Hawthorne's words, but not all. "He has five minutes."

Hawthorne gave him an approving nod. "Haddington and I scoured London and we found Mr. Wycoff in a tavern. We struck up a conversation—"

Mr. Wycoff scoffed. "You threatened me!"

"Words were exchanged," Hawthorne said with a small shrug, "and we may have used some strong language."

"May have?" Mr. Wycoff asked. "You were going to speak to the magistrate and have me dismissed without references."

"Regardless, Mr. Wycoff was nice enough to share some details about Lord Wakefield with us," Hawthorne shared.

"Which are?" William asked eagerly.

Hawthorne turned towards Mr. Wycoff. "Would you like to tell him, or shall I?"

Mr. Wycoff frowned and turned to William. "As you know, Lord Wakefield hired me to return his sister, Miss Holbrooke, to him, but it proved to be a much more difficult task than I imagined."

"Why was that?" William inquired.

"Miss Holbrooke was not the simpering miss that Lord Wakefield claimed that she was," Mr. Wycoff said. "Furthermore, she was hardly alone, and I didn't dare challenge Miss Ashmore again."

Haddington spoke up. "You are acquainted with Miss Ashmore?"

"She bested me at the market, and I found myself curious about her," Mr. Wycoff replied.

"I suggest you forget about Miss Ashmore," Haddington warned. "She is not someone you should be wasting your time or notice on."

Mr. Wycoff bobbed his head. "I understand, my lord. I just found it odd that a woman of her station—"

His words stilled as Haddington took a commanding step towards him. "Miss Ashmore is a dear friend of mine, and I do not take kindly to people asking questions about her."

Mr. Wycoff swallowed. "Consider her forgotten." He turned his gaze back to William. "After I failed to retrieve Miss Holbrooke at the orphanage, Lord Wakefield grew irate and demanded I return to the orphanage at once. I refused, and he threatened to kill me."

"You are not alone in that," William said. "He threatened to kill me, as well."

"It is not the first time I have been threatened, nor will it be the last, but I was tired of Lord Wakefield's pompous attitude, and I quit. I knew that he wouldn't make good on the threat."

"He let you just walk out of his study?" William asked.

"He did, but he refused to pay what he owed to me," Mr. Wycoff said. "Frankly, I was just relieved to cut ties with him."

William furrowed his brow. "How is this going to help us

keep Miss Holbrooke safe?" he asked. "I assume that Wakefield will just send another Bow Street Runner to abduct her."

"I'm afraid it is worse than that," Mr. Wycoff said. "Before I quit, Lord Wakefield informed me that he had hired a band of ruffians to help bring his sister home."

"Why would he do such a thing?" William asked.

"He is determined to bring her home, at any cost," Mr. Wycoff stated. "I was hoping you knew what motivated him, as he refused to tell me, even when I asked him directly."

William shook his head. "He wants her home to force her into an arranged marriage."

"But why is her marriage so important to him?" Mr. Wycoff asked.

"I don't rightly know," William admitted.

Mr. Wycoff glanced between Haddington and Hawthorne. "Am I free to go now?" he asked. "I assume our business is concluded."

"Before you go, can you tell me how you got into the orphanage?" Hawthorne asked.

"Someone unlocked the front door," Mr. Wycoff replied.

"Do you know who that was?" Hawthorne pressed.

Mr. Wycoff gave him an apologetic smile. "I do not, but I know someone was feeding Lord Wakefield information about Miss Holbrooke. That is how I knew she would be at the market and which room was hers."

"Did Lord Wakefield tell you that he plans to kill an orphan every day that Miss Holbrooke is not returned to him?" William asked.

Mr. Wycoff pursed his lips. "He did, but there is little I can do."

"But you are a Bow Street Runner!" William exclaimed.

"It is his word against mine, and his carries much more weight," Mr. Wycoff said. "Besides, if you went to the magistrate, then you would play right into Lord Wakefield's hands.

He is still Miss Holbrooke's guardian, and he is entitled to bring her home."

"By killing innocent children?" William asked.

"I'm sorry," Mr. Wycoff said. "My hands are tied on this one. I am only a Bow Street Runner. I do not have enough clout to go against someone like Lord Wakefield."

"No, you don't," Hawthorne agreed, "but we do."

Mr. Wycoff glanced between them. "For what it is worth, I am sorry that I ever agreed to work for the man." He walked over to the door and stopped. "I wish you luck. I don't believe Lord Wakefield will stop until his sister is returned to him."

After the Bow Street Runner departed, William walked over to the settee and dropped down. "He's right," he declared. "How are we going to stop Lord Wakefield?"

Hawthorne and Haddington exchanged a meaningful look.

"What is it?" William asked.

Putting his hand up, Hawthorne said, "We have discussed this, and we believe we know a way."

"That is wonderful!" William exclaimed. "How?"

Haddington came to sit across from him and carefully met his gaze. "You must marry Miss Holbrooke."

William blinked. "I'm sorry," he said. "Did you just say that I must marry Miss Holbrooke?"

"I did," Haddington confirmed. "It is the perfect solution."

"For whom?" William asked.

Hawthorne stepped closer. "It is obvious that you hold Miss Holbrooke in some regard."

"I do, but that is a far cry from wanting to marry her," William said. "What does this have to do with stopping her brother?

"We can keep Miss Holbrooke safe for a few days, maybe a week, but Lord Wakefield won't relent," Haddington said.

"He will keep coming for her, and how many people will die in the process?"

"How do we know he won't kill the orphans if Miss Holbrooke and I wed?" William asked.

"Once you are married to Miss Holbrooke, there is no reason for Lord Wakefield to pursue his sister," Haddington said. "Her usefulness will have expired the moment you two wed."

"It is the only way," Hawthorne declared. "We have posted guards at the orphanage to keep the girls safe, but it only buys us time."

"What if Miss Holbrooke refuses to go along with this madcap plan?" William asked.

"You must convince her," Haddington insisted.

With a huff, William said, "I believe you have underestimated how obstinate Miss Holbrooke can be."

Hawthorne sat down on an upholstered armchair. "You are unable to obtain a license because you need Lord Wakefield's consent since she hasn't reached her majority yet," he said. "The only option is to travel to Gretna Green and have an anvil priest perform the ceremony."

"That is, assuming Miss Holbrooke even wants to marry me," William pointed out.

"You are a far better choice than Lord Ransdale," Haddington said.

William glanced over at the darkened window. "Do you think it is too late to call upon Miss Holbrooke?"

"Yes, but you should go anyway," Hawthorne said. "If you are able to convince her, then you should leave at first light tomorrow."

Rising, William asked, "What should I say?"

"Speak from the heart," Hawthorne advised.

"I'm not good at speeches," William said. "I have a feeling I'm going to botch it up."

Haddington rose. "I'm afraid that is not an option.

Explain why this is the best way to keep her safe, and if that's not enough, add that it will protect the children, as well."

William muttered under his breath as he walked over to the door. Bringing up the well-being of orphans while proposing didn't seem like the best choice. "Thorne!" he called.

The butler promptly appeared in front of him. "Yes, my lord?"

"Bring my coach around front," he ordered.

"Yes, my lord."

William stepped back into his study. "I do hope this isn't a fool's errand."

"It is only a fool's errand if you are foolish enough to not recognize that you need Miss Holbrooke in your life," Hawthorne said. "Ever since you met her, you have begun to change for the better."

"It's true. You have become somewhat tolerable," Haddington joked.

"Even if I admit that I desire Miss Holbrooke to be part of my life, that doesn't mean she wants me in hers," William pointed out.

"Convince her otherwise," Haddington encouraged.

William's work was cut out for him. Miss Holbrooke was as stubborn as she was beautiful.

Georgie stared out the window as she sat in the drawing room. She could vaguely hear Mrs. Carter and Evie convers-ing, but she was paying them little heed. Her thoughts were solely focused on how she was going to get herself out of this predicament. She concluded that the only way she could keep the girls safe was if she disappeared.

But where could she go that her brother couldn't find her?

She knew he wouldn't stop searching for her, but she only needed to remain hidden the few months until she reached her majority. Then she would petition the courts for her brother to turn over her inheritance.

Evie came and sat down next to her. "I know that look."

Georgie turned towards her. "What look?"

"You are thinking about doing something intolerably stupid."

"I am doing no such thing."

Evie gave her a knowing look. "If I had to guess, you want to run away and hide from your brother in an attempt to keep the orphans safe."

Georgie gave her a surprised look. "How could you possibly know that?"

"Because that is precisely what I would have considered," Evie said.

"What would you do if you were me?"

A mischievous twinkle came to Evie's eyes. "I don't think you want to know the answer to that question."

"I do."

"I would stay and fight," Evie said firmly. "I wouldn't let anyone have that kind of control over me."

"But what about the girls at the orphanage?" Georgie asked. "Charles has threatened to kill them if I don't return home."

Evie gave her a compassionate look. "I know you are worried about them, and you have every reason to, but running away isn't the solution."

"I can't fight my brother. He is too strong."

"You are not alone in the fight," Evie said. "We are working on a plan to help you."

Georgie sighed. "I don't think anyone can help me."

"That is what Lord Wakefield wants you to believe. He wants you to feel helpless and alone, but you must remember that you are not."

Mrs. Carter approached them. "I must agree with Evie, and I rarely do. You mustn't let your brother control your thoughts."

"What about the orphans, though?" Georgie asked. "How will we keep them safe?"

"Lord Hawthorne has arranged for guards to protect the girls," Evie informed her. "No one will get past them."

"That is a relief," Georgie murmured.

The butler stepped into the room and announced, "Lord Grenton has requested to speak to Miss Lloyd. He said the matter is most urgent."

"At this hour?" Mrs. Carter asked, glancing at the long clock in the corner. "Well, nothing surprises me anymore in this house." She met the butler's gaze. "Send him in."

"Yes, Mrs. Carter." The butler spun on his heel to fetch the gentleman.

Lord Grenton joined them a moment later in the drawing room, his eyes roving until they met Georgie's, what appeared to be relief flickering in them.

He bowed. "Thank you for agreeing to see me at this late hour."

Georgie rose. "You said that the matter is urgent."

"It is." Lord Grenton acknowledged the other ladies before he returned his gaze towards her. "May I speak to you privately?"

Georgie turned her attention towards Mrs. Carter for her permission. "Would it be permissible to take a tour of the gardens?"

Mrs. Carter nodded her approval. "Take a lantern. Evie and I shall keep a watchful eye on you from the drawing room."

"Thank you," Georgie murmured as she accepted Lord Grenton's outstretched arm. They walked towards the rear of the townhouse in silence and a footman opened the door. The man followed them outside with two lanterns, one of which he handed to Lord Grenton. He kept the other with him as he took up position by the door.

As they started walking down the path, she noticed that Lord Grenton was unusually tense, his lips set in a grim line, and she worried that he came bearing bad news.

Lord Grenton glanced over at her. "How are you faring?"

"I am not doing well," Georgie admitted. "I keep worrying that my brother will make good on his promise and hurt one of the girls."

"We won't let him do that," Lord Grenton said. "Lord Hawthorne arranged for guards to be posted at the orphanage to keep them safe."

"That was thoughtful of him."

"It was."

"Should we sit for a spell?" Georgie asked, gesturing towards a bench set back from the path.

Without saying a word, Lord Grenton escorted her to the bench and dropped his hand. He waited for her to sit before he claimed the space next to her.

Georgie waited for Lord Grenton to speak, but he remained quiet, appearing agitated. She could hear his teeth grinding, and his hands were fisted into tight balls.

Uncomfortable with the silence, Georgie asked, "How are you faring?"

"I am angry."

"That is understandable."

Lord Grenton shook his head. "No, not just angry. I am furious enough that I want to go over to your brother's house and beat him to a bloody pulp."

"That wouldn't solve anything."

"It would make me feel better."

Boldly, Georgie placed her hand over one of his clenched hands. Maybe she could assuage his anger some. "You are a good man, and I know you will not stoop to my brother's level."

"You have entirely too much faith in me," Lord Grenton said, his hand relaxing under hers. "I don't know what I did to deserve it."

"It isn't about deserving; it's about believing—and I believe in you."

Lord Grenton shifted in his seat to face her, his expression guarded. "Lord Hawthorne and Lord Haddington believe they have found the perfect solution to your predicament."

"They have? What is it?" she asked eagerly.

With a slight hesitation, Lord Grenton replied, "If we marry, your brother loses his control over you, and you would be free of him."

Georgie was stunned, and she just stared back at him. As the shock wore off enough for some thought to return, she said, "There must be another way."

"I'm afraid not. Your brother is your guardian until you reach your majority, and he can do with you as he sees fit."

"Even if we did wed, how do we know he wouldn't harm the girls at the orphanage?"

"Once you marry me, your usefulness expires to him, since he can't marry you off to Lord Ransdale," Lord Grenton explained. "Furthermore, once we are properly wed, we could go to the magistrate and alert them to the threats he's made."

"But not before?"

Lord Grenton shook his head. "If we went to the magistrate now, we would play right into his hands. The magistrate would order you to return home and could even arrest me for kidnapping if I don't allow it."

Georgie bit her lower lip before she nervously asked, "Do you even want to marry me?"

"I would do it to keep you safe."

"That isn't what I asked."

Lord Grenton smiled wryly. "I would be lying if I didn't admit it has some appeal to me."

"Only some?"

"You are clever, quick-witted, and beautiful," Lord Grenton said. "Any man would be lucky to marry you."

Georgie's eyes turned down. "I won't force you into a marriage of convenience, no matter the reasons. It wouldn't be fair of me to do so."

"I am making a mess of this," Lord Grenton remarked, running a hand over his face. "I know you probably wanted a love match, but that doesn't mean we couldn't turn this marriage into one."

Bringing her gaze back up to meet his, she asked, "What if you grow to resent me? This would remove your ability to choose your own bride."

"I could never resent you. You must believe that."

"I want to, but I can't ask you to throw your life away for me."

Lord Grenton turned the hand she still covered with her own and intertwined their fingers, bringing hers up to his lips. Her stomach fluttered in response, and she nearly gasped. "You must forgive me, because I am not good at giving speeches. But I do know that I would be unequivocally blessed to have you as my wife."

She opened her mouth to argue, but Lord Grenton spoke first. "I hope you would find me more preferable than Lord Ransdale."

She huffed. "That goes without saying."

"Then what are your other reservations?" Lord Grenton asked, lowering their hands. "Surely you can agree that we suit."

"I do, but—"

"Isn't that enough?" Lord Grenton questioned. "Just agree to marry me now, and we will work everything else out over time."

Georgie found herself in a terrible predicament. She did want to marry him, desperately. She was already halfway in love with him, but Lord Grenton had mentioned nothing about love or even affection. What if that never grew within him, and she was left to pine after her husband for the remainder of her days?

Marrying Lord Grenton seemed to be the only viable option for her, but how could she agree to such a thing, knowing he was only doing it to keep her safe for a few months? It was her fault that he was in this position, and she wished things could be different—but they weren't.

Lord Grenton tightened his hold on her hand. "You must know this is the only way, Georgie."

She looked at him in surprise. "You said my name."

"I assumed it would be all right, since we are engaged," Lord Grenton said.

"I haven't agreed to it yet."

"No, but you will," Lord Grenton responded. "It is the only way to keep you and the orphans safe."

Georgie knew that Lord Grenton spoke the truth. She would do anything to keep the girls safe from her brother.

With a bob of her head, Georgie agreed. "I agree. We should get married."

A boyish grin turned up Lord Grenton's lips. "I am pleased to hear you say that," he said. "I was worried it would take me all night to convince you."

"It is only logical that we wed."

The grin faded. "Yes, logical," he muttered. "If you are agreeable, we will depart for Gretna Green at first light tomorrow. We can't obtain a license since it would require your guardian's approval."

"I am amenable to that plan."

"Very well, then." Lord Grenton abruptly rose. "It is late, and we have a long trip ahead of us tomorrow."

After Lord Grenton assisted her in rising, he kept hold of her hand. "I will be a good husband to you," he promised.

"I believe you," Georgie responded, "and I will strive to be a good wife to you."

Lord Grenton took her hand and tucked it into the crook of his arm. They were silent as they walked along the path, both retreating to their own thoughts. Georgie hoped she had made the right choice.

They entered the townhouse, and he led her back to the drawing room, where Evie and Mrs. Carter were waiting for their return.

Lord Grenton dropped his arm and turned to face her. "Until tomorrow, Georgie." He tipped his head respectfully at Evie and Mrs. Carter before he departed from the room.

Once the main door was closed behind him, Evie gave Georgie an expectant look. "What did Lord Grenton want?"

Georgie hesitated before revealing, "He offered for me."

"That is brilliant!" Evie declared, nodding in approval. "Once you two are wed, Lord Wakefield has no power over you."

"Yes, that is the consensus," Georgie said. "He wants to depart for Gretna Green at first light tomorrow."

Evie cocked her head at Georgie's lackluster tone. "Do you not want to marry Lord Grenton?"

"I do," Georgie rushed to reassure her, "but Lord Grenton is only marrying me to give me the protection of his name."

Mrs. Carter spoke up. "He is doing the honorable thing."

"Yes, but will he come to regret doing so?" Georgie asked.

"I'm afraid I can't answer that," Mrs. Carter replied, "but I do believe you two have genuine affection for one another."

Georgie shook her head. "I do not presume that Lord Grenton cares for me. He didn't speak of affection or anything like it when he offered for me."

Mrs. Carter gave her a kind smile. "Sometimes it is most difficult to see what is right in front of you."

"And what is that?" Georgie asked.

"Love," Mrs. Carter said simply.

Georgie put her hand up. "I said nothing about love."

"You didn't have to," Mrs. Carter responded. "I can see

how Lord Grenton's eyes light up when he sees you. He appears to be smitten."

"I'm afraid I haven't seen it."

"You will. Just give it time," Mrs. Carter encouraged.

Georgie gave her a weak smile. "If you will excuse me, I have to prepare for our trip."

She departed from the drawing room and hurried up the stairs, having an intense desire to be alone. She stepped into her bedchamber, closed the door, and leaned back against it before slowly sliding to the ground

Was she making the right choice? She truly wanted to marry Lord Grenton, but she was scared—scared that he would never return her affection.

Chapter Eighteen

Logical.

Georgie's words replayed in his head. Their marriage would be logical, yet it was so much more. Why couldn't Georgie see that?

William ran their conversation through his mind as his coach rolled towards Miss Ashmore's townhouse the next morning. He'd had a fitful night of sleep as he wrestled with the fact that he would need to work harder to secure Georgie's affection. He meant what he'd said about turning their marriage of convenience into a real marriage. He would prove to Georgie that he was the man for her by loving her unconditionally.

Love.

Yes, he did love her. The revelation had come in the wee hours of the morning as he stared up at the ceiling. If he was being honest with himself, he'd started to fall in love with her the moment that she first defied him. No one had dared to do so before. She challenged him to live a better way than he had been.

The coach stopped in front of Miss Ashmore's townhouse and a footman stepped off his perch and approached the building. He had just reached the main door when Georgie slipped out with a valise in her hand. The footman accepted the valise and hurried to open the coach door.

Georgie stepped into the coach and sat across from William. She was dressed in a dark blue traveling habit, and her hair was pulled back into a tight chignon, which was mostly covered by her matching bonnet. William had always found Georgie to be beautiful, both inside and out, but he suspected that she was quite unaware of the effect her presence had on him.

"You aren't wearing black," William commented.

Georgie shook her head. "Mrs. Carter didn't think it was appropriate for me to be married in mourning, so Evie let me borrow her traveling habit."

"You look lovely."

"Thank you," Georgie murmured.

"I thought it would be best if I remained in the coach, in case anyone was watching," William explained.

"That was wise, my lord."

William lifted his brow at the use of his title. "I thought we agreed we would call each other by our given names."

"No, you decided that. I have yet to decide if I wish to be that familiar."

"We are on our way to Gretna Green to be married, and sharing a coach unchaperoned," he said. "I can assure you that we are past formalities."

"You are right. I am just rather nervous."

"About our marriage?"

She nodded slowly. "I just wish my mother was here to see my wedding."

"I feel the same," he said. "Although, I know my mother would have loved you. You have taken what she held dear and tended to it with care."

"It is easy to love those girls."

William shifted in his seat as he asked, "Do you think your mother would have approved of me?"

"Not at first," Georgie said, "but you would have grown on her, just as you did to me."

"Was that a compliment?"

"Perhaps."

William grinned. "You are terrible at giving compliments."

"I am not," Georgie defended.

"Allow me to give you a compliment," William said, leaning forward in his seat. "Your beauty radiates from the depths of your soul and envelops everything you see through your eyes."

Georgie gave a noncommittal half-shrug. "That was slightly better than mine."

"It was much better," William bantered.

Georgie grew silent. "Did you mean it, though?"

"My compliment?"

She nodded.

"I meant every word," William said. "I have never met someone as beautiful as you are, Georgie. You must know that."

He watched as a blush crept up her cheeks, something he knew he would never grow tired of.

William leaned back in his seat. "I should warn you that it could take up to three days to get to Gretna Green," he said. "It depends on the road conditions."

"Are we traveling at night?" Georgie asked.

"I would prefer it, as it would be faster, but it depends on whether the driver believes it is safe or not," William replied. "I did, however, tell our driver to get as far from London as possible before we stop to rest the horses.

Georgie glanced out the window. "I must admit that I will feel some relief once we are out of Town."

"By the time your brother realizes you are gone, we will be too far ahead of him. He will never be able to catch up."

"I am happy to hear that."

"Will you tell me about yourself?" William asked. He had a sudden desire to learn everything he could about his betrothed. No detail would be too small.

Georgie gave him an odd look. "What do you wish to know?"

"What were you like as a child?" He paused. "I'm sure that I could guess."

"Well, go on, then."

With a knowing look, he said, "You were a stubborn child, and prone to getting into mischief."

A playful twinkle came to her eye. "I did have my share of adventures," she responded. "I never thought it was fair that girls were taught needlework and boys were taught to fight."

"Did you wish to fight?"

"No, but it would have been a useful skill to have learned."

"For what purpose?"

The twinkle dimmed. "I could have fought back against my brother. Perhaps show him that I am not as weak as he perceives me to be."

"You are far from weak."

"Am I?" Georgie asked. "I can't even protect myself. You are only marrying me to keep me safe."

William held her gaze for a moment. "I am marrying you because I want to," he said fervently.

Georgie gave him a look that implied she didn't believe it, but she didn't press him. Instead, she asked, "What were you like as a child?"

"I got into a lot of fights," he said.

"Truly?"

He chuckled. "I don't know why that surprises you. I meant what I said before, that I don't like a lot of people."

"What is it that you don't like?"

"They always find a way to disappoint me."

"Have you thought, perhaps, that your standards are too high?"

"No," he replied. "I have never once considered that."

Georgie gave him an amused look. "Everyone makes mistakes; it is what makes us human. You cannot define someone based upon a mistake."

"I don't have time for incompetence of any kind."

"There is a difference between incompetence and an honest mistake."

"Not to me."

Georgie reached up and fingered the strings to her bonnet. "Have you considered that you push people away unintentionally?"

"Why would I do that?"

"So you don't get hurt."

"That is rubbish."

"Is it?" Georgie asked, lowering her hand. "If you keep people at arm's length, then you don't give them the chance to hurt you."

"I daresay that you are reading too much into this."

"I might be, but I do think you need to give people the benefit of the doubt."

William leaned over and opened the window, allowing fresh air to circulate in the coach. "I gave you the benefit of the doubt, and look where it got me? I'm on my way to Gretna Green to be married." He tried to soften his words with a sardonic smile.

Georgie laughed, as he'd hoped she would. "And I am grateful for that."

"I do have friends, though," William said. "I became friends with Lords Hawthorne, Haddington, Hugh, and Graylocke when I was at Eton. We have remained close ever since."

"I am acquainted with Lord Hawthorne and Lord Haddington, but I have yet to be introduced to Lord Hugh or Lord Graylocke."

"We shall have to rectify that soon enough."

"I haven't seen any of my friends since I went into mourning for my father."

"I am sorry to hear that."

Georgie waved her hand dismissively in front of her. "It is the plight of women of our station. We must mourn our loved ones for the appropriate length of time," she said. "Even though it wasn't under the best circumstances, I did enjoy working at the orphanage as headmistress."

"You won't be able to hold that position once we are married."

"I know, but can I assist in finding my replacement?"

"I wouldn't have it any other way," William replied. "I must say, it won't be easy to replace you."

"We will find another lady, just as your mother intended."

"I am not just talking about that. You brought new life to the orphanage when you became its headmistress."

Georgie gave him a grateful look. "You are being awfully complimentary this morning."

"I only speak the truth."

The coach hit a rut and Georgie reached out to steady herself. "I see that the roads are in fine condition," she mocked.

"I told the driver to take the fastest route to Gretna Green," William shared. "It would appear that we are on a less-traveled road."

"Do you think we will meet highwaymen?"

"I hope not," he said.

"We were robbed by some when I was little," Georgie shared, excitement tinging her voice. "We were traveling to our country house, and our coach was stopped by two masked men."

William arched an eyebrow. "Weren't you scared?"

"I am not sure why, but I wasn't," Georgie replied. "My

father turned over his coin purse without incident, and the men disappeared into the woodlands that lined the road."

"Did they rob him at gunpoint?"

"I never saw a pistol, but my mother had ushered me behind her skirts."

"You were most fortunate that no one was injured."

Georgie bobbed her head. "We were, but it was an experience I will never forget." A small yawn escaped her lips, and she brought her hand up to cover her mouth. "I apologize, but I didn't sleep much last night."

"Neither did I," William admitted. "Why don't you close your eyes, and I will wake you up when we let the horses rest?"

"I don't dare sleep in front of you."

"Do not be embarrassed. We are soon to be married."

Georgie pressed her lips together, not appearing convinced. "What if I snore in my sleep?" she asked. "What will you think of me?"

William chuckled. "You do realize that we will be sharing a bed after we are wed."

Georgie's mouth dropped open. "I… uh… just assumed that we would be sleeping in different bedchambers."

"I meant what I said about wanting to make this a real marriage," William said, "but I see that maybe we should ease into it."

"I think that would be wise."

William resisted the urge to chuckle again at her expense. He didn't want to embarrass her further, but he had no intention of always sleeping in separate bedchambers. He would need to strive to be patient with her, though. He didn't want to rush her into anything she wasn't ready for. That wouldn't be fair to her, or him.

In time, he would win her over.

Hopefully.

Georgie felt the coach stop and glanced out the window. They were at a coaching inn. She turned her attention to Lord Grenton, who had just fallen asleep. His arms were crossed over his chest and his head was drooping.

"Lord Grenton," she said.

When that failed to wake him, she leaned forward and touched his knee. "William," she said, "the coach has stopped."

His head flew up and his tired eyes met hers. "I apologize for falling asleep."

"You have no reason to apologize," she assured him.

William glanced down at her hand on his knee, and she quickly leaned back in her seat, hoping he didn't consider her too brazen.

"Wait here," he ordered as he reached for the handle. "I will see why we stopped."

After he exited the coach, Georgie heard William shout up to the driver, but she didn't hear his mumbled reply.

The door opened and William said, "The driver doesn't believe it is safe to travel these roads at night. He says we should rest here until first light."

"You want me to stay at a coaching inn?"

William gave her a bemused look. "Is that an issue?"

"I have never stayed in a coaching inn before," she admitted.

"I can assure you that it is preferable to sleeping in the coach," William said as he held his hand out to assist her. "It is only for one night."

Georgie tentatively placed her gloved hand into his and exited the coach. She looked at the aged brick structure, which had a thatched roof and a crooked sign over the door: The Rotten Pig.

Lovely.

She stepped forward, only to sink into a patch of sticky mud. Gads, her boots were ruined. Could this night get any worse?

William leaned closer and asked, "Would you like me to carry you inside?"

"I can walk," Georgie said firmly as she pulled her feet out of the mud. "I just need to be more careful where I step."

William remained close. "It would be best if we pretended that we are already married."

"For what purpose?"

"I have no intention of letting you out of my sight," William replied. "It isn't safe for an unaccompanied woman to rent a room in a coaching inn."

Georgie reluctantly agreed that he had a point, and she had no desire to be left alone in this foreign place. "I suppose you are right; but I refuse to share a bed with you."

William smiled in a way she supposed was intended to be flirtatious. "We'll see, my dear."

Georgie felt her cheeks growing warm and ducked her head. "You shouldn't say such things," she insisted.

"Am I not allowed to tease my fiancée?" he asked.

"There is a time and a place for such things, and this is certainly not it."

A man stumbled out of the coaching inn, burping loudly as he did so. He glanced in their direction, showing no signs of remorse, and tipped his head before continuing on.

"Dear heavens," Georgie muttered. "What manner of men come to coaching inns?"

"You don't want to know the extent of it. It's why you won't be leaving my side."

William led her inside, stopping in the entry hall when a tall, stout man met them at the door.

"Good evening, sir," he bellowed. "What can I get for you and the missus this evening?"

"I would like a room and for supper to be brought up," William replied as he retrieved some coins from his waistcoat pocket.

The man accepted the money. "You are in luck, because we only have one room left. You'll have to share a bed. That won't be a problem, will it?"

William slipped his arm around her waist, and Georgie felt herself tense. "Not at all," William said. "My wife prefers it that way."

The man nodded approvingly. "I'm Edgar Vance, the innkeeper here. This fine establishment has been in my family for generations, and we take pride on being respectable." He pointed towards the main hall. "The men can get rowdy in the evening, however, so be mindful not to leave your wife unattended."

"I have no intention of letting her out of my sight," William said, placing a kiss on her cheek.

Mr. Vance smiled. "Ah, young love," he declared as he produced a key from his pocket. "If you will follow me, I will show you to your room."

As they followed the innkeeper through the main hall, Georgie asked in a hushed voice, "Was the kiss on the cheek truly necessary?" Her face felt like it was on fire.

"I thought it was."

Georgie couldn't maintain eye contact with him and chose instead to look over the hall. Long tables filled the room, and men of all ages sat on benches along them. Most seemed to be staring at her, even as they drank from their tankards, and she leaned into William.

"Is it my imagination, or is everyone staring at me?" Georgie murmured.

"They are most definitely staring at you," William replied. "Just remain close and I will keep you safe."

His words gave her a sense of relief, and his scent—sandalwood, if she hazarded a guess—didn't hurt, either.

They walked up a rickety set of stairs and down a dimly lit hall. The innkeeper came to a stop in front of a door and unlocked it, then opened it and stepped inside.

William allowed Georgie to step in first and she glanced around the darkened room. A bed sat against the wall with a small side table next to it. The green paper on the walls was faded, and no drapes hung over the lone window.

Mr. Vance lit the candle and placed it onto the side table. "Will the room do?"

"It will," William replied.

With a bob of his head, Mr. Vance said, "I will see to your supper being brought up." He walked over to William and handed him the key. "I would recommend keeping the door locked, considering how beautiful your wife is."

William accepted the key. "I shall heed your advice."

Once the innkeeper departed, William locked the door and slipped the key into his waistcoat pocket. "I know this is not quite what you are used to."

"You seem to forget that I have been living at the orphanage." Georgie walked over and sat on the bed. "Although, this mattress leaves a lot to be desired."

"It will only be for a night," William said.

Georgie glanced at the worn floorboards. "I assume you will be sleeping on the floor," she said.

"Unless you would prefer that I share the bed with you," he remarked.

"I believe we have already established that I do not."

William approached and asked, "May I sit next to you?"

"On the bed?" she asked in disbelief.

"There isn't anywhere else to sit," William replied in an amused voice. "I promise that I will behave."

Georgie nodded. "I shall take you at your word, my lord."

As William sat down, he said, "I don't ever want you to 'my lord' me again. We will be married soon enough."

"So you keep reminding me," Georgie murmured under her breath.

"Are you having second thoughts?" William asked with a concerned glance. "Because I dare say that it is too late for those."

"I am not," Georgie said. "I know what is at stake."

William moved back on the bed until his back was resting against the wall. "I cannot wait to see the look on your brother's face when he discovers that we are wed."

Georgie allowed herself to smile. "He will be furious."

"I have no doubt about that," William said. "I am half-hoping that he will challenge me to a duel."

"You can't be in earnest!"

"I am. I do not take kindly to being threatened."

"Do not let your pride rob you of your tomorrow."

William shifted to face her. "You are assuming that I will lose," he said. "I will have you know that I am an excellent marksman."

"I don't doubt that, but my brother will find a way to cheat." Her eyes shifted towards the walls. "The papered walls remind me of my grandmother's estate. We used to spend our summers in Brighton with her."

"You were close with your grandmother, then?"

"I was," Georgie replied. "She would have me accompany her when she visited her tenants. She wanted me to become acquainted with them so I could fully understand my responsibilities when I inherited her estate."

"I hadn't realized you would inherit an estate, as well."

"It isn't grand, mind you, but it is important to me."

"I would imagine so."

Georgie leaned back and rested her back against the wall, matching William's position. "I know it would be rather unorthodox for a married woman, but would you mind if I oversaw my grandmother's estate?" she asked hesitantly.

"It is your estate, Georgie," he said. "Why wouldn't you run it?"

"Not once we are wed. Everything I have becomes yours."

"No, it becomes 'ours'," he corrected. "There is a difference; and I already have an estate to run."

"Do you truly mean that?"

William held her gaze. "Your happiness means a great deal to me. You must know that."

Georgie searched his eyes, and warmth filled her heart. How could she not fall in love with this man?

A knock came at the door, startling her out of her thoughts, and William jumped up from his seat. He walked over to the door and asked, "Who's there?"

"I have your supper for you," a girl's voice said.

William unlocked the door and opened it. He accepted the tray and set it on the side table. He fished a coin from his pocket as he returned to the door. He handed it to the girl, and her eyes lit up.

"Thank you, sir," she gushed before hurrying away.

William closed the door and locked it. He walked over to the side table and looked at the tray. "Supper consists of bread, cheese, and meat."

"I must admit that I am so hungry that I care not what I eat," Georgie acknowledged.

He picked up the tray. "Shall we eat in bed?"

"I suppose we must."

After William put the tray down on the bed, he carefully sat down and reached for a piece of meat. "I am hoping that this tastes better than it looks." He took a bite and chewed for a moment before a disgusted look crossed his face. "You might want to avoid the meat," he advised.

Georgie laughed as she reached for some cheese. "I do appreciate you trying it first."

"It is the least I can do."

A comfortable silence descended over them as they ate,

but it was interrupted by periods of loud, boisterous shouting coming from downstairs.

"Are all coaching inns like this?" Georgie inquired.

William nodded. "I'm afraid so."

"I hope I can get some sleep with all this noise."

William brushed the crumbs off his hands as he said, "It may be loud, but you need not fear. I will keep you safe tonight."

Safe.

Georgie did feel safe around William. He felt like home.

Chapter Nineteen

The following morning, just as the sun peaked over the horizon, William led Georgie through the narrow hall and down the rickety stairs. His eyes roamed over the main hall, which contained only a lone man resting his head on one of the long tables, appearing as if he'd had entirely too much to drink the night before.

They were greeted by the innkeeper near the entrance. "Good morning," Mr. Vance said, holding a basket in his hand. "I trust that you slept well."

"We did," William lied. The floor had been astonishingly hard, but his racing thoughts would have prevented a restful night even if he had been comfortable. He had to admit that he was rather eager to marry Georgie, to make her his own.

"I have the basket that you requested," Mr. Vance said as he held it out. "My wife filled it with food, and even included fresh biscuits that she baked this morning."

Georgie accepted the basket and smiled. "That was most gracious of your wife. You will have to thank her for us."

"It was the least we could do," Mr. Vance replied, returning her smile. "The sun is just coming up now. I hope you have safe travels."

"Thank you," William said.

He assisted Georgie into the coach, sitting across from her as the footman closed the door behind him. The coach jerked forward, and they were alone again. Not that William minded. He preferred it that way. He didn't think he'd ever been more content than when he was with Georgie.

She stared out the window, unaware of his attention. Her hair was hidden beneath the bonnet, but a few pieces escaped and curled around her forehead. She was a beautiful woman, and only seemed to grow more so as he spent time with her.

Georgie glanced at him, and he realized that he had been caught staring. He quickly turned his attention towards the basket next to her. "I do hope Mrs. Vance did not pack any of that meat from last night."

She took the linen covering off the basket and shifted through the contents. "It doesn't appear so." She removed a biscuit and took a bite, and her face lit up. "This is delicious!"

William leaned forward and helped himself to one. "Mrs. Vance seems to have quite the knack for making biscuits," he agreed once he'd eaten it.

"That she does," Georgie responded as she brushed the crumbs off her hands. "How much longer do you think before we arrive at Gretna Green?"

"We made good time yesterday, so with any luck, we will arrive late this evening. But that is assuming we don't make any unnecessary stops."

Georgie nodded in approval. "I believe I will breathe a sigh of relief once we are wed."

"As will I."

"I keep looking out the window, half expecting to see my brother," Georgie admitted.

William gave her an encouraging smile. "There is no way he could have known what we planned to do."

"I know, but sometimes, when things are going too

perfectly, I worry that it might come crashing down around me."

"Nothing will happen to you, I promise."

Georgie waved her hand in front of her. "I know I sound foolish—"

"You don't, and you never need to worry how you sound around me," William said. "I want you to be able to speak your mind."

"You say that now, but I tend to have the most outlandish thoughts."

He lifted his brow. "Like when you sold your gowns at the market?"

"Those funds were used to buy the girls new dresses," she defended. "I would do that again if I had to."

"You won't ever have to sell your clothing again," William said.

Georgie smoothed down her traveling habit. "I will need a whole new wardrobe, since newlyweds aren't expected to be in mourning, and all my other gowns are gone."

"I am sorry that you won't be able to mourn your father properly."

"My father has only ever wanted me to be happy," Georgie said.

William hesitated for a moment before asking, "Are you happy?"

Georgie's face softened. "I am."

"That does please me to hear."

She surprised him by asking, "Are you happy?"

"I suppose I am."

Georgie arched an eyebrow. "You don't sound very convincing."

"I haven't been content for so long that I forgot what it was like to be happy." He sighed. "After my mother died, I just felt lost, like there was no purpose to my life with all of my family gone. I was miserable, and it was entirely from my own making. But…" His words trailed off. How could he adequately express what he felt in his heart?

"But?" she prodded.

"I have a new purpose in my life."

"Which is?"

"You," he replied. "I know we are getting married under special circumstances, but I hope to make you so deliriously happy that you never regret marrying me."

As he waited for her to respond, William felt the coach slowing down, eventually coming to a stop. He glanced out the window.

"Why did we stop?" Georgie asked.

"There is a cart blocking the road," he said, reaching for the handle.

"Can't we go around it?"

"There doesn't appear to be room to do so," William replied. "Let me go speak to the driver."

William had just opened the door when four men on horseback appeared, racing towards them from the woodlands that sat back from the road, guns drawn. He closed the door and reached under his bench. He pulled out a metal box and opened the lid, revealing a pistol.

"What's happening?" Georgie asked nervously.

"Highwaymen," he said.

They heard pistols discharging, and William knew this was going to be a battle for their lives, not the peaceful exchange of a purse Georgie had experienced as a child. As he went to aim his pistol out the open window, he recognized one of the riders as Lord Wakefield.

"Blazes," he muttered under his breath. "It's worse than I thought."

"How is that possible?"

"Your brother is the one leading the charge," he informed her.

Lord Wakefield reined in his horse and pointed his pistol

at the coach, a smug look on his face. "Toss your pistol out the window," he ordered. "You are surrounded, and your servants are dead. There is no one to help you."

A glance through the opposite window confirmed this. William turned his attention towards Georgie. "It will be all right."

"How?" she whispered, her breath quickening.

"You must trust me."

She placed her hand on his sleeve and swallowed. "Always."

"Your pistol, Grenton!" Wakefield shouted, his attitude blasé despite the seriousness of the situation.

William reached through the window and dropped the pistol to the ground.

"Now get out of the coach," Lord Wakefield directed. "Do so slowly, and bring my sister along with you."

William wanted to tell Georgie that it would be all right, but his words caught at the back of his throat. He didn't want to lie to her, but he didn't want her to be scared either.

As he wondered what he could say to her, she pressed her lips against his. She leaned back slightly, her warm breath on his lips, and said, "I didn't want to regret having never kissed you."

"We will get through this," he promised.

William could tell that Georgie didn't believe him, but she remained quiet. He opened the door and stepped out, then reached back in to assist her out, shielding her with his body.

Lord Wakefield huffed. "There she is," he declared. "Do you know what great lengths I've had to go to get you back?"

Georgie stepped up next to William, their shoulders brushing together. "I care not."

"You should, because all these deaths are on you," Lord Wakefield said, waving his pistol in the air. "If you had just done your duty and married Lord Ransdale, none of this would have happened."

"I don't want to marry Lord Ransdale."

"I'm afraid you don't have a choice in the matter. He wanted you for his bride, and I was more than happy to give you to him."

"Why would you arrange a marriage for me?" Georgie asked. "Father would never have done such a thing."

Lord Wakefield snorted angrily. "Father was weak! He couldn't do what needed to be done."

"Father was twice the man that you will ever be," Georgie declared.

Her brother's eyes narrowed. "You will pay for that."

"I don't care. It is the truth."

Lord Wakefield dismounted, keeping the pistol in his right hand, and stalked toward Georgie, his features distorted by anger.

William drew Georgie behind him, holding her there with his hands on her arms. "You will not lay a hand on my fiancée."

Lord Wakefield's steps faltered. "It won't matter when you are dead," he said as he raised his pistol.

Georgie pulled free from William's grasp and rushed to stand in front of him. "No! I won't let you kill him."

"What are you doing?" William asked in a hushed voice.

"I'm saving you," Georgie said over her shoulder. She turned her attention towards her brother. "If you promise not to hurt William, I will go with you."

Lord Wakefield chuckled dryly. "I'm afraid you do not have a choice in the matter. Besides, I can't leave behind any witnesses."

"What if I gave you my inheritance to leave us be?" Georgie asked, grasping at hope.

The man before her scowled. "That money was gone long ago."

"What do you mean?"

"I spent it."

"All of it?" Georgie asked. "How is that possible?"

Lord Wakefield scoffed. "I do not have to explain my actions to you!"

"What of Grandmother's estate?"

"I sold it."

Georgie gaped at him. "Why would you do such a thing? You stole my inheritance!"

"No!" Lord Wakefield shouted. "It rightfully belonged to me. You are just a woman."

"Regardless, Grandmother entrusted her estate to me, not you!"

Lord Wakefield took a commanding step towards her, but Georgie held her ground. "You forget that I do not answer to you," he snarled. "I will do as I please."

"What happened to the money?" Georgie asked.

"It is expensive to run an estate, and I ran into some trouble," Lord Wakefield said.

"Did you gamble it away?"

Lord Wakefield looked at her in disbelief. "What did you ask me?"

"Did you lose my money gambling?" Georgie asked slowly, emphasizing each word.

"I did, and more," her brother spat, "but Lord Ransdale has generously agreed to take care of my debts once you marry him."

"Lord Ransdale would want to marry me even though I thoroughly detest him?" Georgie asked, clearly appalled.

Lord Wakefield shrugged. "It doesn't matter to me what his reasons are," he said. "He could lock you up in an asylum for all I care."

"How could you care so little for me?"

Lord Wakefield's eyes blazed even as his voice became ice. "You have always been just a nuisance to me. I could no more love you than I could a nail in my boot." He brought the pistol up. "Now move aside."

Georgie remained rooted in place. "And if I refuse?"

"Then I will make your fiancé's death as painful as possible," Lord Wakefield growled.

William put a hand on her arm. "It is all right," he said quietly. "You need to stand aside."

"How can you ask me to do that?" Georgie asked with a glance over her shoulder. "I won't do that!"

Gently, William turned her to face him. "Whatever happens, I want you to know that I have no regrets."

Tears came to her eyes. "You were supposed to marry me," she breathed.

"I know, and nothing would make me happier."

"How sweet," Lord Wakefield mocked. "Are you done saying your goodbyes?"

William released Georgie's arm and took a step to the side, creating distance between them. "This isn't over," he told her brother. "I have friends who will see that justice is done."

"I'm willing to take my chances," Lord Wakefield said as he aimed his pistol at him.

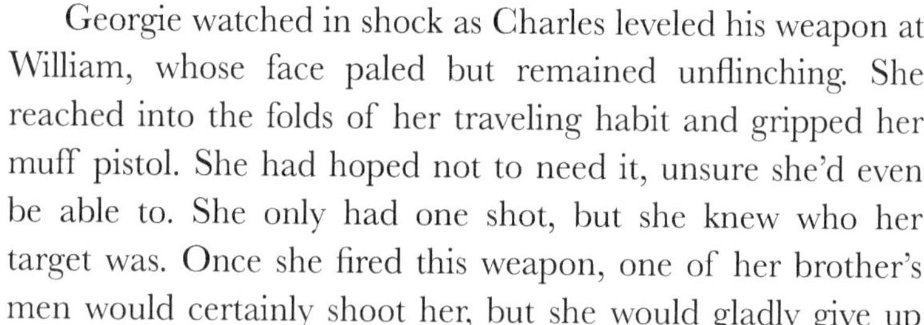

Georgie watched in shock as Charles leveled his weapon at William, whose face paled but remained unflinching. She reached into the folds of her traveling habit and gripped her muff pistol. She had hoped not to need it, unsure she'd even be able to. She only had one shot, but she knew who her target was. Once she fired this weapon, one of her brother's men would certainly shoot her, but she would gladly give up her life for William's.

As she slid the gun past the folds of fabric, she heard someone shout, "Halt!"

Two riders emerged from the trees, and she immediately recognized them as Lords Haddington and Hawthorne.

They trotted past Charles's men, their faces as serene as if they were on a leisurely ride. They reined in their horses and dismounted, holding the reins loosely in their hands.

"It's about time you got here," William said, some of the color returning to his face.

Charles scoffed. "Have you two come to die alongside your friend?"

Lord Hawthorne shook his head. "No, we have come to bargain."

"With what?" Charles asked. "You are outnumbered!"

"Not for long," Lord Hawthorne said, and as if on cue the sound of a gun discharging was heard in the distance, followed by one of the men falling dead off his horse, the beast running wildly the other way.

The other two men turned their skittish horses towards the woodlands, their pistols pointed towards the trees.

Another shot was fired, and one of the men reached for his heart before sliding sideways into the dirt.

Lord Haddington spoke up. "I would say that evens things up a bit."

"But you don't even have pistols!" Charles cried incredulously.

"We have them, but I do not think we will need them," Lord Hawthorne replied. "As I said, we are here to bargain."

"Why would I bargain with you?" Charles asked.

"Because if you don't, you will die," Lord Hawthorne asserted.

Charles tightened his hold on his pistol. "Not before I kill Grenton," he declared. "This man has caused me nothing but trouble!"

"I would argue that you created your own problems," Lord Haddington remarked. "You were the one who got involved with the wrong people."

"What would a dandy like you know about that?" Charles shrieked.

"Quite a lot," Lord Haddington replied. "You frequent The Queen's Parlor, a notorious gambling hell, and are extraordinarily terrible at cards."

Lord Hawthorne chuckled. "That is putting it mildly."

"It's true," Lord Haddington said. "You should have stuck to parlor games. Gambling hells cheat and spit out people like you."

"Regardless, it will all go away once I deliver my sister to Ransdale," Charles said, turning determinedly in Georgie's direction.

Lord Hawthorne held his hands out widely. "I'm afraid I can't let that happen. My wife has grown rather attached to Miss Holbrooke, and she would be devastated if I let anything untoward happen to her."

"I care not for what you or your wife want," Charles snapped. "Georgie is mine, and I will do with her as I please!"

"You should know that we took the liberty of going to the Court of Chancery and speaking to Lord Reynolds. He was very concerned with your ill-treatment of your sister," Lord Hawthorne said.

"Very concerned," Lord Haddington agreed with a bob of his head.

"Insomuch that they granted me guardianship over her until you go to court," Lord Hawthorne continued.

"You are lying!" Charles exclaimed.

"He's not," Lord Haddington said. "I watched the judge sign the document myself. I should note that Lord Reynolds is a friend of ours."

Charles growled. "You will pay for this."

"Who?" Lord Haddington asked. "Will Hawthorne pay, or me? You might want to be more specific in your threats. They can be rather confusing."

"Yes, they can," Lord Hawthorne said, glancing at Lord Haddington. "I thought he was threatening me, but then, he was looking at you."

"Be quiet!" Charles shouted. "You two are imbeciles!"

Lord Hawthorne tutted. "That wasn't very nice of you to say. Here I thought we were being civil to one another."

"I tire of this game." Lord Haddington reached behind him and retrieved a pistol. "I don't want to have to shoot you, Wakefield, but it is becoming very tempting for me to do so."

Charles kept his pistol aimed at William. "If you shoot me, I'll kill Grenton."

"That is, assuming I don't kill you with my shot first," Lord Haddington said.

"No one is that good of a shot," Charles huffed.

"I am," Lord Haddington responded without hesitation.

One of the horses whinnied, drawing Charles's attention.

"I would just give up, Wakefield," Lord Hawthorne said. "If Haddington doesn't kill you, then our sharpshooter will. Either way, it ends poorly for you."

A line of sweat appeared on Charles's brow. "Why did you two have to get involved?" he grumbled. "This has nothing to do with either of you."

"Because you threatened our friend," Lord Haddington answered. "We do not take kindly to that."

Lord Hawthorne also reached behind him and pulled out a pistol. He pointed it at the remaining horseman and ordered, "Get out of here."

The guard nodded and kicked his horse into a run.

"You are outnumbered and outplayed," Lord Hawthorne said. "This is the moment when you should realize you have lost."

"If you haven't realized it already," Lord Haddington mumbled.

"I will do no such thing!" Charles exclaimed.

Lord Haddington sighed. "I knew he wasn't very bright."

As Charles's finger twitched on the trigger, Georgie brought her pistol up and aimed it at her brother.

"I will kill you, brother, if you do not lower your pistol," she threatened. "I won't let you hurt William."

Charles started, then smirked. "You don't have the guts to kill me."

"You don't know me at all," she insisted. "You have never even made an effort to do so."

"I know all I need to about you. Your lady's maid tells me everything that I need to know."

Alice? Georgie's lips parted in surprise. "I don't believe you. You're lying!"

"How else would I know that you ran off to that orphanage? Or that you would be at the market on that particular day?" Charles mocked. "It was easy to convince her to turn on you when I offered her money to help her mother."

"You exploited her!"

"No, we helped each other," Charles said. "You need to be more careful who you trust."

Lord Hawthorne spoke up. "There are three pistols pointing at you, Wakefield, as well as a rifle. You need to decide if you want to walk out of here alive."

Charles lowered his pistol to his side. "I know when I am bested," he said, raising his chin, "but you have only won the battle, Hawthorne, not the war. This fight is far from over."

"I don't think you're going to like what happens next," Lord Hawthorne said. "I'm going to help Miss Holbrooke petition for the return of her inheritance."

"You can't do that!"

"I can, and I will," Lord Hawthorne replied. "I won't rest until you are in debtor's prison. It is no less than you deserve."

Charles gritted his teeth as he turned to Georgie. "This is all your fault! You have ruined me!"

"No, brother, you have ruined yourself," Georgie said.

Glaring at her with open hatred, Charles raised his pistol, but before he could fire, Lord Hawthorne and Lord Haddington each discharged their pistols.

Georgie watched her brother fall to the ground in a heap as if from afar. A range of emotions welled up inside of her: shock at what had happened, and sadness for what their relationship should have been. But those fell quickly away in the face of how relieved she was that he was dead. He could never hurt her again.

William cautiously approached her, his eyes brimming with concern. "Are you all right, Georgie?"

She blinked. "I am," she said, bringing her gaze to meet his. "I must admit that I mostly feel relief that he is dead. Is that so wrong of me?"

"Not at all." He opened his arms wide, and she rushed into them. She wrapped her arms around him and closed her eyes. She had finally found where she belonged. After all the pain and deceit, she felt the warmth and safety of his arms and how they held her as if he had done so all her life. She was home.

He rested his chin on her head. "No one will ever hurt you again. I promise you that."

"I believe you."

After a long moment, he asked, "What do you want to do now?" He leaned back far enough to look her in the eye. "Do you still want to marry me?"

"I do."

"You don't have to," William said. "You are now free to pick your own suitor and have a love match."

She lowered her arms to her sides as doubt crept in. "It sounds as if you don't want to marry me."

"That's not what I am saying. I just want you to be sure." His eyes searched hers, but she couldn't read them. They were guarded. "Are you sure, Georgie?"

Georgie blinked back the hot tears that were starting to form in the back of her eyes. She didn't want to cry in front of him. "I thought I was, but I don't want to force you into marrying me."

"Force me?" He chuckled. "I'm afraid you've misunderstood me. I *want* to marry you!"

"You do?" she asked, feeling nervous hope build back up inside of her.

William gently brushed a hand along her jaw and cupped her cheek as he leaned closer. "I want to make something clear. I am not marrying you out of obligation. Maybe at first I was, but everything is different now. We are different now. I want to marry you because I'm afraid I can't live without you," he said. He took a deep breath. "The truth is, that I am in love with you."

"You are?" Her voice quivered on the simple words.

He smiled. "How can I not be?" he asked. "You have taken my desolate existence and replaced it with hope for a brighter future."

"I love you, too," Georgie breathed.

His breath hitched, and for a moment they were silent.

"I suspected that you cared for me after that kiss, but I didn't dare presume that you loved me," William said. "I hoped as much, though." His eyes dropped to her lips. "May I kiss you?"

She gave a slow nod even as her gaze darted to his mouth and then back to his eyes. "You may."

That was all the encouragement William needed. He caught her lips fiercely with his own, and she kissed him back with equal fervor. This wonderful man was her future, her everything.

They were lost in each other for a moment, and then Georgie thought she heard Evie ask, "How long do we let them kiss?" Was her mind playing tricks on her? Why would Evie be all the way out here, so far from London?

"Not much longer," Lord Hawthorne said as Lord Haddington snorted. "I want to go home to my wife and change out of these dusty clothes."

William broke the kiss and leaned back just enough to ask, "Marry me, tomorrow?"

"How would we accomplish such a feat?" Georgie asked. "We have no coachman to take us the rest of the way to Gretna Green." Her eyes involuntarily made their way to the slain servants, and she hastily turned back to William.

"We'll go back to London. Now that Hawthorne is your guardian, he will grant you consent to marry me by special license," William said.

Lord Hawthorne nodded. "I will allow it, but only if you two agree to stop kissing."

"I'm not going to agree to that, but I will refrain from kissing her around you," William responded.

"Very well," Lord Hawthorne sighed, feigning to be put out.

William slipped his arm around Georgie's waist and turned to face his friends. "Thank you for following us. I hate to admit that you were right."

"They were?" Georgie asked.

Evie stepped forward with a rifle in her hand. "I saw your lady's maid sneak out of the townhouse after you were asleep and followed her to your brother's house."

"Why didn't you say anything?" Georgie asked.

"We didn't know exactly what your brother would do: if he would send hired men, if he'd come personally to retrieve you, or whether he'd even do anything at all. No one was able to discover anything, either, though we tried. We decided it would be best to simply follow you and help if needed," Evie explained.

"I must assume you were the sharpshooter in the woods," Georgie posited.

"I was," Evie replied. "We were a little down the road when we heard gunfire. After conferring a moment, we thought it would be best if I remained hidden."

"Thank you," William said. "You helped save our lives."

Evie gave him an appreciative nod before saying, "We should get you home."

Georgie's eyes flew to her brother. "What do we do with his body, and the others?" she asked. "We can't leave them out here."

"You're right," William agreed.

"I will take care of it," Lord Hawthorne said as he mounted his horse. "The constable in the village over owes me a favor."

William turned towards their vehicle. "I don't suppose anyone knows how to drive a coach?" he asked.

"I do," Evie said, stepping forward.

"Absolutely not!" Lord Haddington declared. "You are not going to drive that coach!"

Evie put a hand on her hip and frowned. "Whyever not?"

"Because I will."

"I can drive the coach, Reginald," Evie argued with a fierce glare.

Lord Haddington walked over to the coach and stepped up to take the driver's seat. "What would the townsfolk think if they saw a woman drive a coach?"

"What would they think if they saw a lord driving a coach?" Evie countered.

"You can ride in the back with Grenton and Miss Holbrooke," Lord Haddington said, reaching for the reins.

"I think not," Evie retorted. "I will ride next to you."

"If you think I am going to let you sit next to me, then you have another thing coming!"

As Evie and Lord Haddington squabbled, William leaned over and kissed Georgie on the cheek. "I will love you today, tomorrow, and for as long as I live," he whispered in her ear. "Just promise me that we will never be like them."

Georgie giggled. "I promise."

Epilogue

One week later

Grenton whistled as he walked down the pavement. He was getting odd looks from the people he passed, but he didn't care. He was in a jovial mood, and nothing was going to change that.

He had been married for about a week, and he had just met with his man of business about a wedding gift that he had just secured for his wife. He couldn't wait to see the look on her face when he presented it to her. Unfortunately, that was going to have to wait, since he'd agreed to meet his friends at White's.

As he approached the gentlemen's club, a liveried servant opened the door, and he stepped inside. He saw his friends in the back of the room and raised his hand in greeting. He skirted the tables and joined them.

"Good afternoon, gentlemen," he greeted cheerily.

Hugh gave him an apprehensive look. "Who are you, and what have you done with my friend?"

William laughed. "I do believe that marriage agrees with me."

"Oh, please; you have only been married for a week," Hugh huffed as he brought his glass to his lips. "Just wait until the novelty of it all wears off."

A server approached the table and replaced their empty glasses with new ones.

Hawthorne reached for a glass and said, "It is good to see you looking well. We haven't seen much of you or Lady Grenton lately."

"We've been busy," William smirked.

"Will you be joining us at Lady Westgate's ball tomorrow night?" Hawthorne asked.

William nodded. "It will be our first event as a married couple."

"Run, Grenton," Hugh muttered. "Once you start attending these events with your wife, you will never be able to hide away in your study during them again."

"I find that I am tired of hiding away," William admitted.

Haddington spoke up. "I am pleased that you have finally found some happiness."

"I have, and it is all because of Georgie. She's brought love back into my life," William said.

"Gads, Grenton," Hugh muttered. "You should write sonnets with all of that sentimental talk. At least that way, I wouldn't have to hear it. It's nauseating."

William grinned. "You are just jealous because you have no wife."

"That is by choice, my friend," Hugh countered. "I will not fall prey to the parson's mousetrap."

"Do you not require an heir?" Haddington asked.

"I intend to spend all of my money before I die," Hugh said, holding his glass up. "I want to enjoy it."

"Says the man who still resides with me," Hawthorne joked.

Hugh shrugged. "I just haven't found an estate that agrees with me; or a townhouse, for that matter."

"May I ask what you are looking for?" Haddington asked.

"I don't rightly know," Hugh said.

Haddington chuckled. "It is no wonder that you haven't found it yet."

"Perhaps you should get a wife to help you decide?" Hawthorne suggested. "Dinah would be thrilled to help you, as you are currently lacking in that area."

Hugh shuddered. "I don't need, or want, a wife. They are nothing but trouble."

"Not if you select the right one," William said.

Haddington took a sip of his drink, then said, "I do agree with Hugh. I do not see myself being saddled with a wife."

"Not even if it is the lovely Miss Ashmore?" William asked.

"Even then," Haddington said, though his response was a second delayed and lacking conviction.

William decided to take pity on his friend and rose. "If you will excuse me, I need to go see Georgie."

"But you just got here," Haddington remarked.

"True, but I have a gift that I need to give to her," William revealed as he pushed in his chair.

Hugh rose as well. "I will walk you out."

After they exited White's, William walked over to his coach and asked, "Would you care for a ride?"

"I'll walk. The place I like to game at is only a short walk from here." Hugh's eyes grew serious. "I am glad that you are happy. You deserve it."

"As do you."

"No, I don't," he said lightly, shaking his head and looking skyward.

Before he could respond, Hugh set off down the pavement, his hands in his pockets. William would need to seek out his friend soon to discuss his despondent behavior.

William stepped into the coach and felt it merge into the traffic. He thought about Georgie and a smile came to his face, as it always did when he thought about her.

Earlier that day, they had gone to the orphanage to help the girls with their lessons. Georgie was still insistent that she should act as a headmistress until a new one could be found. He tried to reason with her, but it wasn't much of a fight. He loved that she cared so much for the children. He knew his mother would be pleased.

He reached his townhouse and hurried up the steps, pleased when Thorne greeted him at the door.

"Good afternoon, my lord," Thorne said, opening the door wide.

"Where is my wife?" he asked.

"She is in the library."

"Very good," William said as he rushed up the stairs and down the hall. He stepped into the library and saw Georgie on the settee, a book in her hand. "Good afternoon, wife."

Her eyes lit up when she saw him. "Good afternoon, husband," she said as she set her book on the table in front of her. "You are in a fine mood today."

He sat down next to her. "That I am. I have a wedding present for you."

"Another one?" She fingered the coral necklace that hung around her neck. "I don't think I need any more jewelry."

"It isn't jewelry."

She eyed him curiously. "Whatever could it be, then?"

William removed some papers from his jacket pocket and unfolded them. "Something that I know is special to you."

"You don't need to keep buying me things, William," Georgie said. "I am content just being your wife."

"Just one more gift; especially since I went to a lot of trouble to secure this surprise for you."

Georgie relented with a smile. "One more gift, then."

He handed her the papers and waited for the moment

realization dawned on her face. She lowered the papers and said softly, "You bought my grandmother's estate."

"I did," he said.

Tears appeared in her eyes as she asked, "How is this possible?"

"I had my man of business meet with the owners and negotiate a fair sum for the property," he replied.

"I can't believe you did this for me."

"I would do anything to see you smile," William said. "After all, it is only fair, because you are the reason I wake up with a smile every morning."

A tear rolled down her cheek and he reached forward to brush it aside. "I didn't think it was possible to be this happy," Georgie murmured.

"I hope you don't mind, but I had another desk placed in my study so we can manage our estates together."

"That is a brilliant idea!"

William reached for her hand and brought it to his lips. "I don't care what our future holds; as long as I am with you, that is all that matters."

"I couldn't have said it better, my love."

The End

Is Love worth the gamble?

Lord Hugh Calvert has managed to disgrace himself again. He gambled and won a small fortune, as he usually does, but this time the pot included a ward. He has never been responsible for someone other than himself. Perhaps it would be best if he just turns the care of his new ward over to his mother, washing his hands of her. But he hadn't anticipated that Miss Wymond would be so intriguing… or so beautiful.

Miss Marielle Wymond has lost her entire family and is forced to rely on the good graces of her guardian until she reaches her majority. When he gambles with her life and she is sent to live with Lord Hugh, she wonders what fresh misery she will be subjected to.

Will her new guardian be as terrible as the first one? What will she
do if he's worse?

Also by Laura Beers

Proper Regency Matchmakers
Saving Lord Berkshire
Reforming the Duke
Loving Lord Egleton
Redeeming the Marquess
Engaging Lord Charles
Refining Lord Preston

Regency Spies & Secrets
A Dangerous Pursuit
A Dangerous Game
A Dangerous Lord
A Dangerous Scheme

Regency Brides: A Promise of Love
A Clever Alliance
The Reluctant Guardian
A Noble Pursuit
The Earl's Daughter
A Foolish Game

About the Author

Laura Beers is an award-winning author. She attended Brigham Young University, earning a Bachelor of Science degree in Construction Management. She can't sing, doesn't dance and loves naps.

Besides being a full-time homemaker to her three kids, she loves waterskiing, hiking, and drinking Dr. Pepper. She was born and raised in Southern California, but she now resides in South Carolina.